T0157982

Rite Of The Path

A Three Dimensional Love Story

Book One

Laura Lang

AuthorHouse™
1663 Liberty Drive
Bloomington, IN 47403
www.authorhouse.com
Phone: 1-800-839-8640

Published by AuthorHouse 12/05/2012

ISBN: 978-1-4567-5393-1 (sc)
ISBN: 978-1-4567-5392-4 (e)

Library of Congress Control Number: 2011904110

This book is printed on acid-free paper.

Contents

The Path

Keep Straight the Path of your feet,
And all your ways will be sure
Do not swerve to the right or to the left;
Turn your foot away from evil.

Proverbs 4.10

This book is dedicated to all that are seen and unseen . . . to the many souls who have touched my life with both joy and sorrow, as both are necessary, for one cannot exist without the other. L

For my mother, whose faith and encouragement was instrumental during the process of writing this book.

"All truths are easy to understand once they are discovered; the point is to discover them."

Galileo Galilei

Inner Strength
Chapter One

1992

Eden had been fast asleep. Then slowly, the flutter of the early morning activities downstairs disrupted her fanciful dream and brought her quiet mind back to consciousness. What was it that she was dreaming about? She wrapped herself up in her new quilt, an early birthday gift from her grandmother Rebecca, who she affectionately called Nana Becca, and tried to remember her dream, but it was no use. It was gone, but the sensation of it lingered a bit. Opening her eyes slowly she looked at the beautiful bright colors of the quilt. Some of the squares represented the seven creeds Eden tried to live her life by. She knew many hands had worked hard on her gift. All the church ladies in quilting club had helped make it special and meaningful for Eden. For that, she was truly touched and grateful. She had been taught at a very early age not to take the kindness and generosity of others for granted.

Eden could smell breakfast being prepared by her mother Rachel and she was sure her dad was already dressed and having his first cup of morning coffee, undoubtedly reading the paper. "Eden, honey are you up?" her mom called from the bottom of the steps. "Yes mom, I'm up." Eden answered through the half opened bedroom door, stretching and yawning at the same time. "Breakfast in five minutes dear . . . you don't want to be late for school." Her mom put that in for good measure. This same repartee had taken place from first grade to twelfth grade. Eden was glad things would be changing, but she knew the change would be hard for her parents.

School was over for the summer and senior graduation had been last weekend. It had been a proud moment in Eden's life, but Eden still had some unfinished business to take care of. Like cleaning out her locker and picking up letters of recommendation. Today was the last day the school would be fully operational. It had been set aside for everyone who had procrastinated, including the teachers. Forcing herself up, she made it out of bed and headed to the bathroom carrying her underwear, jeans and a tee shirt. She brushed her teeth and washed her face, pausing to to look at herself in the mirror. In a few days she would be eighteen and by the time autumn rolled around she would be far away at college. Combing her hair always took the most time. It was long, falling below her waist, heavy with natural curls and pale blond. Eden considered her hair her best feature, but in fact her eyes were what no one could get past. They were inherited from her grandmother. Large and pale crystal blue, they were magnetic. At least most of the guys at school thought so. Even so, Eden never let their compliments or passes have much effect on her. She couldn't, not the way she had been raised. She had her grandmother, and her mom to keep her focused. She always wore a purity ring that had been especially created for her, by her grandmother. It was made of white gold and held a bezel set diamond in the middle of it surrounded by two doves in yellow gold on each side of the diamond. The ring was in the style of a band and Eden wore it on her left hand ring finger. It was there to remind her that one day that finger would hold a wedding band and a commitment to go along with it. The ring was a symbol of what Eden herself believed was the right way to stay focused on her own commitment.

Raised within her church community she had taken an oath of celibacy on her own when she was thirteen. At almost eighteen she had not betrayed her oath because it meant something to her. She would stay committed to her oath, until the time came for her to marry. Eden had seen up close and personal, the evidence of what happened to girls in her school who had sexual relationships with guys in their early teens, and she didn't want to follow in their footsteps. Throughout her young life Eden was led more by logic and sensible reason than her emotions. In fact she had never been so diverted or interested in any member of the opposite sex that her rational thoughts could be altered, at least not yet.

Grabbing a hair elastic, she made her way downstairs to the kitchen. As she expected, her dad was nose deep in the Hadleyville Gazette, glancing at his watch, he said plainly. "Thirteen minutes." He was such a stickler for punctuality. Eden kissed him on the head and went to her mother by the stove and kissing her on the cheek, took a piece of buttered toast off the paper towel on the counter. "Don't have time for breakfast, have to run." Eden said. "Edie dear have something more to eat." Her mom insisted. "Mom I can't I have to go, all the teachers will be gone before noon and I have those letters of recommendations to pick up, Mrs. Clark might have them but if not I'll have to track them down, plus I have to clean out my locker." She said picking up her glass filled with milk and taking a long drink from it. "Saying grace would have been appropriate Eden." Her father reprimanded her. "Dad I said it silently." Eden replied. In truth she had said a short one silently. "Have you given any thought to our talk?" asked her dad, looking over the rim of his eye glasses. "Yes . . . I'd really like to go to Smithfield in Washington State dad . . . but I will consider Laramont in Maine." Eden replied, not wanting to get into a whole discussion about college right now. "It's going to depend on the scholarship funds." Her dad quickly interjected. Her mom put down a plate of scrambled eggs and toast in front of her dad. "Edie, we don't want you to go that far away." She told Eden. "Mom, I've been in New England my whole life, I'd like to go somewhere else." Eden stated in her own defense, a slight pout forming on her lips. She grabbed her red hoodie and putting it on, added, "I promise I'll think about it." She meant it, as she had thought about it quite considerably already. "They have a beautiful coast line and a strawberry festival every year!" Her mom called after her, as Eden walked through the hallway to the front door. "Ok, mom, bye . . . see you later . . . I'll think about it, I love you both." Eden called back to them, as she opened the front door, and walked onto the front porch. She was happy to be outside. She loved her parents but sometimes they could be so clinging.

Eden closed the front door and ran down the steps. She would miss living here. She loved the front of her house with the two tall oak trees flanking each side of the lawn, which her father was fanatical about. Her mother's rose bushes ran along the entire wraparound porch. Today she was acutely aware of everything around her. The early morning sun highlighted the veins of the new spring leaves and the last of the dawn's dew drops sparkled on each blade of grass. Eden took a deep breath and made her way down the street. Her neighborhood was a spattering of old Victorian houses, mixed in with more modern split levels and capes. The grand dames which reminded one of days gone by, fascinated and intrigued her. Here they had been handed down generation to generation and were like old heirlooms that held the hearts of their inhabitants. Hadleyville was one of the first towns settled in New England and home to many a historical site.

As she turned on to Hadley Circle, she looked up at the Victorian that still housed some of the Hadley's today. She was the grandest one of the neighborhood, and had been completely remodeled several times. Eden imagined many times what it would be like to live in the Hadley Estate as it was called. Her father said he wouldn't want it if he could have it for free, as the winter heating bill would surely put them in the poor house. John Moore Hadley had settled the town in 1635, Hadleyville High was named after him. Officially it was named John Moore Hadley High School, but everyone called it Hadleyville high. Eden knew that wherever her travels in life would take her, Hadleyville would always be her true home.

Picking up her pace, she arrived in town square in record time, passing Barney's Coffee Emporium at seven twenty. Looking through the window she waved to her friends Nia and Leah who were twins and were waiting in line for drinks. It was at that moment that she spotted a little girl pull away from her mother, and run into the street. For Eden time seemed to stop and she saw everything in slow motion, as the light turned green, the girl's mother turning and running after her child. Eden knew she could get there faster, and she did. With speed that would significantly change the course of history for all three of them, Eden stood in front of the oncoming traffic and mentally kept the cars from moving. Taking the little girl by the hand, she recovered her to her mother who was grateful beyond words. This miraculous event took several moments in real time and yet, Eden was unmoved by her speed and instinct and her clarity of thought.

As she made her way to the side walk, someone came running up to her. Trying to keep time with her speedy pace he introduced himself. "Hi! I'm Josh." The young man tried to get her attention, but Eden was focused on getting to school. "I saw what you did back there, that was incredible!" He told her. "I wouldn't go that far." She replied. "I'm Josh, I'm in your English lit class." He said with visual excitement. "I know who you are." Eden answered him, with a slight smile. "You moved with lightening speed." He told her, his voice still filled with awe at what he had seen. "How did you do that?" he asked walking along side her. "I was just close enough, that's all . . . it was no biggie." Eden replied simply. "Are you kidding?" Josh asked not dropping the subject. They had arrived outside the school steps. "Look, Josh, if you're hitting on me, you're wasting your time." She said walking up the steps. He stood waiting until she turned around at the top . . . he knew that she would. "Hey, no hard feelings, I'm sure you're really nice." She said smiling and then entered the building. Joshua smiled back at her but she was already inside. He was pleased with himself. She was the one . . . she was the one. He felt it and he knew it. Now he had to tell Daniel.

Joshua hoped that the miracle had not sparked any curiosity among anyone else that possibly saw what happened. Daniel had told Joshua, miracles happen many times a day throughout the world and yet most humans are not aware of them. Daniel went on to explain that humans don't pay close enough attention. When Joshua asked Daniel why there was so much crime and atrocities against mankind, Daniel's response was brief. "It is the balance of nature and the gift of one's own free will to choose. "Choose?" asked Joshua, "Yes, choose between good and evil." Daniel answered stoically. Daniel was not one for many words, but his words were well placed when he spoke. Daniel's reputation communicated for him, he was The Path's leader in The Highest Realm. Daniel could negotiate with one look. He had done this for Joshua; he negotiated Joshua's second chance.

Now it was all about Eden, that was Joshua's responsibility and he must see it through to the end. His future and Eden's future depended on him. Joshua wondered why he had been given a second chance. What had Daniel seen in him? He had done awful things . . . had been a total disappointment to his parents, disrespected them, even stole from them. Joshua thought about the choices he had made, and knew that his choices had led him to where he was now. Perhaps it was that Joshua truly regretted his actions, or maybe it was that he had pleaded for forgiveness from his maker. Whatever it was, it was not for Joshua to question, he needed to rise to the occasion and fulfill his obligation to The Path and . . . that was harder then it sounded.

As Eden made her way through the corridor toward the guidance counselor's office, she thought about Sienna, who had disappeared last year. The two girls had been close since elementary school but, when Eden and Sienna were in Jr. High School, they had a falling out, not surprisingly it was over a boy. It was over Will Johnson. Will had a crush on Eden all through seventh and eighth grade. To Eden he was just another kid in school. She knew he had a crush on her, but she was too young and uninterested to really care. More than that she was raised under very strict guidelines and she knew the rules and expectations of her family and church. Even if she had wanted to go out with Will, she had made a promise to the church, her family and herself to abstain from sex until she was an adult. If she got involved with any boy, eventually it would lead to sex, it always seemed to with girls she knew at school. It certainly had with Sienna and these thoughts were filling Eden's mind today as she walked through the school's corridors. Eden hadn't wanted to deal with the pressure to have sex from anyone. She had been raised to maintain certain principals and those principals had been established in her from birth.

The issue was that, Sienna was wild over Will and he couldn't care less. Using very poor judgment Eden convinced Will to ask Sienna to the eighth grade school dance. He didn't want to at first. He wanted to meet Eden there and spend the time with her, but Eden told Will she wasn't even sure she would be going. Eden had always been up front with Will about how she felt about him and dating, but to Will she was the ultimate challenge. He could wait. She often told him, "You'll be waiting a long time." So, taking Eden's advice he asked Sienna to the dance. Will's dad picked Sienna up the night of the dance, and then dropped them both off at the school gymnasium. Sienna looked beautiful, dressed in a burgundy satin A-line dress, with delicate spaghetti straps. The dress highlighted her auburn hair and hazel eyes, with pearl earrings that dangled just below her earlobe that were her mom's, Will took a second look.

However, when Will arrived there and saw Eden, he left Sienna and stayed around Eden, never leaving her side, wanting to dance with only her. Eden had a reserved and cool air about her which transfixed Will most of the time and this was no exception. Sienna was devastated and pulled Eden into the girl's bathroom. "Why are you trying to take Will away from me?" she yelled at Eden. "I am not trying to take him away from you . . . what are you talking about?" asked Eden perplexed. "The whole night he's only been hanging around you!" Sienna continued with her tirade. "Sienna, everybody is hanging around each other . . . it's not what you think." Eden replied trying to stay calm. Sienna stormed out of the bathroom only to find Will standing there leaning against the wall of the gymnasium. "What's going on?" he asked knowing full well, as he could hear everything they were saying especially Sienna who had been screaming. "Why did you ask me to come with you tonight?" Sienna asked him, coming straight to the point. Will paused for a moment and then replied, "Eden asked me to." Sienna flew into a rage and stormed back into the bathroom, bumping into Eden on her way out. "You lied to me, you call yourself my friend, and you're a liar!" Sienna yelled. "You're right I did ask him to bring you . . . because I know how crazy you are over him." Eden said in her own defense. To that Sienna did not have a comeback. She simply turned away from Eden. "It was wrong of me to do that, I guess I should have asked you first." Eden admitted knowing that now, there was nothing left to say.

Eden turned and left the gymnasium with Will following close behind. Taking the stairs she made her way to the pay phone on the first floor of the school. Eden searched her bag for change as Will watched her. "Who are you calling?" asked Will. "My dad." Eden replied. "Why?" he asked as he pulled out a quarter from his pants pocket. "I want him to pick me up." Eden answered, taking the quarter from his hand and depositing into the pay phone. "Why are you going home?" Will responded not wanting her to leave. "I'm not feeling well, I just think it would be the best thing to do right now." She replied looking up at him, knowing by his expression he didn't want her to go. He walked her outside and stayed with her until her dad pulled up in the parking lot behind the school. "You're not the one who should be leaving . . . anyway I wish you'd stay . . . I mean who cares about Sienna anyway?" Will said quietly, as he tried to hold her hand but Eden pulled back. As Eden got into her dad's car, she paused to look up at Will. "This has nothing to do with you, this was my mess up, and it's my fault this happened."

Will watched as Eden drove away from the school and from him. She had been the most beautiful girl he had ever seen tonight and now his chance was ruined. A bitter resentment began to grow inside Will as he returned to the gymnasium and to the dance. He was the one who was losing as far as he was concerned, from both sides. Before this night he hadn't even thought about Sienna one way or another, but now he decided he was going to make her pay. As time would prove, he was going to make them both pay, Sienna more than Eden.

Through on onslaught of seniors running here and there, trying to finish up all the stuff that they had procrastinated on till today, she walked into the crowded office. A group of students were already there, but when Mrs. Clark saw Eden she handed her a large envelope, and wished her luck. "Eden there are three letters of recommendation in the envelope." She told Eden. "Thank you Mrs. Clark." Eden replied, as she handed her back a small envelope which contained a thank you note inside. Next she headed for the third floor hallway and took out the last remaining reminders of senior year from her locker. Shuffling stuff around and pulling out books and magazines, she came across a hair barrette that Sienna had given her a long time ago. Memories of their friendship came rushing back to her again, as she picked up the barrette and held it in her hand. Eden began to mentally relive the moments of her past.

Taking her back to a time, when a year ago, Eden's parents had gone away over night to Ridley Wells, for her aunt and uncle's anniversary party. The two girls were now seventeen. They were suppose to spend the night at Sienna's house, but at the last minute Sienna told her parents that she was going to stay with Eden, at her house. The fact was that Sienna had become a challenge to her parents in the past two years. They had lost control of her coming and going a long time ago. When Sienna had to give her baby up for adoption, she had become a totally different person. In fact Eden had struggled to keep the friendship going, in spite of Sienna's sometimes erratic behavior.

After watching a movie and girl talk, Sienna told Eden she had a surprise for her. Opening the outside zipper of her backpack, she pulled out a small metal case, similar to the size of a business card holder. Sitting on Eden's bed she opened it carefully. "What is that?" asked Eden, with hesitation. "It's coke stupid." Sienna replied pulling a tiny make shift straw from her bra. "Coke, like in cocaine?" Eden asked her. "Yes, like in cocaine." Sienna answered her obviously annoyed. "Sienna, you can't bring that stuff in here." Eden answered her with complete shock and restrained anger. This was her parent's house, what was wrong with Sienna? "Eden you are such a baby, half the kids in school do coke." Sienna replied after carefully arranging the powder into thin, neat little lines. Eden opened the door to her bedroom. "Sienna, you have to go and take your drugs with you." Sienna looked up at her after inhaling some of the powder through the straw into her nostril. Some of the powder stuck to the tip of her nose, so she took her index finger and collected it and then rubbed it into the top of her gums, inside her mouth. It disgusted Eden to see what had happened to Sienna. "You have no idea how good this stuff is, Dante gets only the best stuff." Sienna said as she let her head fall back in relaxation. Eden stood by the bedroom door, waiting for her get up and leave. "Who is Dante?" Eden asked stunned. "My boyfriend." Sienna replied, rather arrogantly. "Your boyfriend? Since when do you have a boyfriend?" The surprise in Eden's voice was more than evident. Sienna looked at her slyly. "You have no idea who I am E." Sienna said in a hushed voice, using her nickname for Eden. Eden held her ground, "I'm sorry Sienna, but you have to leave." Eden demanded. Sienna looked at her, stood up and walking over to her, back handed Eden across the face. "I'll leave when I'm good and ready." Sienna growled back at Eden, her eyes looked crazed. Suddenly there was a knock at the front door downstairs and Sienna quickly shoved Eden out of the way.

"That's Dante." Sienna said and headed downstairs to open the door, that's when Eden took the metal case and the straw and shoved it in Sienna's bag throwing it down the stairs hitting Sienna on the back. Then quickly she closed her bedroom door and locked it. With strength she didn't realize she had, she pushed her bureau against the door, and grabbing her house phone she dialed 911. Eden's heart was racing, as she instinctively knew she was in danger. Sienna pounded on the door crying, "please E let me in, I'm sorry I hit you . . . please open the door, he's going to kill me." Sienna whispered, her voice sounded desperate and scared.

As Eden talked to the dispatcher she looked out her bedroom window and saw several men all dressed in black on her porch, slowly they made their way across the street to a black limo. Eden had wanted to move the bureau and let Sienna inside, but her instinct told her not to. One, she knew she could no longer trust Sienna and two, they were obviously outnumbered. Seconds later she saw Sienna following them with her head down, behind Sienna was a tall man who turned, and looking up at the window caught Eden's eyes, with his. His hair was jet black, his face pale. He smiled at Eden and she pulled back from the window. "Hurry please, someone has broken into my house and I am here by myself." She told the dispatcher. Hadleyville had its own police force and just as the black limo drove away with Sienna in it, a squad car turned the corner onto Sparrow Lane. Eden told the police as much as she knew and asked to be taken to her grandmother's house.

They canvassed the area around the house and found nothing and no one, they wouldn't . . . everyone had left in the black limo as she had told them. Eden knew she couldn't stay alone. She would go to her grandmother's house and stay there until her parents came home the next day. In the meantime, Eden was convinced that Sienna had been the bait that had been used to get to her. But why? Who was Dante and what interest did he have in her? Would he now hurt Sienna . . . more then he already had? Eden knew the answer before she asked it of herself. Of course he would.

Eden thought back to her friendship with Sienna and believed that Sienna had blamed her for what happened with Will Johnson. She went over the events again in her mind of the eighth grade dance and the years that followed. It was as if she was channeling her past through the energy contained in the hair barrette, clutched in her hand.

After the dance, Will had tried to recover his friendship with Eden, but he was unsuccessful. Eden had lost all interest in Will as a friend, she no longer trusted him. Although she didn't ignore him, she didn't go out of her way to talk to him either. She had an uncanny sense that given the opportunity he could cause her pain. Although he had apologized, for spreading the rumors about sleeping with her, Eden knew that he would possibly turn on her again, if he didn't get his way.

Eventually he started dating Sienna, telling her that he was an idiot, a fool to chase after Eden. That Sienna was far more beautiful than Eden, and smarter and sexier. The more Will would tell her how stupid he had been to like Eden in the first place, the more Sienna gave in to Will sexually, a little at first, then his sexual demands increased and Sienna was in fear of losing Will if she did not comply. Will was just ensuring his future, to keep getting what he wanted. He would sneak in to Sienna's bedroom window every night, while her parents slept upstairs. He made love to Sienna, and fantasized about Eden.

A few months had passed since the dance, when Sienna approached Eden and began talking to her. Both girls apologized to each other and regained their friendship. Sienna trying on occasion to convince Eden that Will was a really nice guy. Eden reaffirming her belief that Sienna should proceed with caution. Sienna didn't tell Eden about the sexual nature of her relationship with Will until the day she went to the store and purchased a pregnancy test, and it read positive. Both girls were now fifteen years old. Sienna had been seeing Will for well over a year. Her parents knew that she liked him a lot. He was always over the house with Sienna after school playing video games or watching a movie, and then he would leave and go home. That was what he did in front of Sienna's parents, they didn't know what he did when they went to sleep.

When Sienna told Will she was pregnant, he lashed out at her. Yelling how his father would kill him. Sienna retorted that if he had worn protection every time this would not have happened. She turned to Eden for support, crying her eyes out on Eden's shoulder. Eden told her inevitably she needed to tell her parents. Eden also told her she needed to make Will go with her. Eventually that's what took place, but not before weeks had passed and fights between Sienna and Will erupted into all out battles as to who was the one to blame.

Finally, Will went with Sienna to talk to her parents, and then Sienna and her parents went with Will to tell his parents. Will was right about his father, who heard the news and punched him in the face knocking him off the kitchen chair leaving Will with a bloody nose. Will's mother was in a hysterical crying jag, as Sienna's parents looked on. They were equally upset but chose to be more contained in their reaction. After all it was their son who was sneaking into their daughter's bedroom window night after night. Will's mother shot back, it was their daughter that was letting him into the room night after night. It was decided that Sienna would have the baby and give it up for adoption. Will's parents would shoulder the burden of Sienna's medical expenses and doctor visits. They would also pay for the delivery and birth of the baby and future expenses until the time the infant was adopted.

Everyone failed to take one very important fact into consideration, and that was how Sienna would feel after giving birth. Sienna agreed because she saw no other way around the situation, but when the time came, could she give up her baby and never look back? If she were able to give her baby up what effect would it have on her? She would be sixteen when she gave birth, could she move on and know that it was not just the right decision for herself, but also for her child?

Eden put the barrette in the pocket of her hoodie and cleaned out the rest of the papers, books and an old sweatshirt out of her locker. She dropped off the rest of the thank you cards at the school office and walked down the front steps outside the school. She had signed up to tutor second graders during summer school, so she'd be going back in a week. Mrs. Clark had suggested it to Eden before spring break, saying it would be beneficial to her, as she liked younger children so much, this would be a great opportunity. Eden was planning to take child development as a second major, so this would be great experience.

When she saw Joshua leaning against the railing of the school steps it heightened her curiosity. He smiled when he saw her. "I thought you'd like company walking home." He said casually, his voice was light and easy. "How do you know I'm going home?" Eden asked. "I don't, just thought you might like company." He repeated, a touch of his nervousness in his voice rising to the surface. "Well, I am on my way home, so it might be nice to have company." She answered being polite, somewhat accepting his gesture of friendship. "Would you like me to carry those books for you?" Joshua asked, trying to make conversation. "Oh no, they're not heavy, thanks anyway." Eden answered nonchalantly. They walked a few blocks without talking very much.

Eden felt comfortable with him, she didn't really know why. She had seen him in school, at the library and in English literature class, but had never talked to him. He kept to himself as she did . . . that is until today. "So where do you live?" she asked casually. "Across town, near Grayson Falls." Joshua answered, quietly. Eden knew that wasn't the best area of town, but she wasn't going to judge him, for one it wasn't up to her to judge anyone and for two, she liked him. Suddenly they were both silent again, Eden broke the silence. "So, what will you be doing come September?" she asked him. "Probably working with my dad." He replied. "What does your dad do?" her voice indicating sincere interest. "He's a locksmith, and a really good one too." Joshua responded, excited at the memory of his dad. "What are you going to be doing?" he asked her as he took in her beauty. For Joshua, Eden was the most beautiful girl he'd ever seen, there wasn't one thing about her that he would change if he could. To him she was perfect in every way. "Going to college . . . somewhere, I haven't decided yet." She told him rolling her eyes and shaking her head slightly. "My parents want me to stay near them, like Maine, New Hampshire . . . but there's a part of me that would like to go far away." Her voice sounding pensive. "Well," replied Joshua. "Maine is far away." Eden laughed, she thought that was cute. He didn't take offense though, Maine was far away. He had an uncle that lived near Sebago Lake and for him that was far away from Hadleyville, Massachusetts.

They had been walking for an awhile and he hadn't gotten the chance to ask her out. "Well, this is it . . . I'm home." Eden told him. He pretended he didn't know where she lived. "This is where you live? Wow your house is beautiful." He said looking at all the rose bushes. "It's not my house, my parents own it." Eden corrected him, as she began climbing the steps onto the porch. Oh no, he thought, he had missed his chance. He blamed himself for getting carried away in the wrong direction. "Thanks for the company." She said smiling and disappeared into the house, much the same way she did at school today. He had made some head way but not much. However, he hadn't wanted to scare her off and he needed to talk to Daniel anyway.

A plan had to be put together, after all this could not get messed up. There was no room for mistakes on his part. He'd walk back to town and get his bike, which he had left chained to the bike rack behind the school. Eden was usually so illusive, but today had gone well and he felt confident that his next attempt would go even better. She certainly was a beauty that's for sure.

Her lips were full and had a natural pink color to them and her eyes, wow he had never seen such amazingly beautiful blue eyes before on anyone. They had a haunting quality about them that captivated him. But, the thing that fascinated him the most was her hair . . . the color was like golden wheat, with a shine to it that glistened in the sun like silk. Joshua longed to touch it, not to mention the shape of her face and her skin. Yeah he was smitten, but more than that, he had a job to do. It had been awhile since he had seen Grayson Falls, he wanted to visit . . . but he needed to ask Daniel first. He reasoned it might not be plausible until after his work with Eden had been completed.

When Joshua arrived at the clearing by Glen Cove, Daniel was transitioning from his spirit essence to human form. He waited several seconds before he approached Daniel. Once Daniel had fully transitioned, Joshua bowed his head and Daniel placed his hand on it. Then Daniel spoke saying, "Give me good news Joshua." "I have found her sir." Joshua answered him. "Are you sure she's the one?" Daniel questioned. "Yes sir, quite sure." Joshua replied definitively. "Have you come up with a plan?" Daniel inquired pensively. "Yes sir, I have." Joshua told him. "Very well, this is all in your hands Joshua, I have complete confidence in you." Slowly, Daniel walked away from Joshua and began to transition back into a thin white mist and evaporated into the atmosphere. That's how it was . . . this was up to Joshua to figure out.

Joshua rode his bike back to Sparrow Lane. Pulling up beside the curb, he wrapped his bike chain around a tree and then attached his bike, locking it. He walked up the steps and paused . . . then he knocked on the door. Rachel, Eden's mom opened the door. "Hi," said Joshua. "I'm Josh is Eden home?" he blurted it out, making Rachel know he was nervous. "Yes, she is, why don't you have a seat in the den and I'll get her." Eden's mom said. "You have a beautiful house, Mrs. Evanharth." He said as he walked through the entrance. Rachel led him into the family room. Glancing around, he saw a fireplace with pictures of Eden and her family on the mantel. "Thank you Josh, we like it." Rachel replied. "Make yourself comfortable, I'll get Eden."

Taking his backpack off and laying it on the carpet he sat down on the couch. Facing him were glass paneled French doors that led outside to a garden, he got up and looked out at all the flowers. It was obvious that The Evanharth family liked flowers and gardening, he thought to himself.

When he turned Eden had walked into the room. "What are you doing here?" she asked hesitantly but not annoyed, mostly just curious about him in general. Nervously, Joshua put his hands in his back pockets. "I wanted to know if you wanted to see a movie?" he asked trying to be casual. Eden paused for a second. "Why?" she asked him. Joshua laughed, and then responded. "Because, movies are cool and I hate going alone." She sat down on the couch and saw his backpack. "Do you take this everywhere?" she asked, nodding in its direction and diverting the subject. "Yeah, most of the time . . . lately." He replied. He sat down next to her, but not too close. "So would you like to go?" he repeated. Eden turned to face him. There was something she really liked about him. He had a head full of curly light brown hair and hazel eyes, which were deep and mesmerizing. "I don't go out on dates." Eden responded, her words said one thing, but her tone implied something else and Joshua noted a slight pout forming on her lips. Joshua sensed it and responded accordingly. "It's not a date . . . it's just two people watching a movie together." His voice was filled with warmth, which melted around her. Eden felt a kind for empathy in Joshua that she had never felt or sensed in any other male before, except her father and Uncle Eli. She believed that if something were to happen, Joshua would go out on a limb for her and not expect anything back in return.

Eden thought for a moment, there was such a close connection that she felt towards him for some odd reason . . . after all, it was only a movie. "What time?" she finally asked. Joshua was lost in his thoughts, thinking about how pretty she was and how he wished things could be different. "What was that?" he asked coming back to reality. "What time is the movie?" Eden asked again with a little laugh attached, realizing how nervous he was. "Oh, it's at eight." He replied shocked that she was even interested. "Ok, I'll meet you there." She said caving in. They were both secretly surprised she would consider it, given who Eden was.

Joshua got up and tried to remain calm, but he was overjoyed. "Great!" He exclaimed with excitement written all over him, picking up his backpack. "Which theater?" Eden asked completely composed, walking him to the front door. "The Fandango in town square." Joshua replied smiling broadly. "Ok, so I'll see you there later." Eden said, trying to hide her own excitement. Joshua smiled and said, "Cool I'll see you outside the theater then." Eden watched him through the window as he unlocked his bike and rode away.

Why she agreed was of equal shock to her. In all this time she had never met anyone that she would consider going to a movie with, not a guy anyway. For some reason Joshua was very different, from most of the guy's she knew at school. Even at church, the guy's gossiped more than the girls. Joshua had a special way about him, it was not in his looks, but behind his eyes there was a familiarity and closeness that she felt. A common ground that was emotional and tangible. She trusted him, but still she didn't know why so, she decided to call her friend Nia, who she had seen talking to him several times at school.

Surprisingly, Nia didn't have much to say about Joshua, except that he was nice and he had moved to Grayson falls after the school year began. If he lived in Grayson Falls why was he going to school in Hadleyville? Eden pressed on for more information, but Nia remained tight lipped, saying only that he was a nice guy and Eden would have a good time with him. Nia cut off the conversation telling Eden she needed to go. Eden's intuition told her there was more here than Nia was communicating, but decided to let it ride . . . it was only a movie.

After Nia hung up with Eden, she immediately drove to the clearing, she knew Joshua would be on his way back to the clearing, he needed some rest before tonight. "She called me about your date tonight." Nia told Joshua as he arrived at the clearing, hiding his bike behind some tall bushes. "It's not a date." He replied thinking Nia should know better. "Well, what else did she say?" He asked, resting his hands on his waist. "She wanted to know about you in general." Nia replied. "What did you tell her?" he asked slightly concerned. "As little as possible . . . just that you moved here less than a year ago and you're nice." Nia told him. "Wow . . . that is as little as possible." He commented. "Then I told her I had to go." Nia added. "Thanks for letting me know she called you." Joshua replied. "What's this all about Josh? Is she becoming one of us?" Nia inquired trying to expel more information from him. "I really can't go into it right now, but you'll know soon enough." Joshua replied looking around, waiting for Daniel to appear. "Thanks Nia, we'll talk soon." Joshua said indicating the conversation was over. Nia walked back to her car, knowing full well that changes were happening in The Path. Joshua was proud of Eden, she was nobody's fool. She did her homework. It was a good thing Nia knew how to handle the conversation. Joshua would take a long needed rest and freshen up before tonight.

Although he was young, he was still only spirit essence, allowed to take human form for the sake of his task. It took a lot more energy to stay in human form than in spirit essence. He was tired . . . excited at the very thought of seeing Eden tonight, but he needed to get back to The Highest Realm to rest.

He stood waiting for Daniel to allow him to transition to spirit essence. Joshua couldn't transition on his own yet. He needed Daniel to do it. Basically he needed Daniel for everything. He also owed this second chance to Daniel. His fate rested on how he proved himself with his task, and Eden was his task. She was beautiful, but she was still a task. Eden was an assignment, which Daniel entrusted to Joshua, who had fallen below grace and approval. This was necessary for The Council Tribunal who intervened when there was a disagreement between the two entities. Daniel fought for Joshua to be allowed into The Highest Realm and Dominic Marchette fought to take Joshua's soul back into the gallows of The Dominion and the followers of Satan. Now Joshua had a chance to serve on the side of The Highest Realm with Daniel. Daniel had the power to handle the Eden situation on his own, but that is not how great leaders lead. Daniel had chosen Joshua because he believed Joshua deserved a second chance, but Joshua would have to do the work. There was no short cut to righteousness, as far as Daniel was concerned. Daniel built his entire army on that belief and if Joshua was to be part of his regime, he would have to prove his capabilities. This was Joshua's dragon to slay, if he was to be allowed entrance into The Highest Realm permanently. However, Daniel knew things were likely to get quite sticky, and like most great leaders he would be at the battle.

Her hair was still damp when she went downstairs to dinner, having showered. "Why don't you say Grace tonight Edie dear?" Eden lowered her head and her parents did the same. Saying grace, Eden thought about Joshua, about his eyes, about what was behind them. "Thank you Heavenly Father for this bounty we are about to receive, amen." "That was quick Eden." Her father mentioned somewhat surprised. Eden smiled and replied. "I guess I'm hungry." As her mom passed her the mashed potatoes. "Thomas, Eden is going out on a date tonight." Her mom announced. Her father looked up over the rim of his eye glasses again, a gesture he often did. "Oh?" he asked, "with whom?" Eden knew by his tone that she must answer the question with specifics, which she didn't have but she'd try to muddle through. "He's a boy from my English literature class . . . but it's not a date, it's just two people watching a movie together." She stated as if it was of no importance. "What's his name?" her dad asked. "Joshua." Eden replied passing the bowl of mashed potatoes to him. "Joshua what?" Eden looked up and said, "Gee, I don't know his last name." Her dad shook his head slightly. "It's ok Thomas, they're only going to the movies . . . then she'll find out his name." Her mom was right on top of it. "I'll drop you there and pick you up." Her dad said. "Dad, I can drive myself there and back." She said feeling like a ten year old. "Eden let your father drive you, then he can meet Joshua . . . what's his name." Her mom intervened, in that "I know what's best" voice.

There were times when Eden felt smothered, this was one of them. "Sure dad." She acquiesced. "I told him I'd meet him there at eight o'clock, well maybe a little before, the movie starts at eight." She explained. "Why isn't he picking you up?" Her dad was so persistent. "I don't think he has a car." Eden replied. Now finally, the subject was closed for the time being. After dinner, Eden helped her mom clean up. Everyone was quiet, her mom was thinking as she loaded the dishwasher, Eden was thinking, and her dad was in the family room having his coffee . . . . thinking. Her non date with Joshua was a big deal, for all three of them. This started the day Sienna went missing, this over protectiveness. She really couldn't blame them; she had never been on a real date and she was more nervous than they were.

Even though Joshua said it wasn't a date, she knew it was and she was happy about it. She did like him, even though she didn't know him. He was comfortable to be around and easy to talk to. She would invite him to her surprise birthday party, if everything went well tonight. The one her grandmother was planning. She had heard her mother over the phone, little bits of conversation here and there, and she had figured it out. She would still do her best acting, so that her grandmother would not be disappointed. Her aunt and uncle and her cousins would be there along with Leah and Nia and some other friends from church. Eden was excited about it, she would be turning eighteen, a milestone . . . but tonight and the expectation of seeing Joshua again was really giving her butterflies in her stomach.

Eden knew she was an outcast in school and didn't make friends easily. All through High School there were only two other girls that she knew, besides herself that didn't date. They were the twins Nia and Leah. The similarity was that they were raised like Eden and attended the same church. Sienna had also attended the same church, but her commitment level wasn't on the same level as Eden's, but then again Sienna didn't have Rebecca Evanharth for a grandmother. Eden also suspected that some of the guys in school thought she was gay, or definitely a geek anyway. There were some guys that thought she had slept with Will after all. Sometimes it bothered her, but she rose above it, by excelling in other things, like her grades. However, something about Joshua was changing how Eden felt about her commitment and dating. He was special, but she didn't know why.

"For they have sown the wind, and they shall reap the whirlwind."

Hosea 8:7

The Creed
Chapter Two

Time passed and tempers never died down, between Sienna and Will. Sienna would be home schooled by a private tutor to save her constant embarrassment about her growing abdomen. Will was sent off to another school. They communicated for a few months, and then little by little Will stopped coming by and calling. Partly it was their continuous fighting and arguing about keeping the baby. Sienna and Will were too immature to handle the strain of the situation, also the more she felt the baby move inside her, the more and more she did not want to think about giving her baby to anyone. Sienna's parents dug their heels into the ground, if she wanted to keep the baby, Will would have to marry her and support her, and that is not something he felt he could do, or wanted to do.

He didn't work, at sixteen he didn't even have a part time job, and it was unrealistic to think he could support himself never mind a wife and baby. It had been a mistake and a terrible loss of judgment on both their parts, but why make it worse with a marriage that would only end in divorce. The baby deserved better, Sienna's mom explained.

Was it right to take away a promising future from three people? Her, Will and the baby? Sienna knew what her mother said was right, but it didn't stop her from breaking apart when she saw her little boy for the first and last time, briefly after his birth. Sienna went into hysterics shouting, "Give me my baby! Give me my baby!" and had to be put on tranquilizers. When Eden went to the hospital the next day, to visit Sienna, she was heavily tranquilized, lying on the hospital bed staring out the large window in her room. Sienna's mom was there and greeted Eden warmly when she came in. "I'll leave you girls to talk for a while." Her mom said and then left the room. "How are you Si?" Eden asked giving her a kiss on the cheek. "I will never forgive them." Sienna answered. "You'll get through this . . . I know you will you're a very strong person." Eden told her. "Will I Eden, will I?" Sienna broke into tears, sobbing. Eden got on to the bed and held Sienna in her arms. "Of course you will!" Eden exclaimed. "Your life is only beginning, Si . . . you and I well . . . we're still kids ourselves." Eden explained, trying to be comforting. "We still have to get through high school and college." Eden continued smoothing back Sienna's hair as she talked.

"It will be alright . . . sure it's going to take a while but you made the right decision." Eden said encouragingly. Sienna was drifting off into sleep. "Did you see him?" she asked Eden, her voice barely audible. Eden knew she meant the baby. "Yes, I did he's the most lovely baby in the world." Eden replied thinking about her baby brother Benjamin who had died. She was not able to see Sienna's baby as he was not with the other newborns, but in another unit. When Sienna fell totally asleep Eden laid Sienna's head back on the pillow, gathered her things and left. She knew it would be upsetting, but seeing Sienna lying there practically comatose and all those babies through the window in the corridor of the maternity ward, really affected her. The very thought of giving up your own flesh and blood, how hard that must be? Having him ripped from your body and given away to a stranger. Eden could barely comprehend it. She would stop by after school tomorrow and visit Sienna again. Perhaps tomorrow would be a better day, Eden thought as she left the hospital. But, tomorrow would lead to big changes in Sienna's overall attitude. Eventually, her resentments would lead her straight to Dante and the drugs.

In the months that followed, Sienna returned to school, but she had changed in many ways. The girls still spoke, but not as much. Eden noticed that Sienna was now hanging out with a different crowd, some of them would wait for her after school and were much older than she was. Eden thought that Sienna had been through so much that she needed an outlet and this was it. Sienna had begun making new friends. What she didn't know was how very dangerous these new friends were. All Sienna knew was how good it felt when she inhaled the cocaine. She felt alive and happy, like she could do anything. All the thoughts of her baby son that had been taken away from her, would melt away under the effects of the cocaine. Now she couldn't live without it.

He promised to supply her with all she wanted. He told her he would take care of her as long as she swore her alliance to him and only him. This was where she needed to be, with him. It didn't matter that he was older, or that she couldn't introduce him to her parents. They didn't really care about her or her feelings anyway. If they had they would have let her keep the baby. In the end no one really cared about her, not her parents, not Will and especially not Eden. The only one who truly cared about her was him. She put all her common sense aside when it came to him, because he took all her pain away. All the pain flew away like hundreds of tiny birds flying out of a nest, when she was with him. For this, Sienna would do anything he asked.

He symbolized her freedom from the life she was running away from. Sienna was too damaged to realize that he would be far worse than anything she could ever imagine. Lying in his arms he introduced her to something new, it filled her with a warm intoxication of euphoria. Now she was dancing in complete bliss, completely leaving all reality. Sienna had no idea her sex partner had changed until the next morning. Who was this guy next to her? it wasn't him, it was someone else. Pulling the sheet over her naked body she saw the needle marks in her arm. Now it was morning and the harsh reality of her life came crashing down on her. The house was large and cold. The day outside was dark and rainy. Sienna threw her clothes on and ran for the door, pulling on the handle she realized she was locked in. No escape.

Eventually Dante would return, and with him he would bring her biggest nightmare. Sienna would never escape him, the men or the drugs. Her life was that of a slave. Sometimes Dante would unlock the door and hold it open. He would taunt her to leave . . . but her fear of what was outside became larger then her fear of what was inside. For Sienna, the devil she knew was better than the devil she didn't know. Dante broke her down to nothing. He would tell her to leave, that she could leave of her own free will . . . sometimes she would leave, only to return and beg his forgiveness. Sienna could not live without him or the drugs, she knew it and he knew it. He was her Lord and Master. Between Dante, his men and the drugs, Sienna was dying a slow death . . . painfully and torturously. So, when all of Hadleyville was wondering where Sienna was, it was sadly ironic that she wasn't as far away physically as she was mentally, emotionally and spiritually.

So . . . Eden realized it had never really been over. Having gone over this so many times in her mind, she concluded that, Sienna had held on to that deep seeded resentment since the eighth grade dance and Sienna was the bait used to get to Eden that night, her parents were away. Finally Sienna realized that Will never truly cared about her. Then having to give the baby up lead her to a deep and dark place filled with drugs. It was all becoming clear to Eden. Sienna had snapped after they took the baby from her. That was the final blow to her world. Sienna had run away from home last year, leaving behind no traces of where she could be, but Eden knew she was with him, whoever he was. He was the guy with the drugs and who knew if Sienna was still alive, and where she was? That incident with the cocaine in Sienna's backpack, and the sleep over had all been a ploy to get Eden into the car with them.

Eden could still remember Sienna's words, "He's going to kill me." As she sobbed outside Eden's bedroom door. Maybe he had by now. Eden's heart went out to Sienna, but when she disappeared, she had told the police everything she knew and a year later . . . all Eden really knew was that she was very lucky she had locked her door and dialed 911 that night. She was also lucky her grandmother was there for her, she had always been a safe haven to go to, and she still was. Not that her grandmother was a delicate push over by any means, she could be strict and formal, but with Eden there was a much deeper connection. It was the connection of a mutual and spiritual faith that they shared.

Being born as Rebecca Evanharth's granddaughter carried a supreme responsibility. Eden had been taught this by her grandmother since birth. Rebecca Evanharth was one of the founders of The Path, a religious sect of Christians that was founded in England and a fundamentalist in many of her practices and beliefs. However Thomas, Eden's dad refused to let his mother to go too deep into the teachings of The Path where his daughter was concerned. Although Rebecca followed her son's request she did teach Eden some things that she might need some day and she did it by playing games when Eden was young. Eden was highly skilled in meditation and extra sensory perception. She was also well schooled in scripture and could quote whole passages from The Bible and explain their meaning.

Rebecca knew her granddaughter would one day be faced with a decision to follow in her footsteps, or not. She also knew that Eden would be challenged one day and would need a strong foundation. When Eden was born, Rebecca knew that Eden possessed special gifts and internal strength, which not everyone was born with. She recognized this in Eden because she had them as well.

The Path members had a creed to follow and respect, in fact to live by. They were the seven steps that were necessary to belong to The Path. Some of the members were Warriors of God, like Rebecca and were chosen by a higher power before human birth. They lived by higher standards, because it was their mission in life to save souls. All members believed in the practices and had different functions and powers, some greater than others. However all were committed to the seven creeds. #1. Do Gods work here on earth. #2. Always speak the truth. #3. Keep calm your emotions. #4. Respect your body above all else for it shelters your soul. #5. Hold close to your heart your mother and father as they gave you mortal life. #6. Do not take what is not offered. #7. Honor the fellowship of The Path with honesty and faith. Rebecca knew that one day Eden would make the choice for herself, by herself.

When the time was right, Rebecca would be there to guide Eden through the transition. In fact it was Rebecca's decision to tell Eden that she would be the next Warrior of God on her eighteenth birthday. The choice to become part of The Path would be hers alone to make. Eden was born with the abilities and could harness them if she chose to, or let them stay dormant, if she chose not to follow the way of The Path. Either way Rebecca knew that Eden needed to be told, whether or not Thomas approved. By this time, it should have been obvious to Eden's parents, but it wasn't. Sometimes the most obvious things are the most difficult to recognize. Rebecca also knew that The Dominion might make a move to capture Eden, so she called on Daniel, to help in Eden's defense. Daniel responded with Joshua, who needed a task and who also needed to exonerate himself before The Council Tribunal.

There were other members of The Path who knew Eden well, Nia and Leah. As in any organization or military regime, there is a chain of command and Nia and Leah were aware of it. They never spoke to Eden about The Path, because as far as they knew she was an outsider. Even though Eden's grandmother was the highest ranking elder who was mortal in New England.

The twins were both experts in archery and possessed great physical strength. Both were extremely eye catching due to their long red hair, fair complexion and green eyes. Like Eden, they were in all advanced classes in school. They were sometimes teased at school because they wore monochromatic colors on a daily basis. Nia and Leah had a tremendous amount of self confidence, but were demure about it.

Having been raised to appreciate their good looks, they were thankful but not boastful; they did not base their self worth on their appearance. Their core values were to follow The Creed of The Path to the best of their abilities, but even Nia and Leah's abilities could not compare with the powers that Eden contained. Eden's powers were in fact supernatural, similar to someone on the opposite side of righteousness . . . Dante.

Dante was tall and slim with violet eyes and black hair. He wore his hair straight and pulled back. His power came not from his brawn but from his ability to mentally and verbally intimidate anyone he chose to. He was a master at finding the weakness in others and capitalizing on it. He did it so easily, that sometimes it truly bored him. His allegiance was to The Dominion; his superior was Dominic Marchette who had raised him like his own, to worship Satan and the underworld.

Dante stood by the window of an old abandoned warehouse, smoking a cigarette, the night Sienna was suppose to trap Eden and failed. The room was dirty, cold and empty except for himself, two men by the door and Sienna who was tied to a chair. Her face was badly bruised and her lip was split and still bleeding. Dante put his cigarette out under his shoe and walked over to Sienna. As she saw him approach, she trembled with fear, Sienna had every reason to, she was his slave. He knelt down beside her and ran his fingers against her thigh. "Sienna my darling, I am so disappointed in you, I thought you understood your commitment to me and the organization." His voice was low almost sensual. "I now have to question your loyalty and you know that I simply cannot deal with uncertainty." As he stood up, Sienna started to speak but her lips were too swollen. Suddenly Dante screamed. "Did I say you could speak?!" He shouted and kicked the chair over. Sienna's head smashed against cement floor.

He walked over to her but she was unconscious. Dante looked up at the two men who stood guarding the door. "Untie the wench and put her in the car . . . take her over to the property!" Dante yelled, as one of the men untied Sienna and threw her lifeless body over his shoulder. Then they left the building and got into a black limousine parked outside. Dante owned the building, it was a perfect location for drug pickups, money laundering and beating up a wayward prostitute. He rarely did any of the grunge work, that's something his hench men did . . . usually, but this was too personal. Sienna had cost him the perfect opportunity to get the newest member of The Path, she was so new . . . she didn't even know it yet.

He wanted Eden bad. Dante needed to even the score. His plan was simple, easy and would be so satisfying. Sienna had messed everything up and she was going to pay. He knew he still had time but that wasn't the point, he could have gotten her now, today if the stupid little druggie had done her job. He was furious, she couldn't even stay away from the cocaine long enough to trap Eden. No instead she had to snort the coke and slap Eden across the face, which ruined everything. Well, if anyone was going to do slapping it would be him, not some idiot drug addict.

There were so many ways he could punish Sienna and he was going to. She would suffer the consequences of her actions, tonight and all of her tomorrows. Everything in life and death is timing . . . and it was no different for Dante. He still had a year to capture Eden, but it would have been a feather in his cap to get her now. This was Dante's world, and it would be a hot shot in the arm for Sienna . . . eventually.

Eden told her parents what happened when they arrived home the next day, from Gridley Falls. Naturally they were shocked. Thomas called Sienna's parents to see if Sienna was alright. They told Thomas Sienna hadn't been home. Thomas explained that Eden had been pretty much shaken up herself, spending the night with her grandmother out of fear. Sienna's parents said that they had called the police after Eden's phone call to them that night. However, it was not unusual for Sienna not to come home until the next day, refusing to say where she had been or with whom. They were told by the police that they should wait until the next day, as Sienna might very well come home of her own accord as in the past. They were waiting for a detective to come to their house momentarily, as it had been twenty four hours since Sienna was last seen. Sienna's parents asked that the Evanharth's come over to their house to speak with the detective, of course they agreed.

Eden recounted everything she could remember, including the drugs that Sienna had pulled out of her backpack. The detective asked Eden a lot of questions and she was straight forward and direct in her answers. From the description of the men, the detective told the families that it sounded like drug affiliated gang members. "In Hadleyville?" asked Thomas shocked. "Yep." The detective replied. The detective said he would follow up with a missing person's investigation, but this was happening more and more around town. Eden explained that Sienna had referred to the man dressed in black, whose name was Dante, as her boyfriend, but was clearly afraid of him.

Listening to her story and taking notes the detective advised Sienna's parents do get the word out about their daughter. The more people who knew about it, the more chances there were of finding her. What none of them knew was that, everyone who worked for Dante feared him. Those that didn't work for him wouldn't see her because she was under lock and key. Over the next few weeks, posters with Sienna's picture were posted all over Hadleyville and the surrounding towns. Her face was even on the evening news. Her parents held a news conference, pleading for information and offering a fifty thousand dollar reward. The church held prayer vigils every weekend for months, praying that Sienna would be found. Whole neighborhoods were searched and the surrounding woods, but nothing led to her disappearance.

Dante got such a thrill out of it, as he watched it on the news; there she was lying right next to him, while everyone was out looking for her. She was usually so strung out on heroin, that she didn't know what was going on around her. Dante held her head up to show her that she was on television, but her eyes just rolled back in her head. Her body was being eaten away by the drugs and the constant steady stream of men Dante allowed to have their way with her.

Weeks turned in to months and within time, the girl with the auburn hair, hazel eyes and bright smile disappeared into the background. Other news was happening. Sometimes there would be an insert in the news paper, or a picture on the side of a milk carton which read, "Have you seen this girl?" Slowly, Sienna was replaced by some other missing girl, or child, or mother. The missing girl from Hadleyville was no longer the top story of the day, or news worthy.

All these thoughts rambled around in Eden's head, as she helped her mom clean up from dinner. As much as she looked forward to seeing Joshua, and going to the movie, there was a part of her that was still apprehensive. Not just because of how she was raised, but everything that had happened with Sienna. She wished that somehow she could have saved Sienna, but Eden also knew that Sienna was too hooked on drugs to have listened to her. That was obvious when Sienna back handed her across the face. Eden also knew that Sienna had made a horrible choice to get involved with Will and allow herself to get pregnant. Sienna had told Eden that it wasn't a choice to get pregnant, it was an accident. However, Eden had been taught and raised that prevention was the best medicine, and to abstain from situations and people who might cause one to lose their footing . . . wise. Eden's grandmother would often say that, "one's choices now would be their heaven or hell later."

Eden's grandmother had shed some more light on Sienna's pregnancy, in her response. "Apply your mind to instruction and your ear to the words of knowledge." A quote from Proverbs. It wasn't always easy to live up to her family's expectations. Eden often felt they were unrealistic in a world that challenged her on a daily basis. Sometimes, it seemed like the world was going in one direction and she, in a totally different direction. However, there was a force of will and internal strength inside Eden that kept her focused in the right direction. More than her mother and father, Eden's grandmother had not just directed her young life, but had impacted it with The Creed's set of principles. However, Eden had never been in love. In the near future Eden would struggle with one principle in particular. She had found strength within herself at a very young age, but her strength would soon be challenged in more ways than one. Someone was about to come into her life, and quite literally turn her upside down emotionally.

It made Eden smile to see Joshua already there waiting for her outside the Fandango movie theater. He even opened the car door when her dad pulled up to the curb. "Eden, I'll be waiting here to pick you up after the show." Her dad said with a nod of his head in a gesture of "hello" to Joshua. "O.k. Dad." Eden replied, getting out of the front seat. Before closing the door Joshua looked in at her dad and extended his hand to him. "Hi, Mr. Evanharth, it's nice to meet you, I'm Josh Pendleton." He introduced himself properly and Eden could see it impressed her dad. Then he closed the car door. That's when she noticed he had already bought the tickets; he had them held in his hand. "Hey, I'll give you the money for mine Joshua." Joshua smiled and said "No worries . . . why do you call me Joshua?" Eden laughed a little at his comment. “That’s your name isn’t it?” she asked smiling. “Yeah but Joshua is so formal . . . just call me Josh.” He replied holding the door open for her. “When you get to know me . . . Josh, you will see that I am pretty formal.” Eden responded, as they walked inside. “Oh, so I’m going to get the chance to get to know you am I?” He teased her. “Maybe.” Eden said coyly.

“Let’s get some popcorn and drinks.” Joshua said leading her to the concession stand. Eden thought about Joshua, as he paid the cashier and handed her a coke. It was something about his aura, which she was attracted to. Although he was just a kid himself he had a deeper understanding about things-like he already knew her and how to talk to her. This made it interesting for Eden and she was glad she’d agreed to come. They sat in the middle of the theater trying not to block any ones view, sharing the popcorn their hands touched several times.

They watched the movie silently and laughed at the teen comedy. Then somewhere between finishing the popcorn and and the middle of the movie, Joshua took her hand in his as if he had done it dozens of times, that it felt completely natural. Eden had never held a boys hand before. It was new, and had an element of excitement. She turned to look at his reaction several times during the movie, but did not speak. One time he moved closer to her without taking his glance from the screen and whispered, “I’m really glad you came with me tonight.” Eden whispered back, “me too.” The thought did pass Eden’s mind that Joshua might try to kiss her and she wasn’t sure how she’d feel about that. That expectation, turned in to more butterflies in her stomach.

The truth was Joshua wanted to kiss her desperately. He wanted nothing more then to wrap his arms around her and touch her lips with his own . . . but that was not part of the program. He was stepping out of the rules just holding her hand. In the past six months that he had been in Hadleyville and had first seen her he thought she was incredibly beautiful and smart. He had watched her and studied her from afar and had fallen in love with her. His job had depended on finding her. After literally watching every female senior in Hadleyville High, studying their every move, every gesture, he had fallen in love with Eden. Not that he could be with any of them. But, if he could . . . if life had not gone from him, this would be the one girl he could never have, but the only girl he would ever want. Although her destiny depended on him, it would not and could not include him. This was all temporary . . . he kept telling himself.

As the credits to the film began to roll on the screen, people started to get up and leave the theater. Joshua and Eden sat still holding hands. Eden waited for him to release her hand and he didn't want to, instead as they sat watching the screen, he whispered in her ear, "Thank you for this special time . . . I will always remember tonight, with you." Eden turned to look at him . . . it was dark and the music was loud, but she had heard him. She didn't know why or how it happened, but she let go of his hand and put her hand on his cheek. Both of them sat there and then ever so slowly and gently, he leaned toward Eden and kissed her and she responded. The kiss only lasted a moment, but it would have an everlasting effect on Joshua, whose heart was now in Eden's hands.

When it was over, they both stood up and Eden turned to walk toward the aisle. "Wait a second." Joshua said softly and took Eden's hands in his and looked into her eyes. The theater was now completely empty. The screen had gone dark and the theater lights were on. "I don't want you to think, I just go around kissing any girl . . . I did that because of how I feel about you . . . because it is you." He said, desperately trying to find the right words. Eden sighed deeply. "Joshua, I've never even kissed anyone before, you are my first kiss." Her voice was barely above a whisper and filled with embarrassment. "I know." Joshua replied. "You Know?!" Eden asked in disbelief. "Was I that bad?" she gasped, feeling completely humiliated. "No!" Joshua insisted, "You are incredible . . . in every way." He said softly, because he wanted to say so much more, but couldn't. "Look, I know I'm in the minority, most girls my age have already had several boyfriends and you know, all the rest of what goes along with it . . . but I'm . . ." she paused for a second, as Joshua guided her towards him and kissed her again. "Eden, you don't have to say anything else, I know who you are, and that's why I feel this way . . . I know you." Eden looked up at him and then rested her head on his shoulder, as he held her. He was so comfortable to be with. "How is it that you know me? Why do I feel so safe and secure with you?" Eden asked as she searched his eyes. "It's as if I've have known you my whole life." She explained exhaling deeply. Suddenly, the cleanup crew came in and broke the moment. As they left the theater Eden invited Joshua to her surprise birthday party. Joshua accepted the invitation by saying "Thanks, I'd love to go to your birthday party."

Joshua was touched by Eden's invitation. The innocence of how she asked took him back to when he was a small child. Did teenagers actually act this way? Not the kids he hung around with in High School, that's for sure. She was sort of an enigma to him, with the body of a young woman, the face of a goddess and the naiveté of a young child. He was aware that he had fallen in love with her but tried to direct his mind that this was all very temporary.

The truth was he could never be with her, he was not of her dimension. At some point he needed to tell her everything and hopefully she would believe him. However,

Joshua felt it didn't matter, because even if he wasn't a spirit, she was out of his league. His chances of even meeting Eden when he was on earth was slim to none. Now Joshua and Eden existed in different dimensions, but before they were worlds apart as well. If it wasn't that Daniel had fought for him to be part of The Highest Realm, and given him this chance, he would never have even met Eden. Now that he had, he was painfully aware of everything he had lost.

As they made their way outside, Eden looked for her dad's car. They waited for a few minutes and then Eden showed some concern. "This isn't like my dad, he's always on time." "Well," said Joshua, "maybe something came up." Eden looked up and down the street, "Maybe I should call home." She told Joshua. "Well, I could get you home on my bike . . . I have it chained over there." He nodded in the direction of the bike stands. "How?" asked Eden. "Well, it wouldn't be very comfortable, you'd have to balance yourself on the bar." Eden laughed. "No way, riding that way all the way home . . . I don't think so." She responded. "No worries, I'll walk you home." Joshua suggested. Then Joshua looked across the street. "Hey who's that?" he asked nodding towards the parking lot. Eden turned around and saw her Uncle Eli waving at them from his car. "It's my Uncle Eli, come on." Eden and Joshua ran over to him. "Hi guy's get in." Uncle Eli called out. Eden jumped in the front and Joshua took the back seat. "What's going on? How come dad didn't come to get me?" There was a pause and then uncle Eli spoke. "Something has happened . . ." he said as Eden buckled her seat belt and waited, finally she gave in. "Well what is it? Why the suspense?" Uncle Eli rubbed his forehead with the back of his hand and started the car. Then he said simply, "Nana has had a heart attack." Looking over at Eden for her response, he continued. "It happened about eight thirty . . . Ro and I went over there to help her get ready for your surprise birthday party tomorrow and . . . she collapsed." He began driving, as Eden said nothing. She was in shock. "Everyone is at the hospital, I'm heading there now." Finally Eden spoke. "She's o.k. though? . . . I mean she's going to be alright, isn't she?" Eden asked still trying to grasp everything her Uncle had said. Uncle Eli exhaled. "Eden the doctor told your father it was a massive heart attack, you can talk to your dad when we get there . . . it's not that far, a couple of more blocks . . ." Joshua just listened and said nothing, he was in shock too. The great Rebecca Evanharth dying was not a good sign for things to come.

Uncle Eli pulled up to the emergency entrance and both Eden and Joshua got out of the car and ran in. Inside Eden saw her dad, Aunt Rowena and her two small cousins who were twins, Caleb and Samuel in the lobby. Her dad came up to her and she fell into his arms. He hugged her and glanced over at Joshua. "It's nice that you're here." He told Joshua. Joshua just nodded back. Having been down this road in his prior life Joshua felt the pangs of sadness fill him. Remembering that fateful night of the fire and his own death. The separation of this dimension to the next is not an easy transition for the people who stay behind. "Eden, she's not conscious, the doctor doesn't think she'll make it through the night . . ." Thomas began to choke on his words. "Can I see her dad?" Eden's heart was filling with grief as she spoke. "Yes, of course." He replied. "They just moved her into a special critical care unit on the third floor. The nurse told us we can go in one at a time. Mom is up there now, with Father Clemmons . . . I wanted to stay here and wait for you . . . I know how hard this is going to be for you honey." Eden turned to Joshua. He spoke before she did. "If it's ok I'll sit here with these guys and keep them company." Meaning Caleb and Samuel who were only six. "I'm sure my uncle can give you a ride home later." She said as she walked away. "No worries." Joshua replied. When they got off the elevator, Eden noticed the stillness of the critical care unit.

As they walked over to the nurse's station, her dad introduced Eden to the nurse. "Hi, this is Rebecca Evanharth's granddaughter." He said. The nurse, who was tall, imposing and showed signs of a bad temperament, looked up at Eden. "How old are you?" the nurse asked. "I'll be eighteen tomorrow." Eden replied. "Alright, follow me." She began to follow the nurse, and then turned back to look at her dad, "Go ahead honey, they only allow one person in at a time." He repeated as he was in shock as well. As Eden approached the door she saw Father Clemmons outside of the room, quietly praying. The nurse opened the door and Eden could see her mom holding her grandmother's hand. "Eden I have administered the last rights to Rebecca." Father Clemmons told her, his voice sad for many different reasons. "Thank you Father for being here." Eden could not control her tears as she spoke. Eden's mother Rachel came out of the room and hugged Eden. Then Eden went inside.

As she walked into the room and saw her grandmother, Eden's heart broke. She looked frail and in pain. Her eyes were closed, but Eden could see her chest rise in slow unsteady breaths. Nana Becca had a tube coming out of her nose and one in her arm. To the right of her there was a monitor that showed the beats of her heart, they were slow and far apart. Alongside the heart monitor was something that looked like an accordion, which continuously expanded and then retracted. Eden assumed it was for oxygen. She reached over and pulled a chair over to the bed and sat down. In her mind she thought this couldn't be happening. Memories of her grandmother filled her mind, she tried to slow them down but they came fast, one after another. Apple picking in the orchard, baking pies, bed time stories, the time she fell off her bike and had to get stitches, so many memories and how special they all were. The games they played, her Nana's voice singing in the church choir. There were quiet memories too, when they meditated together and practiced silence and breathing. Her grandmother had shared so much with her, special moments that Eden held on to as she sat in silence now.

She took her grandmother's hand in hers and kissed it. Suddenly she felt a hand on her head and looked up. Her grandmother was looking at her. It was shocking at first, but her blues eyes called out to Eden. "I'm here Nana." Eden said softly. Tears began to fall from Eden's eyes as she watched a faint smile come across her grandmother's face. Nana Becca's hand pulled Eden closer to her. Eden knew she wanted to talk; she stood up and placed her head close to her pillow. The words were faint but she could hear them. "Follow The Path child." Eden felt her grandmother take her hand and squeeze it hard. "Nana save your strength." Eden said crying, but her grandmother continued gasping for breath. "For so long I've wanted to tell you everything about me . . . and you, but your father didn't want you involved." It was so hard for her grandmother to breathe, yet she had to tell Eden as much as she could in the few moments she had left. "Eden, you are . . ." her grandmother gasped, "a Warrior of God." Her grandmother was struggling to the end. Eden leaned over and put her ear as close to her as she could without disturbing any of her tubing. "Follow The Path and be honorable to the creed and the fellowship child . . . someone will come to you, trust his words, as he is sent from Daniel." Eden looked into her eyes and asked "Who is Daniel . . . Nana? Nana?" Eden cried, as her grandmother drew her last breath. Eden looked up at the heart monitor, she saw just a thin solid line on the screen and knew what it meant, a frightening steady sound that she would never forget. She placed her hand over her grandmother eyes and closed them, and then she collapsed on the chair and sobbed. As she heard the door open she sat back on the chair and held her nana's hand, desperately trying to compose herself.

The nurse put her hand on her grandmother's neck and then systematically, she turned off all the equipment. "She's gone now, you will have to leave." The nurse said coldly. Eden sat frozen to the chair still holding her grandmothers hand. "I want to be with my grandmother alone." She responded, tears streaming down her face. "I will leave when I'm ready." Eden replied. As the nurse opened the door, Eden added, "Kindly send my parents in." Eden had lost the person she had always been closest to, her grandmother had been the foundation of the family and now she was gone. Adding insult to injury, her grandmother had been preparing for Eden's eighteenth surprise birthday party, but everyone got a terrible surprise. Tomorrow instead of celebrating her birthday she would be mourning this tremendous loss in her life. Father Clemmons and her parents came into the room and recited the twenty third Psalm together, as they stood holding hands.

Joshua waited in the lobby of the hospital until Eden and her family returned. There he gave them his condolences. Uncle Eli drove Joshua back to the movie theater where his bike was, gratefully expressing his thanks at Joshua's being there with them and watching Samuel and Caleb. Joshua rode as fast as he could back to the clearing to see Daniel, who was waiting for him in human form. Daniel's concern was visible. "We don't have much time now Joshua." Daniel told him. "Did Eden mention anything to you?" he asked Joshua. "No sir, nothing." Joshua replied. "My abilities will not allow me to speak with Rebecca until she has fully transitioned." Daniel said, thinking as he talked, his body glowing under the moonlight. "She must be told, the sooner the better." Daniel told Joshua. "What if she doesn't believe me sir?" Joshua asked. "We will pray that she does, in the end we can only help in her protection . . . Eden is her own salvation." Daniel assured him. "Sir I would like to stay in human form tonight and guard The Evanharth residence, may I have your permission?" Joshua asked. "Permission granted." Daniel answered as his body began turning back to spirit essence.

"Sir, how do we know Dante will make a move against Eden?" Joshua was wishful thinking. "He has already done so and was unsuccessful, he is with The Dominion, and Dante will use Eden to conceive a son with powers to use against The Highest Realm and The Path here on earth." Daniel's voice was far off and distant now, and Joshua was alone in the clearing.

And so it was that Joshua rode back to Eden's house, and stood vigil outside of her house. He could hear voices inside, but as the pre dawn hours arrived, the voices quieted. He needed to be close to her for two reasons. One, he knew that he loved her, as purely as possible, and as completely as possible. The second reason was that he was worried about what Daniel had said. In as much, as he wanted to knock on the door he knew he couldn't do it now. It would have to wait till morning. Having just been through the trauma of loss, Joshua knew Eden needed time to absorb the reality of that loss. At least in the morning, he felt he would have a better chance of telling her what his purpose was and who she was and why she was being hunted.

He had so looked forward to sitting down with Eden's grandmother and telling her who he was. More than that he needed to tell Eden who he was. Now with the death of her grandmother, he knew it would be harder. Looking up at Eden's bedroom window, he saw her turn off the light . . . it was three in the morning. Joshua walked around the house and into the garden out back. Everything was quiet as it should be, and he felt comfort being around all the flowers. He put his backpack down and sitting down on the grass he leaned against the bottom structure of the porch. Closing his eyes he rested a while, but sleep was not an option.

As he sat there he constructed in his mind how he would approach his next conversation with Eden. He knew he would have to hard line it, as Daniel had said she needed to be told. It was a direct command, but Joshua agreed with it. Too much time had already been wasted. Joshua never would have imagined that the most beautiful girl, the smartest and the most elusive would be the next Warrior of God. What surprised him most was in the years that he had been mortal, he had never met anyone like her before . . . not even remotely. Then again, his school had been in a whole different area town. There weren't any other girls like Eden on the planet, never mind in Grayson Falls.

In these early morning hours he thought of his own family and how they were. Maybe when all this was over, and he finally became a full fledged angel, he would have the opportunity to see them. Of course it would have to be one sided, he didn't think Daniel would let him appear before them. That was only possible for some humans, who had special psychic abilities. If you did that to a normal human, it could give them a heart attack. Joshua already knew his mother would faint, and his dad would think he had drunk too many beers. His little sister though, she was a possibility. However, unless he took care of the Eden situation, he was going to stay in limbo. He was a floater right now . . . which meant he was pretty much homeless. It was only through Daniel's mercy that he had this chance. He couldn't mess it up, no matter what, Eden needed to be told and she needed to be protected.

Leaning his head back, he looked up at the stars. The night was so clear he could see many of them. He knew it was immature and foolish, but he made a wish. If he could have one, just one . . . alright it was a big one. If there was some way The Highest Realm could bring him back as a mortal, just so he could be with Eden. That's what he wanted more than anything. He knew it was a lot to ask. It was much more than he deserved.

Joshua sat at Barney's Coffee Emporium having his caramel frapachino with whip cream. He was waiting for a respectable time to ride back to Eden's house. It was seven thirty in the morning. He had stayed in her backyard till around six, and then rode to Barney's for coffee. He needed it. Considering the fact that he knew all the Evanharths were up, his plan was to ride back around ten. Barney's was busy even though school was out, he wasn't surprised when the twins, Nia and Leah walked in, they came over to him and sat down. "Hey Josh." Said Leah. "Hi guy's." He replied, taking a sip from his drink. "I guess you know what happened, right?" asked Nia. "Yeah, I was there . . . not in the room, but I was in the hospital with her last night." Joshua responded quietly. "We heard through the grapevine, that she's definitely the next Warrior." Nia said, with ample enthusiasm, which irritated Joshua. He nodded his response. "When are you going to tell her?" asked Leah whispering. "Soon, today . . . actually in a couple of hours." Joshua replied, with slight annoyance. "Really girls, this isn't the place to talk about this." He said standing up and throwing his backpack over his shoulder. "But hey, I'll stay in touch . . . I'm sure I'm gonna need you guy's at some point." He smiled at them, and grabbing his drink he left. Nia and Leah looked at each other. They both knew this had gotten way too personal for Joshua.

When he arrived at Eden's house, it was clear to Joshua by all the flower arrangements, that Rebecca was a well loved part of community. The front door was open and people were milling all around. He spotted Aunt Rowena and asked her where Eden was. "She's probably in the kitchen helping her mom." She answered carrying a tray of pastry into the family room. Pictures of Rebecca Evanharth were all over the front room and and a large collage stood on an easel in the hallway. As Joshua approached the kitchen, the door swung open and it was Eden. She had an apron on and was drying her hands with a towel. It was obvious she hadn't slept all night, but she looked beautiful anyway. "Hi." She said smiling faintly. "I thought I'd stop by to see how you're doing." He told her. "Well, we've all been really busy with funeral arrangements and cooking, my grandmother was very active in the church community." She continued. "She was a very special person . . . a lot of friends . . . you know?" trailing off, she got lost in her thoughts. Joshua knew he had to hard line it. "Eden I've got to talk to you." He said as he followed her outside. Eden took in a deep breath of fresh air and rubbed the back of her neck with her hand, trying to message a muscle spasm. Joshua fought hard not to reach over and message it for her. "What do you need to talk to me about?" she asked looking at him. "About you." He answered. "Look, this is a really bad time for me Joshua . . . I really can't get into all this with you." Eden replied her eyes filling up with tears. Joshua didn't think twice, he just took her in his arms.

Eden could feel his heart beating as she rested her head on his chest. Slowly she pulled away from him, and wiped her tears with the dish towel. "Sorry, I didn't get much sleep last night." Her tone was apologetic. "I have to go . . ." she told him, turning towards the front door. He cut her off. "Eden, this is for your own protection!" He pleaded. "I just need five minutes . . . please?" His voice was just short of demanding, but now he had her attention. "What do you need to tell me?" she asked, her eyes looking deeply into his. "Did your grandmother ever mention anything to you about The Path?" he asked her quietly. Eden was pensive, thinking about last night. "Yes, she did what about it?" Then before he could reply, she added. "Joshua I really can't do this right now, you have to understand." Suddenly, they heard Eden's mother calling her from inside the house. "Look I have to go; we can talk after the funeral ok? I promise you . . . I do want to hear all about this, I just can't right now." She insisted. As she turned to go inside Joshua grabbed her arm.

"No!" He whispered, then letting go of her, he added, "It will be too late." He wouldn't let this pass. Walking down to the front lawn, she knew she had to listen to him. "Tell me what you have to tell me." Eden asked him, her tone was calm, patient. "You are The Chosen One, a Warrior of God and your life is in danger." He was glad he finally had said it, but even to him, it sounded ridiculous. Eden looked at him intently, and then asked "Who has sent you to me?" "Daniel has sent me." Joshua replied. Eden looked down at the lawn and tried to concentrate on her grandmother's last words. "Alright, I can prove it to you . . . truly I can, I can take you to Daniel, but it has to be soon." Joshua said interrupting her thoughts. "Just think back to the day you saved that little girl, Eden remember?" He asked, putting his hands on her shoulders.

Looking into her eyes, he tried to get her to focus. "I know none of this makes any sense unless, you put everything together. "Don't you remember how you saved that little girl?" he continued. "You have special gifts that most humans don't have." Joshua explained. "Eden search inside of you, seek the truth." He went on. "Eden you have come to mean so much to me . . . I have been watching you and studying you for months . . ." Eden cut him off, visibly shocked. "You have been watching me?!" her voice elevated. "I know that sounds sick, but it's not for the reasons you may think, I was sent here to find you and help you against The Dominion . . . and mostly to protect you from Dante." He said and kissed her on the forehead.

"Eden, I know this all sounds insane, but your grandmother was a major supporter for the fellowship of The Path." He continued. "Ok, ok . . ." Eden cut him off. "I'll meet you outside the Library at six thirty tonight." Eden relented, walking back toward the house. "Eden?" he called out to her, she turned and looked at him. "Please have someone drive you there." His voice sounded concerned. She nodded and waved to him from the doorway. "Eden!" Joshua called back again, and running up the stairs he handed her a pink envelope. "I know this is probably inappropriate, but I bought it anyway." He told her. Eden took the envelope and looked up at him. "Thank you Joshua." She replied and kissed him on the cheek.

As he walked away, he knew that she would show up and then he would take her straight to Daniel or bring Daniel to her. Joshua truly feared for her safety and he now realized how much he loved her. She had become everything he was about. He was so caught up in Eden, that thoughts of himself had become almost meaningless. Where he ended up seemed to matter less then Eden's safety and future. Joshua didn't realize it but that was exactly how Daniel expected him to feel. Eden walked into the kitchen and saw her mom pulling a tray of mini sandwiches out of the refrigerator. "Mom I need to take a moment to myself, is it alright if I do?" Eden asked feeling guilty as her mom and Aunt Rowena had been working so hard to get all the food ready. "Sure, go ahead honey, I've got it under control." Her mom replied, putting the tray down on the table. Eden made her way up to her room, maneuvering herself through the increasing crowd of visitors, all expressing their sympathy to her as she passed them.

In her room she was finally able to open the envelope. He had remembered it was her birthday. The cover of the card had an angel on it with white wings and long blond hair. The inside read; Happy Birthday to an angel of a girl. It was printed in pink script, but Joshua had written something below it in his own hand. She was very familiar with the quote. "Love is patient; Love is kind; Love is not envious or boastful or arrogant or rude. It does not insist on its own way; it is not irritable or resentful. It does not rejoice in wrong doing, but rejoices in truth. It bears all things, believes all things, hopes all things, and endures all things. Love never ends." It was signed simply, Joshua.

"Hatred does not cease by hatred; hatred ceases only by love. This is the eternal law."

The Dhammapada

Dimensions
Chapter Three

Dante had no respect for anyone who could be easily manipulated. However, he thrived on the art of manipulation, he quite simply was a master of it. A perfect example was how well he drew Sienna into the life she was now living. Girls like Sienna were plentiful. Runaways, abused, mistreated and rebellious. Dante got them all to feed his and his men's sexual appetite. Dante controlled the drug and prostitution ring on the entire east coast. He could get whatever anyone wanted . . . and he made you want them, heroin, crystal meth, smack, cocaine, uppers, downers and of course marijuana was a given. He had all the controlled substance drugs that doctors try and keep tight on prescriptions. He would joke about it and say they were uncontrolled substance drugs. Sienna fell into this category of girls. Who were made to truly believe they needed Dante, until they realized too late that he was hell on earth. Worse than that was the fact that these young women came willingly to him, by way of his drones.

The mansion was noted for its extravagant parties among the wealthy and promiscuous of Claremont. The word would go out to the drug runners and the drug runners would drop hints to their more attractive users. Which is how Sienna made her way to the compound, she walked through the front door of her own free will. Before the evening was over, she had been captivated by Dante's ability to make her feel wanted, and beautiful. She would keep coming back for more until one day she never left. Now Dante kept her alive for his sexual appetite, which was extensive. It was clear to Dante that Sienna wouldn't be around much longer; she was out lasting her usefulness. He would soon have a replacement, though it would not be Eden. His soldiers would find someone who would easily take Sienna's place. The promise of drugs, champagne and an opulent lifestyle, pulled young girls in to the trap as easy as bees to honey.

However, Eden was in a different category entirely. Eden was going to carry his son and for those nine months, special care would be given to her, so that his future would be well developed and healthy. The child would drink his mother's milk for one year and then be taken away to be raised as Dante had been. Eden would be used for a relatively short time before she would be put to death. Nine months to carry Dante's son and one year of nursing. Death was the separation of choice. It was quick, and easy, cutting the ties of mother and child without any complications. Dante now pulled himself off of Sienna and filling a syringe he injected the lethal dose into the vein in her arm. Soon she would be completely unconscious, maybe dead. Who knew? Who cared? Not Dante. Dante dressed and left the room locking Sienna inside.

Two hours away from Hadleyville, was the town of Claremont, well known for its hills that rose high above the city and the enormous mansions that were built before the turn of the century which were surrounded by large amounts of acreage. These homes were never for sale. They were passed down to relatives and stayed within the namesake of the family. Dante had inherited the home from the man who raised him Dominic Marchette, who was still the head of The Dominion in the United States. The Dominion began and was formed in Europe in the fifteen hundreds. Dante was in the direct line to be the new head of The Dominion in America, which was thriving in the drug culture. Drugs were the prominent trade for The Dominion, which had all of the market share, except in Russia, which had been hard to penetrate. Eventually however, strong associations would be made, opening the way for The Dominion, but it was still a challenge to be met. Although Dante had other siblings, they had their own territories, in Asia and Europe, all the way up to the Russian border. Dominic favored him, perhaps it was because he had paid such a high price for him, or maybe because of whom his biological parents were he was favored.

The organization drew its strength and money from drug trafficking, as well as prostitution. The Dominion had enormous wealth and power throughout Europe as well. All members were expected to contribute a monthly stipend; the amount was determined by your station within the organization. Once you were accepted in, there was no leaving it. There were those who had tried and the consequences were horrific. The Dominion was the purest definition of evil there was and torture was their specialty.

Any mercy shown by any member meant that you were weak and could no longer be trusted. It was an indication that you no longer accepted Satan as the true and rightful ruler of the universe. The Dominion's main goal was to take down the spiritual followers of The Path. Both organizations existed on the same spiritual and mortal plains. One faithful to Satan, the other faithful to God. The battle over good and evil raged on a daily basis. Satan ravaging souls and

The Path trying to save the ravaged souls. Which is, what helped create The Council. Council members were unique in one way. They were immortal, having traded their souls after death for eternal life.

The Council kept both the Path members and the Dominion from completely destroying the earth. They did this by fear of expulsion from the earth. The Council believed that no mortal could be completely all good or all bad one hundred percent of the time. They made the call as to how far was too far, as good mortals do bad things sometimes as well, depending on the situation facing them at the time. The Council kept the balance. If you did not accept their recommendation they could take your soul while you were still living. That was not only a terribly painful process, but you had no chance of getting back. Your soul would be cast off into oblivion.

They were warriors of the middle dimension and they were also void of deep emotion or caring. They were humans which had died but offered their soul for life everlasting on earth. They simply no longer felt emotions like a human and did not physically age like a human because they were no longer mortal. To help them make the transition, all memories were erased by removing their souls, and therefore all their judgments were unemotional and analytical. The Path followed the light of God, The Dominion the underworld, and The Council stayed neutral to the best of their ability. Because it was often necessary to have an intermediary, The Council charged a high fee to both sides of the dimensions. It was hard to be in a constant battle were one side predominated . . . The Dominion was more likely to go over the edge and cause all out wars between both spiritual entities. The Council also had more soldiers then both groups put together. Their strength lied in the fact that

The Council had the best negotiators of all three dimensions because of their objectivity and unbiased sense of reason.

In the case of Sienna, Rebecca and Daniel had fought on her behalf to save her from Dante while she was still a mortal. Lead Council negotiator Talus Rand brought the matter to the intervention tribunal and they rejected it, based on Sienna's nature to rebel against authority. However, The Path would have the first attempt for her eternal salvation after her mortal death. It had not been an easy negotiation for Talus. He had rebuked the recommendation the first time, stating that Sienna had consciously made her own poor choices. Daniel and Rebecca were unrelenting, stressing that being Dante's slave, she had already been living in hell. Eventually Talus reconsidered and suggested that the tribunal revisit their decision. Talus could be very hardnosed, as he did not necessarily favor one side over the other. His objective was to be fair. It is what The Highest Realm paid him to be. Yet he had a great amount of professional respect for Daniel, which is why he changed his original view.

Like her mother before her, Rebecca had gifts and skills that she excelled in. She was passionate and fearless in exorcisms. This was her area of expertise and she was unwavering in her fight against evil. Sometimes exhausting herself as one exorcism could take days. Having brought The Path to America from London, she was a main supporter. The Path also had anonymous supporters who helped fund the organization. It was not unusual for Sunday mass to be occurring, as in any other Christian Church. While deep below the basement of The Hadleyville Fellowship Church, Rebecca would be in the midst of a full scale exorcism. Those who chose The Path had a special calling and sought it out through different means. Some wanted only to be financial supporters, fearing they could not commit to the intensity of The Path and its creed. However no one's wealth could compare with that of The Dominion.

The Council members were made up of unsung heroes dating back to the fifteen hundreds, who had died in battle. As time passed the rules of acceptance broadened. Then women were added to be Council members based on their mental and physical capabilities and how they died their mortal death. Murdered victims who had led worthy and respectable lives on earth were generally considered first. Also men and women who had not left children behind were chosen first due to the uncomplicated nature of their background. Simply put, it was much easier to erase their memories, than those who had offspring. The agreement was simple, no memory of the past, and eternal life on earth with few exceptions based primarily on your performance, and your soul was your collateral. It was not for everyone; however those who accepted the terms rarely regretted their choice.

Those who had longevity in The Council were highly revered as they possessed strength of character that would not bend under the stress of The Dominion and The Path who battled constantly for mortal souls. For this reason Leaders of The Council like Talus Rand had supernatural abilities to use at their discretion. He was considered to be an asset as he had been a member for over a hundred and fifty mortal years. He was disciplined, objective and highly skilled in negotiations although he could be easily angered if members of The Path or The Dominion became too emotional and failed to listen to his sound judgment. In every way he kept his private life extremely private and unemotional. There was a time in his early days that was not the case. However, he had outgrown his immaturity and was now beyond reproach.

On the east coast he was able to keep battles between the two dimensions to a minimum, which was appreciated by The Highest Realm, whose lead angel warrior in the spirit world was Daniel. Daniel of course fought on the side of The Path along side Rebecca who was his earthly warrior. They believed that all souls are worth saving . . . aren't they? As all mortals have freedom of choice, sometimes good mortals do bad things. Their human nature and ability to separate good from bad can be confusing. This is where The Council would reside, in the depth of collision between good versus evil.

The drugs ran through Sienna's veins like wildfire and she yelled out in pain. Suddenly a vision appeared before her. At first she believed it to be a hallucination as she had had so many. After all her brain was damaged from all the drugs Dante had filled her with. "I'm only giving you what you want." He would tell her. Abdicating himself from the responsibility. The vision came closer and she was able to see that it was Eden's grandmother. But how could that be? The vision spoke to her in sounds that she could clearly understand. "I am here to assist in your journey, child." It communicated to her. "First you must pray with me and renounce Satan." The vision came closer until it was standing next to her. "Pray with me Sienna so that your soul can be saved." Sienna looked away, her mind unable to comprehend what was happening. "I cannot be saved; he will not let you save me." Sienna replied. Again the vision spoke to her. "Sienna do you know who I am?" the vision asked. "Yes, you are my mind going mad." Sienna responded to the vision. "No, my dear . . . I am the spirit essence of Rebecca Evanharth." The vision replied. "I know you are in much pain, you are dying, you must ask God for his forgiveness." Sienna's body began to convulse and she did realize that she was dying. She looked up at the spirit and called out, "Father in Heaven please forgive me for all my sins and release me from my bondage." Her body convulsed one last time and she gasped. Closing her eyes her spirit began to leave her body, floating up, above her body which still lay on the bed. As she floated above it, she felt no pain, no fear, and no remorse. Her spirit and soul were now set free. She took Rebecca's hand and they evaporated in to the atmosphere. She was now a spirit essence of tranquility and peace. She had been saved by Rebecca Evanharth.

In the grand ballroom downstairs Dante sat alone, planning his strategy for the capture of Eden. He looked up at the ceiling. "Oh go ahead and take her, she has out stayed her welcome anyway." I guess that was the lethal dose he thought to himself. Dante also felt no pain, no fear and definitely no remorse. He did not have the empathy to feel or view Sienna's death as his doing. To Dante she was just a stupid girl who found a way to escape what she thought was a horrible existence. If she wanted to really know what horrible was, he had taught her a lesson . . . the cost was her mortal life. He was simply doing what came naturally to him. Was it natural or was Dante trained and brainwashed to be this way? His adopted father was the definition of cruelty and had brought up all three of his sons to follow in his footsteps. In order to survive Dante would need to do as his father expected or pay the consequences himself. Often spending whole days being tortured for his inability to follow direction.

As a small child he was often whipped and beaten, starved and tortured. However, eventually he would rise above the other two sons to have a quick sharp mind, which easily zeroed in on his prey. His motivation was power and something else . . . a deep rooted anger from having been abandoned. Dante would externalize his pain and abuse others, using his charismatic and hypnotic strengths to lure the most unassuming and non threatening victims. Here was his greatest strength; his undeniable ability to make you like him, until he owned you, then it was too late.

If there was one thing that would prove Dante worthy of control of the entire United States, it was his ability to capture the next Warrior of God, Eden Evanharth. He knew that this quintessential move would elevate him above his adopted father Dominic Marchette.

There was another reason for Dante's quest to capture Eden, besides impregnating her. Payback to his past. Eden's blood line went back to his own mother's blood line. The mother who had abandoned him. Revenge is sweet . . . sweeter still for the forces of evil. He could capture Eden and not hurt a hair on her head until she turned eighteen. Whether or not she accepted her position, as a Warrior of God, was irrelevant to Dante. It was more or less the same. True it would certainly be more of a battle of wits and strength which was always fun, for competition, but he would still enjoy the sheer pleasure of capturing an Evanharth who he could bear a son with. Not just any Evanharth, but an eighteen year old virgin.

Being the son of parents who had beauty, strength and one who was immortal, Dante was one hundred years old and looked less than half his age. He attributed this to the foods he ate and staying out of the sun as much as possible, which was fine for he was nocturnal by nature. His skin was pale and smooth, his body thin by most male standards, but muscular. His hair jet black, because he colored it that way . . . his eyes a beautiful intense intimidating violet. To see him was shocking and then alluring and then . . . devastating. He drew you in with a faint smile and a hypnotic quality. Few knew his game until he had already won. He ran his men much in the same way Dominic did, by fear and intimidation. Most regretted their membership, but had seen the effects of trying to escape. Some like Peris, his captain actually enjoyed his work and was handsomely rewarded, with both money and women. However it meant total immersion into The Dominion and alienation from prior family and friends. Not that Dante trusted Peris, he trusted no one and made a point of spying on all his men. Most having lost their lives at one point or another. But Dante always had new recruits; money did amazing things . . . humans often sold their souls for it. But drugs had always been Dante's avenue of choice.

Though he never took drugs of any kind, or alcohol, it gave him even more manipulative tactics and had made him and his family very wealthy. If Dante had anything to complain about was that after being a mortal for one hundred years, he was bored. He had longing, and that bothered him. For being who he was, it was not something he should feel. Ambition at any cost, power and control was his Mantra . . . but longing was an emotion which brought about an uncomfortable notion. The notion that he was slightly human. Yes he was born mortal, but he had spent years, fighting the mortal side of his being, after all, his father was immortal and that was what he strived towards. Internally his mortal side fought and raged against his will to be immortal, on a daily basis.

1892

Mortamion Delmont had been living high up in the castle above the village of San Michelene, in northern France. Waiting, waiting for five years for his beloved. Now the days were finally getting closer. He and his brother by Council law had taken over the castle from The Marchette family. The castle had a reputation of evil and it had been decided that The Marchette's had brought too much trouble and sadness to the small French village. Mortamion was happy to go there as he knew one day his love would come back to him. Mortamion had to wait until Lillianna turned eighteen so she would be free from her debt of time. The year was 1892, the first of May, he counted the days.

Thirty to be exact. With Talus and a fleet of his soldiers Mortamion, who was mortal with protective powers would soon be joined with his true love. His soul had been reborn in the body of a six year old boy, eighteen years ago. He was now twenty four and Lillianna would soon be eighteen . . . but their souls were two hundred years old. A hard concept for a mere mortal to grasp. Certainly a hard concept for his adopted brother Talus to grasp. Talus thought the idea of being mortal undeserving of his respect from the beginning.

His men and Talus followed his command, even though they were still Council members and Mortamion was in transition. He would hold his command and authority until Lillianna was free. Mortamion knew the transition would be harder for Lillianna, for her soul had been placed in the womb of a mortal. Whereas his soul had been placed in a child who had died and was then revived. He could continue to know and see his parents. Lillianna would not have the same ability. Her parents would never understand that all these years, she had been someone else. They would not understand that her soul needed and longed to be with Mortamion, whom she had lived with as a Council member for two hundred years previously.

George and Carlotta, her mortal parents would never approve of her marrying a man who they did not know and that would take her far away from them. Mortal women did not have the same freedom or advantages as men, who could come and go as they pleased. It had been decided by The Council, that Lillianna would have to vanish. As hurtful and insensitive as it was, the alternative seemed too complex and potentially harmful to all parties concerned, to do it another way.

Not to mention that both she and Mortamion were desperate to see each other and had lived together for so many years. Their threshold for courtship would not withstand the burden of time necessary in a mortal family. They had already been apart from each other for almost eighteen years . . . another week, another day, another hour, another minute was inconceivable.

It was a delicate situation and The Council did not think George and Carlotta Evanharth would be able to understand. So, high above the small dairy farm Mortamion waited, for The Council to give him leave to fetch his soul mate. For five years Mortamion waited, until he could come down the mountain and take Lillianna back to his world.

Lillianna Evanharth was born knowing who she was. Her soul had lived hundreds of years before. As a child she understood that she belonged with a man she had desired for many years. The older she became, she realized that her time was her penance for wanting to be mortal. The Council had given her protective powers while she paid that penance. She was never to fall ill to childhood diseases or get ill with fevers as her two sisters. She was the picture of health and well being. The friars at the mission that stood not far from the dairy farm, believed her to be blessed and indeed she was. She had been blessed by the middle dimension to be mortal again.

Having lived and worked for The Council, she had given up her soul and wanting it back meant paying a price. A price of time and sacrifice. She knew him as Jon Pierre Tanrey. His new name would not be revealed to her until her penance was almost finished. He would know her as Sophia Bassett, until The Council revealed her new name of Lillianna Evanharth. Their bodies would be different, but their personalities the same, with the added depth of their souls, now attached they were true mortals. Feelings, emotions, love, hate, need, want, hunger, thirst, sickness, pain, both physical and emotional and the ability to procreate was their eternal goal . . . and to share it all with each other. So, as a dairy farmer's daughter she waited and grew into womanhood, knowing that one day he would come for her. The only problem was that he knew it, and she knew it and The Council knew it . . . but George and Carlotta Evanharth well that was a different story entirely. To George and Carlotta and her two sisters Elise and Margot, she was Lillianna Evanharth, their daughter and sister.

Lillianna Evanharth was born to George and Carlotta Evanharth on May 31st, 1874. She was a beautiful baby, with large blue eyes and delicate blond hair. Lillianna was the first of three daughters born to the dairy farmers, in a secluded village named San Michelene in northern France. George had been on vacation from London when he met Carlotta and fell madly in love with her at a summer wine festival. He proposed within the week. Carlotta's parents allowed her to accept as long as she stayed on in their home on the dairy farm, with her new husband, as she was only sixteen and he twenty six. George agreed as the sultry beauty with the porcelain skin and hour glass shape had captured his heart. He married Carlotta and then left for London to finish out his affairs.

During his time away Carlotta discovered she was pregnant and fell ill from his absence, hearing the news he rushed back to San Michelene and to her. George left his job in London as a printer and began to learn how to run a dairy farm, eventually inheriting it from Carlotta's parents. Two years after the birth of Lillianna, Elise was born, named after Mrs. Stevens, the wife of Mr. Stevens who owned the printing business in London, where George had become a partner. Having risen from a house servant, George found favor with The Stevens family when he protected the family during a robbery. Mr. Stevens came home to find that George had saved the lives of his wife and daughter against three thieves who had broken into the home. Mrs. Stevens insisted, that Mr. Stevens teach George the printing business, which would lead to his partnership.

At twenty six he had the income that afforded his travel to France and to his destiny, Carlotta. A year later, Margot was born, who was appropriately named after Carlotta's maternal grandmother. Lillianna was understood to take after George's side of the family, having the bright blue eyes, creamy complexion and golden curly hair. Elise and Margot were the images of their mother, tall and voluptuous, and dark haired. Lillianna was shorter and more gamine like, then her younger sisters. To look at her there was such purity and light that she carried around her and a stillness of complete tranquility. These early years were happy ones. The farm was doing well and Carlotta and the girls helped their father with the farming chores. The years passed and George never went back to England to visit. As busy as he was, he was also in his own paradise content to be surrounded by his beautiful ladies. There was always something to do, as Carlotta was the best baker in the province and helped maintain the farm with her proceeds from baking. There was always a christening of a new baby, birthdays and anniversaries to celebrate, and of course the farm with orders to be filled for all these occasions. Such was their life.

The village of San Michelene was nestled in a valley surrounded by rolling hills. High above those hills stood a castle. Hundreds of years old with a reputation that kept people away. The inhabitants were known not to want visitors and were rarely seen. The Marchette family lived there and it had been rumored that they ate small children. It was an old wives tale that the small village still believed in. So, all children under the age of seven were kept under careful watch. The castle had been in the Marchette family since it was built in the sixteen hundreds. It was surrounding by forty acres of land, and encircled by high iron fences that were too tall to climb. The reason for the old tale was due to something that had happened in the early seventeen hundreds. A child had gone missing and the Marchette family was suspected by the local authorities to have something to do with it. Nothing was ever proven. When the officers went to investigate the Marchettes, they found nothing to indicate that the Marchette family had any connection in the child's disappearance.

There was no sign of any child or woman for that matter. The officers left the castle without incident. The child, a little girl was never found. Keeping with the tradition of the village, the girls were never far from their mother's sight. Carlotta had been raised with this fear and George took it quite seriously. George adored his family. He had grown up orphaned from the age of five. So having his four beautiful women round him was a blessing he not only craved but appreciated. Until he had met Carlotta, his only connection to family had been the Stevens. They had welcomed him, into their lives and he wrote to them weekly telling them about his new life as a father, and a dairy farmer. However, it didn't stop him from thinking about his parents. Although he was only five when his father died, he had memories of his young life with them.

He remembered his mother Nora Kincaid, as a young vibrant woman with pale skin, blue eyes and curly blond hair. His memories though muddled in some respects, were quite clear in other ways. He could still remember her smell, like fresh clean laundry and English lavender. The sound of her voice and her heart beating as he laid his head on her chest. The wonderful comfort of being held and rocked in his mother's arms took him back to his short lived childhood.

His memories of John Evanharth, his father, were mostly of the sadness and loneliness he felt watching his father mourn his mother who had died of pneumonia.

He was told many times by the nuns in the orphanage, his father died of drink, but George believed it was from a broken heart. The nuns had not been there to see the total devastation in his father's eyes, when he lost Nora. George had, and he remembered all of it. Being only four years old he did not know how to show support to his father. He would go up to his father while he sat in Nora's rocker, and sitting at his feet, George would rest his head against his father's legs. His father would sometimes pat his head, or run his fingers through George's hair. His son had the same golden curls that Nora had and sometimes George's father would cry uncontrollably. George could see so much of his mother in Lillianna. It was obvious that she resembled him, but to George she was the spitting image of his mother. Even the way she ran her fingers through his hair when she sat on his lap . . . felt strangely familiar. Her smile was his mother's smile. When he looked at all three of his daughter's they brought him the greatest joy, but none more than Lillianna.

As years passed on the dairy farm, the three sisters grew into young women, sought after by many suitors. But, Carlotta and George were always in clear sight. They also wanted to keep the girls close to them as long as they could. When Carlotta's mother died, Lillianna was seventeen, Elise fifteen and Margot fourteen. A year later Carlotta's father passed away, he no longer wished to live on without her mother. Though they were busy, and did have company, many of Carlotta's family members lived in other parts of France, visiting only for the holidays. Their most frequent visitors were the friar's who lived in the mission above the meadow. George supplied them monthly provisions, which he would collect on his trips into the city. The friars would offer George a small stipend for his services but he never accepted. Once a month Carlotta would cook a pheasant or a turkey and take it up to the mission as a token for their blessings.

Other than that, life for George and Carlotta revolved around their three daughters and the simple life of dairy farming. What they had not prepared for was that when children grow up, they leave and make separate lives for themselves. For George and Carlotta this transition would not only happen abruptly, but quite disturbingly and painfully.

The patterns of clouds painted images across the sky. Lillianna was mesmerized by them as she lay on the blanket of green grass. Her blue eyes creating characters in the blue and white above her. Tomorrow her sister Elise would be married, Lillianna knew she would not follow the footsteps of her sister. Margot would be next to marry as she was already betrothed. Lillianna was all too aware of her future, already knowing her destiny, she knew who she would be, before she was born. Through the bequest of The Council, seeking back her soul, her soul was placed eighteen years ago in her mother's womb. Now it was time to face her future. Her blond hair blew gently in the wind, the soft cotton flounce of her skirt rising to her knees as she stood. Her only thoughts now were of the pain she could not erase from her mortal family. Lillianna was part of two worlds. One in which she had lived for two hundred years and one that she had lived eighteen years. She looked into the distance and saw his presence coming towards her. She longed to feel him again.

He walked towards her, the tall grass parting in the soft breeze before him. His black hair pulled back, his long coat blowing off his shoulders from the speed from which he walked. The thunder of his steps resounding below the earth, as he neared his beloved. Barefooted she ran to him, her long blond hair billowing behind her. As they connected she fell into his arms, and he lifted her up bringing her lips to his. His kiss ignited the passion she had missed all these years. She wanted to become one with him again, as in the past. She caressed his face with her small hands and stared into his green eyes which captivated her senses. He was by any definition striking, his features chiseled and strong, were handsomely rugged and the circumstance of good breading surrounded him.

He carried her back to his world, to his time, where she needed to be, where she craved to be. "Mortamion . . ." she whispered, kissing his lips as he held her in his arms. At the edge of the meadow, he placed her on his horse and then mounted. His arms folded around her as he held the reins. Slowly they made their way through the thickness of the forest and began the long climb to the top of the mountain.

Suddenly, a large of gust of wind blew across the small valley. George who was milking looked out at the sky, as the milk can tipped over spilling on the floor of the barn and on to his boots. Carlotta stopped to pick up the pieces of the flower pot that had shattered into the sink as she was washing dishes. Closing the window she too looked at up at the sky. Soon it would be time for dinner. Carlotta removed her apron and laid it on the back of a kitchen chair. Walking onto the porch she pulled the long rope hard, ringing the bell attached to it several times. She looked out toward the meadow. The wind had taken her newly washed cloths off the line and it was scattered across the grass. Margot was recovering them. George walked towards Carlotta smiling, as he entered the house. "The wind took all the extra milk for your custard." He said. Carlotta kissed him on the cheek.

"I think I still have enough left from this morning." Carlotta replied, still standing by the bell she was transfixed by the wind and the meadow. Elise was in her room packing for her wedding tomorrow. Margot was walking towards Carlotta, her arms filled with laundry that had been blown off the line and been scattered in the field. Carlotta rang the bell again. The sun was beginning to set. Now the wind had died down and there was a strange stillness in the air. Carlotta called out to Margot, "have you seen your sister?" Margot reaching the porch shook her head. "No, isn't she helping Elise?" she asked. George was at the sink washing his hands. As he dried them he walked over to his wife, who was still on the porch starring out at the meadow. He kissed the side of her head. "Don't worry she'll be along." He said. Carlotta knew better, her instinct was that of a mother. Where could she be? After all it was her birthday, thought George.

Tried and true since the beginning of time, mothers can sense things about their children. Carlotta was no different and she followed her instincts as they always led her to the truth. She knew that she would never see Lillianna again. She felt it inside herself. George realized his wife's concern, because he shared it. It was a farm rule, when the bell was rung, it meant you needed to come back to the house. His daughter's had grown up with this rule and had always followed it. It was uncharacteristic for Lillianna not to follow her upbringing. George tried to keep a level head and not panic . . . maybe she was at the mission. That was it of course, a few more minutes and she would be home.

"Who could refrain that had a heart to love and in that heart courage to make love known?"

William Shakespeare

Lillianna and Mortamion

Chapter Four

As she stood on the balcony of the castle, she could see the lanterns flickering in the blackness of night. They twinkled like stars darting back and forth in the atmosphere. He came up behind her wrapping his arms around her waist. Kissing her shoulder and then her neck, she turned her head to find his lips, kissing him deeply. "Happy birthday my love." Whispered Mortamion. She looked out once again at the small village of San Michelene. "I feel bad for them." Lillianna said sadly. Mortamion turned her body toward his, and looked deeply into her eyes. "Would you have rather stayed with them?" he asked. "No, I could not have given you up . . . ever." She replied taking his hand in hers and kissing his palm. He took Lillianna in his arms, "I want only to be with you." He told her. She clung to him kissing him, " . . . and I with you." She whispered. Lifting her up, he carried her onto the bed. Holding her in his arms he laid down beside her. She was worth everything to him, his life and his soul. Their bodies folded into each other like ocean waves cascading onto the shore, they consummated their love as mortals for the first time. Now they knew the difference, as if they were one heart, one being.

Making the choice had not been easy, having been Council members for so long, becoming mortal was risky, but now they knew the true magnitude of their love. It had all been worth it. The time and struggle and the wait. He had always cared for her . . . something not natural for Council members, but he had never felt these feelings before that consumed him. They told him he could never live without her again. She returned his love and passion with a new awakening that cemented their commitment to one another. Lillianna too had never felt this feeling of oneness or wholeness before. She enveloped him in her love, vowing eternal gratitude to The Council for granting them mortality. If life ended for them at this moment in time she knew that she had lived her true life within his arms, this was worth giving up eternity, to feel this kind of fulfillment was worth the price immortality.

Some would believe them to be selfish . . . but what two lovers who are deeply in love are not? Mortamion and Lillianna truly believed that their love would carry them through the challenges that would face them . . . and in their love all would be healed, all would be absolved. Through insurmountable odds, they would survive. In truth, they knew no other way to think or feel, for that was the enormous measure of their love for one another. Lillianna was his queen and Mortamion was her king and between them they would create their own kingdom, as mortals on earth.

The darkness seemed to close in on George and Carlotta. As night fell the countryside was ablaze with lanterns and candles, lighting the way for the hopeful discovery of a frightened and lost Lillianna. Many hours had now gone by since her disappearance. The legal authorities of San Michelene could not be contacted until morning. The hour of midnight had passed and many of the volunteers came back to the Evanharth house and gave their commitment to start a new search in the morning. Carlotta and Elise were comforted by Elise's future mother in law, while her future father in law and fiancé helped George search the nearby woods. Margot helped by keeping the soup and coffee hot and plentiful. Carlotta knew she would never see Lillianna again. Her instinct told her so. Carlotta believed that a man had taken Lillianna, a man from another world. Carlotta had not shared this with anyone else, not even George. The development of Lillianna's disappearance cast a great sadness on Elise who was to be married the next day.

It was agreed by all that the wedding would be held until Lillianna was found. George made his way around the large gathering in his kitchen to his wife. He held her in his arms. "We will find her, I promise you." He told her, his voice was hoarse from calling Lillianna's name. Carlotta could not speak, there were no words for her pain and desperation. Hopelessness filled her veins, but George still held on to the possibility that Lillianna was not just alive but that she was near. He turned to the friars and neighbors that had come from other farms, to join the search. "Please everyone if you can, come tomorrow morning and help us search." He asked, shaking the hands of the men who had helped tonight.

A new search would begin at dawn which was only six hours away. George and Carlotta would take their carriage into town and fill out an official report at the authorities' office. In the darkness George and his family walked up the hill to the mission that was decorated with wild flowers, some from his own garden, in expectation of Elise's wedding. There with the friars and many of the villagers, they prayed until the light of day. As exhausted as George was he had a plan to find Lillianna and he would carry out his plan. His plan required a trip up the mountain, to the old Marchette castle. George knew that he must go with the town's legal authorities to gain entrance, but in his heart he felt that there is where his daughter was. He couldn't logically explain why he thought so and why he felt it, perhaps it was just his instincts that were leading him there. George would never know about Carlotta's intuition, until much later on. It would prove not to have made a difference if he had known it from her lips, as he would come to the realization on his own.

They had slept in each other's arms all through the night, and well into the morning. Mortamion awoke abruptly when he heard a knock on the bedroom door. He covered Lillianna's body and grabbed his pants off the floor. He opened the door slightly. His man servant appeared before him. "What is it Louis?" he asked quietly, trying hard not to wake Lillianna. "Sir, the police are at the gate." Louis replied. Mortamion stared at Louis, gathering his thoughts. "Let them approach, only to the front door and I will meet them there." Louis turned to go but Mortamion grabbed his arm, "Louis, no matter what they tell you, do not allow them entrance into the house . . . understood?" "Yes sir, understood." Louis answered and Mortamion released his arm. Mortamion finished dressing, only buttoning his white ruffled shirt half way and putting his black jacket over it. Then he went to Lillianna and kissed her, she opened her eyes and smiled at him. "We have trouble my love." He said, pulling his boots on. "Already?" she asked sitting up. "I can't leave you . . . I won't leave you," She said desperately. "I know." Mortamion replied kissing her and left the room. The property was large and Mortamion knew it would take them awhile to get to the front door. He also knew Noah and Drummond were guarding the front of the castle outside, his two best soldiers. He made his way down the long staircase. Walking into the dining room he saw his brother Talus seated drinking his coffee. Mortamion poured himself a cup. "What trouble have you wrought now brother?" Talus asked smiling. "Nothing worth concerning yourself about." Mortamion answered and left the room coffee cup in hand. "I'm here if you need me." Talus called to him. "Thank you Tal." Mortamion replied, and then returned adding, "I might Tal, but I don't want any violence to take place." Mortamion replied. Outside, Noah and Drummond waited as Louis walked back from the gate with a band of officers and one civilian. As Mortamion opened the door two more of his soldiers approached from the perimeter of the castle. All four soldiers were armed and stood on either side of Mortamion.

Mortamion awaited the men approaching, about fifteen officers led by Louis. This was as he expected. The first to speak was a short man in his forties, with a black mustache that Mortamion found amusing as it curled into circles on the ends. "Good morning." The inspector said. Mortamion standing between his guards chose to nod his salutations. "My name is Inspector Laurent and these officers work with me." His voice was firm but not accusatory. Mortamion handed his cup of coffee to Louis, who stood behind him. "How is it that I can help you?" Mortamion inquired. "Sir, a young woman has gone missing . . ." replied Inspector Laurent and waited for Mortamion's reply. "And what's this to do with me?" Mortamion asked. The inspector cleared his throat. "We have reason to believe she is here." The inspector replied, referring to George who stood behind him and the other officers. Mortamion stared into the inspector's eyes and the inspector began to lose his concentration. "I can assure you there is no woman here, young or old." Mortamion stated in a simple yet direct way, which indicated there would be no admittance into the castle. George pushed his way through the officers, and the inspector. "We want to search your property!" George insisted.

Mortamion's guards held George back as he came within inches of Mortamion. "Do not come one more step further sir." Mortamion warned him, he knew of course this was Lillianna's father he was speaking to. "If you have nothing to hide, permit us entrance!" George demanded. "Under whose authority?" asked Mortamion his manner controlled. "I am her father!" George shouted at him. The inspector pulled George back by his jacket collar. Trying to handle the situation adding, "Mr. Marchette, I assure you, we will not take very long . . . please allow us entrance." Mortamion's thoughts were only to protect Lillianna. "I am not Marchette." He answered calmly. "My name is Mortamion Delmont and I live here with my brother." He felt George steadily watching him as he spoke.

Suddenly, Talus opened the door and came out to join Mortamion. In his hand he held a pistol. "Good morning everyone." He said quite matter of factly. George was beside himself with anguish and all hope of finding his daughter. In truth Mortamion felt badly for him. "Unless you can show me legal cause to search my home, I do believe we are done here." Mortamion said ending the conversation. The inspector looked at George and then at Mortamion. "May I ask where the Marchette's are?" he directed the question to Mortamion . . . as Talus had irritated him. "I cannot answer that, as I don't know, my brother and I purchased the home from them five years ago." Mortamion replied. "I did hear rumors that they went to America," added Talus, loading his pistol with a degree of concentration that made the inspector uncomfortable. "You do not scare me with that." George yelled at Talus. Talus looked up momentarily at George. "I am neither threatening you nor am I menacing, I am simply making my pistol ready." Talus stated looking directly into

George's eyes. "Perhaps sir, your daughter does not wish to be found." Mortamion told George. George said nothing he just stared at Mortamion.

Now he knew. He knew she was here, but how would he gain entrance? "How dare you tell me about my daughter!" George threw himself at Mortamion grabbing his neck with both his hands. Inspector Laurent tried pulling George off of Mortamion as well as his own men, but George's grasp did not release until he felt the butt of Talus' pistol against his temple. Talus cocked it and George finally let go of Mortamion's throat. Mortamion leaned against the entrance trying to catch his breath. Talus backed up slowly but his pistol was still aimed at George. Inspector Laurent asked that he stand down his weapon, but Talus refused saying, "I will not! This man attacked my brother and you are all on private property!" George pulled himself together, only after Inspector Laurent admonished him by stating, "Mr. Evanharth for God's sake pull yourself together man . . . this is no way to find your daughter!"

The inspector turned to leave and instructed his men to do the same. George held back. "Please don't hurt her, that's all I can ask of you?" he pleaded to Mortamion. Mortamion cleared his throat and answered him, still feeling the effects of George's tight grasp around his neck. "If she were here, no harm would come to her, and she would be here of her own free will . . . however she is not here." Only after the entire group of officers left the main gate, with George trailing behind them, did Talus lower his pistol, and he and Mortamion go inside, leaving the four guards outside to keep watch. "He will be back you know." Talus said quietly to Mortamion, but within seconds Mortamion was climbing the staircase, he turned at the top to look down at Talus and smiled, "thank you my brother." Talus shook his head, as Mortamion sped to the bedroom and to the waiting arms of Lillianna. "No violence . . . we'll see how long that will last." Talus replied under his breath.

Lillianna was waiting for Mortamion when he reached the top of the stairs, she ran to him. "Thank you Tanni." That was her personal name for him. She smothered him with kisses as they walked back to the bedroom. From the window, he could see Inspector Laurent and her father George walking down the mountain, their figures disappearing now and then hidden by the trees. He motioned to Lillianna to stay back, and then he walked over to her. She looked into his green eyes that she loved and said, "I know how hard that was for you."

Mortamion sat down at the round marble table not far from their bed. Tracing the design of the marble with his index finger, he said sadly, "Harder still for your father, Lillianna." She ran both hands through her hair and sighed. "He has two other daughters, who are human." She said seeking his assurance. Mortamion reached for her, guiding her onto his lap. "To him you have always been human." Mortamion replied. "Isn't this what we promised each other eighteen years ago, Tanni . . . remember?" Caressing her jaw line he smiled, "of course I do." he replied. "It is very hard to be a mortal." He replied sensing the pain her mortal family was in. Picking her up in his arms he carried her over to the large oval mirror. At the top of the mirror her name was inscribed in gold. Sophia, her name before she became mortal. The gold was wearing off in spots and the mirror itself had lost its reflective quality on the edges.

Placing her down in front of him, she looked like a little girl against his six foot frame. He wrapped his arms around her and crossing them, spoke to her through the mirror. "You do know this will not end, your father will be back," warned Mortamion. "He tried to kill me down there…he himself could have been killed." He told her, clearly concerned.

Lillianna tried to turn her body to face him, but he resisted. "No . . . don't, I want to watch your reflection . . . to take in everything this moment has to offer." These eighteen years had been so terribly long. How much they had sacrificed to finally be mortals. "Tanni, I honored The Council Tribunal, I've lived as a mortal for eighteen years, to prove that I can do it." She tried to turn again but he held her fast. "You are such an impetuous girl." He told her smiling speaking to her through the mirror, his jet black hair falling against her porcelain skin. She could feel his strength and masculinity surround her. It aroused her and she tilted her head back, into the crease of his arm. He began to softly, kiss her neck, then her bare shoulder. He could feel her breathing increase as her skin reacted to her excitement. His lips found her lips as he turned her body toward his, kissing her deeply. "Oh Tanni." She murmured her voice fueled with passion. "Let's have a baby, I want so much to feel what it's like to have a baby . . . your baby."

As he sat down on the edge of the bed, she knelt in front of him and pulled off his boots. He lifted his shirt up over his head, he was not going to deal with buttons now. Mortamion knew that she wanted a baby more than anything and having been immortal she could never conceive. Now that she had passed the test of time, she was mortal, as he was. He had given up living forever into eternity to be human and to grant her this wish. For the first time he would feel the aging process, the aches, the pains, the joys the sorrows that human's speak of and the ability to die one day. "How long have we been together?" she asked, unbuttoning his trousers. "I'm not sure . . . two hundred years, more or less." Now he was unclothed and he returned the favor. Their bodies were beautiful, young and supple. He leaned over and kissed her, "Don't you realize how much your mortal family loves you?" he asked with deep sincerity.

Mortamion was saddened by the fact that her mortal mother and father were suffering, even though George had tried to strangle him. "Sweetheart you and I are now mortal as well and we have sacrificed so much time to be together, I guess I am being selfish." Lillianna said, with a slight pout forming on her lips. "As I am, as well. I have thought of nothing else all these years except this moment with you." Mortamion told her, as he took her in his arms.

They were both silent for a moment and then Mortamion spoke. "Perhaps we can think of a way . . . to include them in our life." He said in a tone that sounded more like a question that he was trying to find the answer for. Lillianna nestled her head in his shoulder. "Yes, perhaps there is a way . . . but right now I want only to be with you my love, only you." She said lovingly. He knew that George knew she was here, with him. This would prove to be very difficult in the future . . . but to hell with it he thought, right now he had Lillianna in his arms loving him and that is all that mattered . . . after all he was only human.

Talus stood outside. Looking up at the balcony, then shaking his head he walked around the estate, surveying it, his pistol tucked in the front of his pants. Give up immortality for a woman he thought never, not him. Talus thought Mortamion was insane . . . no he knew he was insane. He may be his older brother by a couple of years, by law not flesh. The Council granted immortality to those who gave up their souls. One would be surprised at how many dead mortals there are who would give up their souls to live forever.

Talus didn't miss having a soul. Why would he? He died when he was twenty years old and hadn't aged a day in over fifty years. He was given a choice like everyone is. Some mortals are tired, sick and have this idea of The Highest Realm, so they don't hear the message. The message one hears between life and death. The Council can capture your soul, if you want to be immortal. They give you life eternal, for a price. Well to Talus it was fair. Mortamion felt quite differently now, but he knew him before, when he and Lillianna were just dating, as they say in mortal words, when they were Jon Pierre and Sophia. Talus never felt deep sadness, hunger, loneliness, guilt or the big one . . . regret. He was void of most emotions, although he could be prone to a quick temper and easily frustrated. Immortals could feel pleasures of the flesh and physical pain, but healed almost instantly. They had supreme recuperative abilities. So, did Mortamion, he had lived the same way and then something happened. Talus had been told it was past life experiences. What a waste of living he thought, all to reproduce and die. The constant state of war, between The Legions of The Path and The Dominion, got to be boring, but other than that, he liked his existence.

He saw living forever to be the priority, it didn't matter if you loved someone . . . love was not part of the equation. He couldn't grasp this need to feel any emotion on such a deep level. In truth he didn't know what feeling felt like. In his world there was no good, no bad, and best of all no guilt. That by his definition was the disease of all the worlds. Talus worked for the supplier of good and bad, given the time of day, or what part of the universe you were in. Everyone knows that all mortals are good and bad, depending on the circumstances. The job of The Council was to intervene when necessary.

Eighteen years ago he and Mortamion had a conversation, about giving up immortality. Talus asked Mortamion one question. "Why?" In one sentence Mortamion answered him. "I want to know what it feels like to live again." Explained Mortamion. "Brother, you are living." Talus replied. Mortamion paused, and then replied. "There is a difference between living and existing." Well, if there was Talus couldn't fathom it and didn't want to. His life everlasting was contingent on his commitment to The Council. Other than that he was a free agent to do as he pleased and never allowed any complications like women to interfere. Now Mortamion had to deal with all the things and issues that mortals have to deal with like heartbreak and loss.

Soon Talus would be leaving the estate. He had spent enough years with Mortamion to handle himself in battles and negotiations. Now that Mortamion was retired from The Council, anything could harm him, including that woman up there, her beauty alone would cause trouble to any man, mortal or immortal, Talus thought to himself. He knew it was her idea, this change from immortality to human. She had somehow convinced Mortamion to take back his soul. Yesterday that request had been granted. They had both lived as mortals for eighteen years. The Council demanded it. The longer you were immortal, the longer your sentence.

The Council needed to be sure, that they were sure. Both Mortamion and Lillianna knew it would change the way they lived, they just didn't know how much. The Council had let them keep their powers and protective healing abilities while they were in mortal form, paying their penance of time, but now those powers were gone, now they could feel all the emotions of a human, and that's why Mortamion and Lillianna were locked in each other's arms right now. Talus arrived back at the front gate.

He took his time in the soft spring air. Walking toward the front door he glanced up at the balcony window which led to Lillianna's bedroom. Suddenly and ever so faintly, he had a feeling of something. No . . . he thought impossible, he insisted, pushing it away. As he entered the house, his nose picked up a scent. It was deep in the recesses of his memory. Was it food cooking? Talus wandered down the hall and into the kitchen, what a sight!

There stood Lillianna, dressed in her white cotton peasant dress. Her long hair falling well below her waist. She looked amazingly beautiful, thought Talus, as he studied her. She stood at the table cooking bacon and eggs in a pan which rested on a metal wire that held the pan up. Below it were three large candles, supplying the heat. Beside her was Mortamion, eagerly waiting and watching the feast before his eyes. "Where did you get the food?" Talus asked, rubbing his nose. "I sent Louis to the village to buy them." Mortamion answered. "I think we need something they call a stove Tanni." Lillianna said giggling. "Yes dear, all in good time." Replied Mortamion. "Just keep a close eye on those eggs." He said, feeling the pangs of hunger in his stomach. Lillianna was hungry too she hadn't eaten since yesterday morning. "Oh well, I'll leave you both to your glorious meal." Talus said turning to leave, being a Council member he had no use of food. Then he remembered something he had forgotten. After all, being immortal didn't mean being rude. As he stopped at the door way he turned once again and looked at them. "By the way . . . congratulations to you both." His voice indicated a slight air of arrogance, but that was normal for who he was. Lillianna and Mortamion looked up and smiled at him. As Talus walked down the hall to the staircase, he mumbled under his breath, " . . . and good luck, you'll need it."

There was a part of him that actually wanted them to succeed in their quest to live as mortals, but there was also a part of him that thought they were immature and acting like children. Indeed he did wish Mortamion luck. He didn't think Mortamion knew everything he was getting into. He also felt that Lillianna had Mortamion wrapped around her little finger and that annoyed Talus, who highly respected his own ability to be in control, especially with women.

As Louis entered the kitchen, Mortamion looked up at him. Lillianna was hand feeding him the last piece of bacon, as she sat on his lap. They giggled like school children. In a way, they were. "Yes Louis?" Mortamion asked wiping his mouth with a napkin. "I have started the fire in the drawing room, as you requested sir." "Thank you Louis that will be all." Louis slowly nodded his head once and took his leave. Mortamion kissed Lillianna with longing and desire, barely able to separate himself from her lips, he spoke between the kisses and said, "Come here my darling, let us rest in front of the fire." They made their way down the hall to Lillianna's favorite room.

It was filled with furniture that had been in their home in Rome, eighteen years ago when they were still immortal and committed to The Council. Mortamion had it all shipped here for her return. In the middle of the room was their French hand woven Persian yellow carpet with pink and blue flowers. Two gold wing chairs adorned with birds and cherubs were placed on each side of the fireplace. To the right was the settee that matched the chairs. Between the chairs was the golden drum table that they had purchased in England more than a hundred years ago. At the far end of the room overlooking the garden, was a sixteenth century French provincial writing desk and stool. "Something of our past to go along with our future." Mortamion had said.

Two glasses of wine sat on the table. "Oh how wonderful Tanni, look we have wine!" Exclaimed Lillianna in her child like way. They sat on the carpet in front of the fire, and Mortamion made a toast. "To my most precious Lillianna, to whom I give my mortal soul." They tapped their glasses, and drank from the English cut crystal goblets. Then Mortamion placed them back on the table. Lillianna melted into his arms kissing him deeply. "I'm so very happy Tanni, so very very happy." She whispered. "What would make you happier?" he asked her. Lillianna stared in to the fire, and then replied breathlessly, "To have your baby and be a mother." Mortamion caressed her face. "You will have my child, I promise you." He told her. Lillanna threw her arms around his neck. "Thank you my darling . . . thank you." She smothered his face with kisses. They sat happily drinking their wine in front of the fire, watching the flames dance, they were as any young couple who were desperately and hopelessly in love.

It was unfortunate that their happiness was not shared within the organization. Changes in their lives would begin to take place that would leave them both vulnerable. Mortamion knew this, but chose not to destroy Lillianna's moments of bliss until it was absolutely necessary. Right now he wanted to let her have all the moments of happiness that her mortal heart could hold. Her spirit had always been light and joyful like a young child and that's how he wanted her to stay, for as long as possible. The Council had little choice but to grant them back their mortality. They had both been in The Council more than two hundred years. Both knew the evidence of war and death. There were constant battles between The Path and The Dominion. The difference was that unlike most immortals, Lillianna and Mortamion had past life memories.

These memories were the common element that they both shared, though it took them many years to disclose it to each other. There were instances that Council members had some flash of a memory, but not often. However, for Lillianna and Mortamion, their memories of their previous lives were complete and clear. During the Council's review, they were able to convince The Council Tribunal concerning their previous lives. Lillianna's lineage could be traced back to royalty. She believed she was a young Queen Margaret of Scotland who was poisoned by her king out of jealousy, as she was so well liked by the people. Mortamion had memories of growing up in a small village in Northern France called Amiens. He had visions of fighting in the hundred year war and dying in battle. Some of their images were so vivid that The Council Tribunal decided to rule in their favor, but first they must pass a test of time and patience. Their souls would be placed in mortals on earth. Lillianna was placed in Carlotta's womb when Carlotta conceived, after her marriage to George Evanharth. Mortamion's soul was placed in little boy of six, who previously died of influenza. The doctor pronounced the boy dead as his mother The Duchess Delmont knelt praying by his bedside. As the doctor raised the sheet to cover the boy's face, little Mortamion opened his eyes and called for his mother.

The Duchess took to her bed for weeks from the shock, but little Mortamion comforted his mother by playing on her bed. The incident would make The Duchess wake Mortamion up several times during the night, until at the age of twelve he was sent off to Austria by his father to attend boy's academy. When he turned seventeen Mortamion was sent to Oxford to continue his education, lasting only two years, he sent his parents a letter stating that he had, in fact received enough schooling. Now he was twenty four years old and Lillianna eighteen years old in earth years. He had been waiting for her and her for him. Now at last they would be together again, and could live as mortals. She could have her wish of becoming a mother to Mortamion's child. Her vision of motherhood went back to her death as the Scottish Queen who was with child when she was poisoned. Mortamion understood this need of hers because of his own mother's grief, and the devastation she felt over his death during the the hundred year war. Because he could remember so vividly, his empathy grew for Lillianna's plight.

During his time at the estate of his parents he communicated frequently with The Council, telepathically. He was asked by The Council to take his younger brother Talus through Council law, with him and force The Dominion out of the village of San Michelene. It was not uncommon for members of The Dominion and The Path to grant respite and shelter to The Council, as they were what balanced the two worlds of good and evil. The Council wanted the Marchette family out of there. The element of control was in their ability to take your soul away while you were still alive.

The Marchette's were evil, but they would not do battle with The Council at this time. Whenever The Dominion did battle it was when it would be least expected, as they were usually the initiators of battle in the first place and it was always against the legions of The Path. Mortamion and Talus convinced them that the small village must be left alone, as Council members they had supreme control, over both entities. The Marchette family gathered their men and left quietly, for to lose one's soul while alive, was the worst torture a mortal could suffer. Mortamion had stayed on in the castle with Talus and his soldiers and awaited Lillianna's release.

Mortamion was well aware of The Councils disappointment in their decision to leave that way of existence, but now that the time test had passed and they had truly broken all ties with The Council, both he and Lillianna would no longer have any protective or recuperative powers. They were like all humans . . . at risk, by their own choice. This worried Mortamion because bridges had been burnt. He knew as long as his men were with him, he had extra protection, but he also knew that The Council would begin to redistribute them to other captains within the organization. Lying with Lillianna in front of the fire he felt this burden, but he would keep it to himself, he vowed that no harm would come to her while he was alive. He knew in his heart that if he had the chance to go back he would not take it without her. Her dreams were now his dreams and they would stay the course.

Mortamion had sent his head Lieutenant, Landon to a town ninety miles away from San Michelene, to bring back a priest to marry him and Lillianna. In order not to raise suspicion, they would use their previous names for the ceremony. Jon Pierre Tanrey and Sophia Basset. These were their names for over two hundred years, as Council members and would serve them well now, for their little guise. However he had sounded the name Lillianna in his mind for so long, he would have to remember to say Sophia in front of the priest. It was much easier for Lillianna who had always called him by his childhood name Tanni, short for Tanrey. Mortamion would wear his formal dress Council uniform and Lillianna her pink silk gown with the high back scalloped neck a favorite of his, which was already hanging in her closet washed and pressed. How surprised she would be tomorrow when Mortamion asked her to be his wife. He had long since decided he would make her his wife and the mother of his children.

Time had served his research well and they would follow the laws and customs of mortals. In The Council couples lived together without marriage as there could be no off spring conceived by a female Council member. Marriage was obsolete within The Council and few couples stayed together for as long as Mortamion and Lillianna had. Talus was a good example of how most Council members lived or rather existed. By their own nature, relationships often became more trouble than they were worth. Council members did not have the need to feel close to anyone. Their needs were purely physical, Mortamion and Lillianna were the exception to the rule. Much to the distaste of many, they chose to be intimate only with each other, and within the organization most male Council members knew where Lillianna was concerned, it was hands off. So tomorrow their new life would begin and Lillianna would soon have her dream of becoming a mother come true.

Mortamion and Lillianna had acquired a fair amount wealth being Council members. Having had evolved along with The Council over the two hundred years. Both started in the field as soldiers, fighting The Dominion. Lillianna was an expert with daggers, and Mortamion not only had a vast collection of swords, but was one of The Councils best in sword fighting, because of his speed and accuracy. He and Lillianna eventually rose to administration responsibilities, similar to where Talus would be in a few more years. Council members had no fear of death which made them a true force to be reckoned with. Death for a Council member simply did not exist. They were capable of withstanding little sleep and had a tremendous pain threshold. All Council members were well paid for their services, but were on call twenty-four hours a day. Not that they were needed every day but if they were, it was their responsibility to rise to the occasion immediately. Their constitution allowed this kind of commitment, with no sickness, aging or emotional strife, it was easily achieved. Now things were very different, Mortamion already felt tired and hungry and anxiousness, feelings he was not use to dealing with. Probably more so than Lillianna, as she was overcome with visions of motherhood and decorating.

However, she would soon experience many new sensations that she would have to resolve, it was all part of being human. The only non worry they would have was the fact that their finances were in excellent order. As for now, right now they were like millions of couples throughout the universe, and beyond, young and beautiful and in love. Never before would anyone love like this, it was not possible, their love was unique and could never be conquered. This was what they both felt on their wedding day.

Talus stood beside Mortamion as he took Lillianna as his wife. Both men were present, and not surprisingly both men wanted her. Lillianna's grace and delicate features were both astonishing and intimidating. Mortamion and Talus had known her for many years, and her spirit and aura had not changed, but now as a mortal she was breathtaking. To look into her eyes was to get lost in a cavern of such depth, and magnetism that there was little escape. Mortamion being human had no advantage here, but with Talus it was quite another story entirely. Talus was driven and acted on instinct, however he was also still under Mortamion's direct command. That would change in the near future, as Mortamion was no longer a Council Captain, but only a mere mortal.

As Mortamion and Lillianna were beginning their new life as mortals, George and Carlotta's life was falling apart. After a month of not locating Lillianna, Elise and her fiancé asked that they be allowed to marry. George of course gave his permission and blessing. It was not fair to ruin the life of his other daughter and her future and happiness. The wedding took place without Carlotta as she was unable to leave her bed. She was indeed dying from grief and the dairy farm was faltering, as well. However, George was not done, he knew he had to find a way into the castle. He was certain that Lillianna was there. He hadn't formulated a plan yet and the memory of Talus' pistol against his head made him apprehensive to go there alone. Margot was still home and helped George as much as she could, but her main attention was to her mother who needed constant care, as Carlotta rarely got out of bed most days. George only had Margot to help him and a young friar that would help in milking the cows in the mornings.

George began having doubts about his own sanity. Perhaps Lillianna had wished to escape her family . . . how that was possible he didn't know or understand. Maybe Mortamion Delmont knew more than he was saying, maybe he was telling the truth, or perhaps it was a deterrent to keep him away and she really was there. His thoughts drove him insane. The only thing he had to keep him focused was his work as his days would often run into nights.

On one of these nights he crawled into bed and told Carlotta everything that he was feeling. The loss and grief he was going through . . . the pain of maybe losing her as well. He cried, telling her his desperate thoughts and fears. She did not respond, and he didn't expect her to. Finally he fell asleep, literally sobbing into his pillow . . . for the first time since he was a little boy orphaned, he felt completely alone.

George awoke startled, realizing he had slept well past dawn. Carlotta was not in the bed next to him, but he could smell coffee and the scent of food cooking. Dressing quickly he went into the kitchen to find Carlotta up and dressed, cooking breakfast. He came up behind her and wrapping his arms around her, he kissed her gently on her neck. "Go on, sit awhile and eat." She told him quietly, her tone sullen. "The cows have been milked, the grates are filled and the eggs are ready for delivery . . . but the barn is a mess." That was all Carlotta spoke that day, but now George had hope that she was coming back to him. He quietly and thankfully ate his breakfast, as Carlotta began kneading the dough for the bread loaves. From that day on she never again mentioned Lillianna's name.

"The way to love anything is to realize that it might be lost."

G. K. Chesterton

Capture and Redemption
Chapter Five

Joshua stood outside the Library, anxiously waiting for Eden. His watch read six twenty five. He tried to control himself. He found a pay phone and called Eden's house and Uncle Eli answered. "Hi, this is Josh, is Eden there?" he asked. "Hi Josh, how are you doing?" asked her uncle. Trying to stay calm, Joshua took a deep breath. "Oh I'm good." He replied. "Uh? . . you know what? . . . let me see if I can find her, hold on a sec." Joshua could hear the phone receiver being put down. He waited and waited, what was taking so long? It wasn't that big of a house! Finally Uncle Eli was back. "No Josh, she's not here . . . my wife said she took a walk up to the town square to meet you." "When?!" Joshua yelled into the phone. He could hear talking in the back ground. "She left about forty minutes ago . . . what's going on? . . . Josh? Josh?" asked uncle Eli. Joshua had hung up and jumped on his bike. He knew something was terribly wrong, he felt it, but he had no idea where she was or where to begin looking.

After riding around and looking up and down the streets, he saw no sign of her. The square was deserted anyway it was Sunday night, everyone was home, or on vacation. He rode to Barney's Coffee Emporium, there were a few people in there but she wasn't one of them. Finally he rode to the clearing, Daniel was already in human form.

Jumping off his bike he just let it fall to the ground. As he reached Daniel, he heard Daniel say, "Dante has captured her." There were two cloud like visions next to Daniel which was where he was getting his information from. It took Joshua a few moments to learn who they were. They both communicated through very high pitched sounds. It was made known to him that one was Eden's grandmother and the other Sienna. Daniel closed his eyes and listened closely to the sounds. Then he opened his eyes and looked at Joshua. "Dante captured her outside the bookstore, she is being held by him." Again Daniel went in to his trance like state, closing his eyes and placing both hands on his chest. To Joshua the sounds were annoying. Again opening his eyes he told Joshua, "He has her in the house on the highest ridge in Claremont." The two cloud like visions began to disappear.

Daniel looked at Joshua and putting his hands on Joshua's shoulders said, "Joshua we have no time to lose, get her back before it's too late!" "Yes Sir, I will sir." Joshua replied. "Listen to me, you must get her back before midnight, Dante will wait for the other side of midnight to plant his seed." Daniel insisted. "What if Dante doesn't wait sir?" Joshua asked. "He will . . . he will . . . we must pray that he does . . ." he answered Joshua. Daniel's voice was far away as he faded into the atmosphere. Joshua rode his bike to Eden's house. How stupid he had been. What had he been thinking? Beating up on himself, increased his speed. Continuing, his thoughts led him back in time to the fire. Wanton and reckless he had been, then and it seems now too. He could have prevented this, just like he could have prevented the drug addiction and the subsequent fire that took his own life. Why hadn't he acted sooner? He asked himself. Fear, is what stopped him, fear that Eden wouldn't believe him and would cast him aside. Joshua was so in love with Eden that he feared her rejection of him, because her own salvation was hanging in the balance.

Being mortal was hard, why would anyone want to be mortal? He thought to himself. Then he remembered kissing Eden, the feel of her hand in his, the smell of her hair, the touch of her lips on his lips. He wanted a second chance . . . even though he'd never get it. He'd never make it into The Highest Realm the way he was going. Memories took him back in time, to that night, when he was free basing and the chemicals exploded in his hands. He managed to get his mom, dad and little sister out of the house with his screams, which was his only saving grace. He remembered being on fire, the smell of his skin burning as his flesh melted off his bones. Daniel being his sponsor thought he had a good chance of being allowed into The Highest Realm because he fought through the pain to save his family, dying in the process. Joshua had suffered forth degree burns over ninety percent of his body. The chemical explosion had made him a human torch and in moments his whole room was ablaze, spreading throughout the whole house in minutes.

Even if it meant he'd have no peace, no afterlife, he had to save Eden, for the one reason that meant everything to him . . . he loved her. He had never known true love, sex yes . . . he had plenty of that in high school. He had often exchanged sex for drugs and now the thought of it disgusted him. It was all degrading and not worthy of who he truly was, but he didn't know that then. Now, nothing could compare to his feelings for Eden. To Joshua true love meant sacrificing your own love and feelings, for the benefit of the one you loved. Their happiness coming before your own.

Why had he been so wasteful of his time, his money, his relationship with his family? Joshua recalled his death and The Dominion asking for his soul. They scared him. As far as he was concerned The Dominion had already had him once. How the heck else had he been so foolish, throwing away his life for nothing. He wanted his soul. He would keep his soul for that's all he had. After the transfer process he always had the choice to give his soul to a new life on earth for The Path, but not as he was still between dimensions. He first needed to get home to The Highest Realm.

Eden was his direction home in more ways than one. She had become his home while he was here on earth. He turned the corner and he was on Sparrow Lane once again, but now, without Eden. Joshua needed her and wanted her desperately, if only for a few moments more . . . to tell her that she was his true love. He knew he could never build a life with her, that didn't matter. What mattered was saving her, so that she could live the life she dreamed of. That would never change, it would follow him into eternity.

Joshua ran up the steps of the Evanharth house, bursting into the living room. Everyone had gone home except for Eden's aunt and uncle. Samuel and Caleb had fallen asleep on the carpet in front of the fire place. Joshua looked at them and announced that she had been kidnapped. Very straight forwardly, without skipping a beat, he said, "By the Dominion." Her mother was the first to react. "Thomas!" Rachel cried out looking at her husband. "Why didn't we tell her?" she asked him knowing the answer. Joshua looked at Eden's mom and then at her dad, and finally at Uncle Eli. "You guys know about the lineage and didn't tell her anything?" Joshua asked in disbelief. "Joshua, I have been listening about this nonsense since I was a little boy!" Eden's dad was clearly angered. "Sir, it's anything but nonsense." Joshua insisted. "I know where she is . . . but I need help to get her back." Joshua could not believe the denial in her father's face. "I'll call the police, which is what we need to do." Thomas said as he went to the phone and picked up the receiver. "Sir . . . your daughter is with the devil himself and will be tortured, raped and impregnated at midnight, if we don't stop it, the police will never gain entrance without a search warrant and that will take too much time . . . time that we don't have!" Joshua declared, his voice raised. Eden's dad put the receiver down. "Thomas this is not about your belief anymore, it's about saving our daughter." Rachel insisted, almost losing control, but not quite.

Eden's mom looked at Joshua. "What do we need to do?" she asked. "She is in Claremont, I know the house she's in." Joshua explained. "He will transform himself into Satan and she will conceive his son," Joshua hesitated, than continued, "you will never see her again . . . what do think happened to Sienna?" Joshua walked around the room thinking. "All of you need to get as many members of the congregation together as possible to encircle the mansion with prayer." Uncle Eli quickly began making phone calls. "Everyone will need to be dressed in black, no other color, black, black shoes too and wear their cross around their neck . . . please we don't have much time." He instructed.

Eden's mother stopped him as he was leaving. "Wait . . . who are you and why should we trust you?" she asked assertively. "I was sent from a higher being, than myself," he answered, "I was sent to protect your daughter and I was not able to do it successfully." He lowered his head in shame. Than looking into her mother's eyes he continued. "I am not of this dimension, this has been my mission, please help me to complete it successfully, as I have come to care about your daughter very much." With that he turned to leave adding, "I will be back in one hour, be ready." Joshua needed to find Nia and Leah quickly and a plan needed to be put in place. His first stop was at the rectory at the Hadleyville Fellowship

Church, waking the cook he demanded that she wake both Father Clemmons and Father Odell immediately and she did only after he told her that Rebecca's granddaughter had been captured by Satan.

Uncle Eli sent out distress signals to as many members of the congregation, as he could reach. They were all to meet at Eden's house as soon as possible. Meanwhile her parents set forth to fill their car with bottled water, flashlights and candles. Although Thomas was in denial, he was fearful and he had to believe Joshua's tale . . . he had heard these stories for years from his own mother, he still found them hard to accept. He promised to banish his own mother if she involved Eden in any way . . . why? Was his daughter now to pay the price? Did he truly believe this was the devil? No but he believed that this nut case who had kidnapped his daughter, probably believed he was the devil and that's what motivated him to follow the plan. Perhaps no one would show up, knowing the following his mother had, that was highly unlikely. One thing was certain and that was that he had to rescue his daughter. Early on when Eden was a little girl Rebecca had told Thomas and Rachel that she sensed that Eden was a Warrior of God, but they admonished her for these thoughts and asked her never to mention it again. Rebecca had effectively respected their wishes.

The ascension began quickly with cars double parking up and down the streets, where Eden's house was. Father Odell was the first to arrive, with Father Clemmons. They quietly spoke to Eden's parents and Uncle Eli. "This will be difficult." Stated Father Odell with serious concern. "But not impossible." Reassured Father Clemmons. "Do you both know this Joshua?" asked Thomas. "We knew of his coming, through your mother." Replied Father Clemmons. "But we did not know who's child was at stake." Clarified Father Odell. "I wish we had, we would have had more time to prepare." Sighed Father Clemmons. "I am so surprised Rebecca being so much a part of our order could not have known Eden was next in line to be part of The Path." Thomas was struck. "What do you mean?" asked Thomas, his tone angry. Both Father Clemmons and Father Odell looked at each other. "Your mother was part of a fundamentalist order called The Path, which strives to fight Satan here on earth, she was our main supporter and a Warrior of God. Rebecca was a direct descendant of the original founders." Father Clemmons responded. "Rebecca was a powerful warrior, casting out demons was one of her specialties, mortals who are chosen to be Warriors of God, are usually instructed from a very early age in our ways and beliefs." Father Odell interjected calmly as he sensed Thomas' anger. "I am well aware of my mother's lineage and gifts . . . but I did not want Eden involved in all this." Thomas retorted. "Well my son it seems she is, and we must give her all the help and support she needs." Replied Father Odell, reassuringly.

Dante leaned over Eden, his face inches from hers. The chloroform would begin to wear off soon. He slowly and deeply breathed in her exhaling air, pulling back quickly when her eye lids began to flutter. Dante watched her as she started to move and enjoyed her horror when, she realized that she was held down by five steel collars, one around each extremity and one around her neck. Trying to wake up she struggled against the steel restraints. "The less you move the better my dear," she heard him say. Her throat was dry, but she managed to speak. "Who are you?" she asked. Dante smiled. "Oh let's not worry about that my lovely . . . let's talk about you." He taunted. "My name is E-" she started to reply, but Dante cut her off, shouting, "I know who you are! I brought you here you silly girl!" Eden lay silently for a few minutes, waiting.

She expected death at any moment. She prayed that it would not be long and drawn out, but happen quickly instead. As Dante walked around the wooden floor of the room, Eden caught a glimpse of him, as he moved very quickly. "You are my guest, let us say you are a very special guest . . . that is why you are tied down." Dante laughed as he spoke. "You know I don't tie down all my guests just you Eden." She could see him fidgeting with his sleeve. Eden noted that he seemed almost feminine. "No my dear I only like women." He replied to her thoughts. He came and stood next to the bed, so she could really see her captor now. "Oh yes, there have been others . . . but not many that I hold in such tight esteem."

Looking at him, she fixed her eyes on his. They were an intense violet in color, almost purple. He smiled at her, she knew it was deadly. "May I speak?" she asked him. "Well, you are a well brought up girl!" He teased with malicious glee. "Yes, my dear . . . you may speak, speak all you want." He encouraged. "You are Dante." Eden was speaking her thoughts. "Was that a question or a statement?" he asked. "A statement." Eden answered him. "That's very perceptive of you." He told her sitting down on the wooden prison she was bolted to. Gently, he ran his fingers down her face on to her neck, then between her breasts, stopping at her waist. His fingers were long, thin and pale. "There's plenty of time for that," he mused to himself. "You know, you and I saw each other a year ago remember Eden . . . you saw me from your bedroom window." Dante provoked Eden's fear.

Eden knew now what had destroyed Sienna and probably hundreds before her. Her grandmother had tried to warn her, but there just wasn't enough time, so had Joshua, he had tried so hard. Could she have prevented her capture, had she known? . . . she asked herself. Eden didn't think so, not after meeting this manifestation of evil before her, who could also read her mind. Her only hope now was to go along with his plan . . . whatever it was. As long as she was tied down, he held all the cards. Eden closed her eyes and concentrated on the room and its size. It didn't appear to have any windows. "No." Dante said simply. "There are no windows." He confirmed, resting his chin between his thumb and forefinger. "You see," he said. "I am better than any Evanharth." Eden cleared her mind and thought of her breath only her breath. Her grandmother's training was coming to the forefront now. Dante tried to break her mentally, causing her to stop her rhythm, but to do so he would have to use a physical connection, of some kind, as she had been trained well in meditation. It annoyed him, yet it fascinated him at the same time. "Yes, I do hold all the cards, and to be truthful, it does get boring with someone of your caliber." Dante said in a sad voice, of course he was pretending, there was nothing sad about him . . . he was overjoyed with her capture.

"In all honesty Eden, I would like to level the playing field." There was no response, she had not heard him, for mentally she was not there. He would bring her back, walking over to her, he kissed her on the lips. It broke her meditation immediately. "See?" he asked coyly, "I can be a romantic when needed." Dante bent down again, forcing his kiss on her. "You may not want me, you may hate me . . . but none of that matters." He talked while kissing her mouth, her nose, her face. Eden closed her eyes and thought of Joshua. Suddenly Dante stood up. "Please don't tell me, you like that loser, that drug addict, that stupid boy," he shook his head. "I am clearly so much a better choice Eden." He laughed, he was after all having a swell time.

He walked around the room and then came back to the wooden bed and sat down next to her. "You don't know do you?" he asked. There was a long pause, Eden wasn't biting. "Alright if you insist on being stubborn, I'll just tell you." He laughed. "Joshua isn't real . . . you know? He's like Pinocchio, he's not a real boy, dearest Eden." Eden clearly by her thoughts, didn't understand. "I know . . . I know, doesn't it just rot?" he sneered at her, pretending to rub his eyes while frowning. He was reading her thoughts almost as quickly as she was thinking them. Dante stood up and expanded his arms like wings. "He's trying to get his wings…poor boy… you know he wants to be an angel." He teased and then unleashed his fury. "I will see him in hell first, roasting like a pig on the spit!" He screamed. "He thinks he burned the first time, he ain't seen nothing yet deary!" Then suddenly he was still again. "You bring out such jealousy in me my dear." He said calmly kissing her again, this time inserting his tongue in her mouth. Eden controlled her emotions and her disgust, which actually impressed him. "Very well done," he whispered, caressing her face. "I am liking you more and more, but that doesn't really matter for us does it Eden?" he waited for her answer. Then looking down at her, he shouted again. "Does it Eden?!" His spit falling on her. "No, no it does not matter." She replied accepting her situation. "That's better . . . now, after all we are to be man and wife." He said simply, as if it were immaterial.

Eden was using the path of least resistance purposely. Her thoughts were that she was his slave and there was no fighting the situation. Dante questioned her on it. "Really Edie, I am finding it hard to believe that an Evanharth would give up so easily?" he asked slyly. "Well, I am bolted down and though you seem to think because I am an Evanharth I have special abilities, I am not aware of any." She replied. "Oh I see you want to play? Or you think me stupid?" he asked leaning over her again. "You are a little vixen aren't you?" he taunted her, running his hand up her leg. "No I am not a vixen and I know you are not stupid . . . but I think you should be honorable and give me a chance at my survival or kill me." Her voice was raspy as she spoke. "Kill you? Kill you? you are going to give me a son first. Eden that's what this is all about darling, death comes later, much later." He again was taunting her, slowly breaking her spirit, as he had Sienna. "Please don't put yourself on the same level as Sienna, there was a stupid girl if ever I saw one." Dante's voice was more analytical now. "I mean after all, she came to me . . . they all come to me. Actually you came to me too. O.K. so I used a couple of tricks . . . because I could." Eden was silent again . . . separating her mind from all random thoughts. "Oh no! here we go again, what am I to do with you?" he asked, almost sounding sincere. Dante bent over her and slapped her hard across the face. "That's better! We'll have no more of that!" He watched as the side of her face turned red. "Well . . . it's still not as bad as the one Sienna gave you a year ago . . . remember when I saw you through the window?" his voice dripping with sarcasm. The room was silent. Eden wasn't talking and Dante wasn't talking. Dante was getting bored, which he hated more than anything. He had not made Eden cry, which brought her up a notch on his belt as far as her spirit was concerned. After all she was a Warrior of God, he was up for the challenge, of which he'd imagined many times.

"Actually this is not as much fun as I expected," said Dante. "It's not appropriate to have you chained down like an animal . . . is it my dear?" With a wave of his hand the bolts loosened and then opened. Dante walked over to Eden and ran his fingers through her hair. Eden slowly sat up, rubbing her wrists. Dante grabbed the back of her hair and pulled it back hard; he stopped short of snapping her neck. He kissed her hard on the mouth, Eden was again repulsed by it. She herself was surprised at her self control and lack of emotion. Dante read her and chuckled, than smiling he walked towards the door. "You cannot know how happy I am to have you here, Eden. I will be back." As he opened the door he turned and faced her. "I choose you to be the mother of my child and you will bear my son." Dante was gone locking the door behind him. Now Eden knew that everything her grandmother had spoken on the night of her death and all that Joshua had said was true. But, why hadn't anyone told her in all these years? Eden believed her father not wanting her to know about her lineage was a poor excuse, but then she did not know about her brother Benjamin and the details of his death, as no one ever spoke of it. It didn't matter now anyway as she was in the thick of it. As her grandmother often said, "the past cannot be changed, one can only learn from it and move forward." How was she to move forward from this?

Was she stuck? To be tortured and used for reproductive purposes? Her own self worth told her there was no way she would let it happen without a fight to save herself. She thought about the words. "A Warrior of God." She said it out loud. Eden looked out a tiny crack in the stone wall. She tried to see the night sky. But the crack was too small. There was no time better than right now to start praying. Kneeling down she faced the crack. "Father who art in Heaven hallowed be thy name," she began, "make me an instrument of your will, and if it pleases you give me the strength to conquer this evil I am faced with. Father I put myself in your hands do with me what you will, I dedicated myself to you and will follow The Path, if it is your will to make me a warrior so be it, I am your servant now and into the afterlife." Someone was coming, she could hear movement. The lock turned and Dante entered the room. He had changed his clothes.

Draped in a black cloak, he moved about the room. Eden stood against the wall, her eyes watching his every move. As he neared her, fear rose up in her throat but she controlled it. "Where are you my bride?" Dante studied the room carefully. Was it possible that he couldn't see her? how could this be? she thought. "Come now my dear little wench . . . you know I'll find you eventually." Why could he no longer read her thoughts? Dante began to levitate around the room. Eden did everything she could to stay out of his way. She continued moving, never stopping, and then . . . she felt the heat. The temperature in the tiny room rose like an inferno. Even though she was invisible, she was still flesh and bone. The heat was suffocating, she started coughing. "There you are." Dante sat on the wooden bed that she had been chained to, triumphantly pleased with himself. "Look I don't want to destroy you just yet . . . after all you need to give me a son first." Dante stood up resting his hands on his waist. "Eden if you continue, I will only make it far worse for you, I promise I can." He glanced up at the ceiling. "Do you know where your mother is Eden, or your father?" Dante asked her grinning.

"I can bring them here and we can all play a little game, if you'd like." He was playing hard ball. Eden had no way of really knowing what he was capable of, but she knew she didn't want her parents hurt. Slowly as she willed herself, she became visible again. "Good girl!" Dante exclaimed. "And you said you had no powers!" He hugged her and then sent her flying into the stone wall. She felt her head hit hard against the brick and slid to the floor. "Oops, . . . sorry sometimes I don't know my own strength." He mused. He reached down and extended his hand to her, she took it and then pulled as hard as she could, smashing him into the wall face first. He stood up, his face bloodied and smiled. "I see you like to play rough, let the games begin." He came at her with fury, but stopped abruptly when he heard a knock at the door. "Who the hell is it?" he yelled. "Sir, it's Peris." The voice answered. Dante was breathing heavy, so much in fact that his cheeks were reacting to his inhaling and exhaling. "Don't worry my love, I will be back to deal with you . . . I love rough housing with my women." He kissed Eden and left the room, locking the door behind him. Eden wiped the blood off her mouth from Dante's kiss on the sleeve of her sweater, then she focused on mentally opening the lock, but she couldn't do it.

She realized that Dante had put a spell or incantation on it, in preparation for this moment. Leaning against the door she heard voices, one was Dante's and one she didn't recognize. "Sir, the guests are beginning to arrive and are waiting for you." Peris said. "Peris, have you forgotten who you are speaking with?" Dante sneered. "No sir, of course not . . ." Peris responded. "Then get out of my sight, I'll come down when I'm ready." Dante said turning to go back into the room where Eden was, and then he looked back at Peris. "What is it you're holding?" he asked him. "The lady's dress and crown sir, you asked that I bring them to you." Peris answered apologetically. Dante snatched them out of his hands and then dismissed him with a wave of his hand.

He unlocked the door and entered the room. Eden was sitting on the wooden board she had been bolted to. Dante threw the dress and crown of roses at her, sending some of the petals flying through the air. He was feeling discomfort from his injury and wanted to make her pay for it now, but there were people waiting for him and a party going on, that he was hosting. "Put those on!" He shouted. "Trust me our battle is just beginning." He scowled. He gently ran his fingers across his face, then looking at them he saw he was bleeding. "It has been a long time since a woman has made me bleed . . . take careful notes Eden, you will pay, you're lucky I heal quickly." He said as he left, once again locking the door.

Eden knew from what she had heard that she was to be some sort of sacrifice and this party was being held to celebrate it. The dress was long and white, and was obviously meant to be her wedding gown. Eden put it on, in hope that if she could get out of her prison she might be able to escape. However, it had now occurred to Eden that escape might not be an option. She very well might have to fight Dante and lose her own life in the process.

The plan was simple . . . in theory. As the church members surrounded the castle and prayed, Joshua would sneak into the mansion and find Eden. It wasn't a brilliant plan, it was the only plan. How else could they stop Dante from taking her as his sex slave? Joshua had to get Eden out of there. He had no idea when Daniel would show up. He didn't know anything except he needed to get Eden out before midnight. Fire torches surrounded the grounds leading up to the front gate of the mansion. Men waited on the gravel driveway to instruct guest's where to park. Slowly cars began to arrive, making their way along the long winding dirt road. The evangelical members followed Joshua's instruction to circle the the grounds. Hidden by the tall trees and forest cover they moved in slowly.

Dressed in black they remained hidden by the night sky. As he watched from high up on one of the trees, Joshua saw that all the guests wore costume masks and held invitations. He quickly devised a plan to stop one the cars, with a ploy that they had to pull over on the side of the road for inspection before proceeding. With the help of Eden's dad and Uncle Eli, they pulled Dante's guests out of the car. Joshua took the mask off of the driver and the invitation from one of the women who spit at him. They tried to yell but Uncle Eli and Eden's dad whacked them on the back of their heads and dragged them onto the ground. Once in the forest they were gagged and tied to a tree. They would be held there guarded by the church members, until Eden's escape. Joshua was able to make it into the mansion, amongst a crowd entering at the same time. Although the invitation was inscribed with a woman's name, Joshua was fortunate that the guards at the entrance did not seem to be checking names.

Inside men walked around carrying trays with flutes of champagne. It was hard to distinguish who was who, as everyone wore a mask, some more elaborate than others. Joshua took one of the flutes and made his way through the large rooms. He knew Eden wouldn't be at the party standing at Dante's side. She was being kept somewhere. But where? Upstairs or downstairs? As he passed people and made eye contact, he nodded as if to say hello. Suddenly, someone stopped him. A man dressed in a black cape with a hood. It was the guard who had taken his invitation. His eyes peered into Joshua's eyes. "Are you looking for someone sir?" asked the guard. Joshua could only remember the first name on the card. "Yes, my aunt Eugenia." Joshua responded. The guard looked down at his stack of cards and flipping through them stopped at one. "She's gone off somewhere." Joshua said with a slight air of annoyance. Glancing at the card, Joshua added, "Yes . . . see right there Eugenia Anderson and guest." Joshua read the card out loud. "Well," replied the guard satisfied. "I'm sure she's around here somewhere, would you like me to help you find her?" he offered. "Oh no." Joshua responded assertively. "I'm sure we'll find each other." "Very well, sir . . . the festivities will begin in forty five minutes and you will be directed where to go." The guard then turned and made his way through the crowd.

Joshua entered the crowded ballroom, noting that everyone was dressed in black, including himself. He casually looked for doors or steps that might lead somewhere. He knew he was being watched so he was careful not to be too obvious. He decided to join the crowd at the buffet tables, as a distraction, but when he got up close he had to control himself from gagging. What he saw repulsed him.

Joshua left the buffet table and tried to hide his disgust. A slaughtered baby lamb fully intact adorned the center of the table, its dead eyes looking up at him, a wreath of red roses encircling its head. It wasn't that the sight of a dead lamb was the worst thing in the world, it's what it signified. He knew that Eden was to be the slaughtered lamb. He looked around at the guests from his masked face. They all looked like normal everyday people, yet they were beasts, all of them. He had to find Eden and quickly. Suddenly a bell rang and everyone stopped eating and talking. It was the host of the gruesome fest, the king of darkness.

Dante came into the room and people around him actually bowed. He was not that impressive, but his eyes had a hypnotic quality, so Joshua avoided eye contact. Dante was dressed in a long black robe, around his waist was a corded belt, hanging off the belt was a crucifix upside down. His hair was jet black, his skin pale, his eyes intense violet in color. Joshua thought him not so tall, but he demonstrated an imposing attitude. Joshua could not say he was unattractive, his features were strong, with a regal quality. He might be handsome in a ghoulish sort of way. Dante smiled and Joshua could see that a young woman could be easily swayed by him, even an old woman. Dante had a certain magnetism that could pull you in. If you were weak, dysfunctional, addicted to anything you were his type. Joshua knew that if he was still alive and doing drugs, he would be prey to Dante. He would more than likely, have been one of his hench men. Joshua was happy he was already dead. What could happen? he asked himself, he'd die twice. Dante was making his rounds, so Joshua kept moving away from him, backing up, until suddenly he felt a step behind him, almost falling backwards he caught himself.

Then Dante began to address the crowd openly. Joshua realizing his opportunity, carefully made his way down the steps. He found himself at a dead end. It was dark so he couldn't see clearly, he removed the mask and looked carefully at the walls. Something on one of the walls looked odd, so he ran his hand across it and the wall swung open, it was a door in disguise. Behind it was another set of stairs, leading up. He climbed them and came to a narrow hallway. Several narrow, inverted doors ran along the hallway and as he walked he heard voices so he tucked himself into one of the doorways. Two men were walking in his direction, laughing. Joshua held his breath as they passed. "Did you see her, she's gorgeous, I'd like a piece of her." One of them said, the other replying, "She can't be touched until after the baby is born, you even try and Dante will slice your throat and eat you for breakfast, he won't even bother to cook you." When they were out of sight Joshua silently moved down a few more doorways, putting his ear against the doors hoping to hear something, what he didn't know . . . just something to lead him to Eden. His instinct told him she was here, behind one of the doors.

Downstairs in the ballroom the festivities continued. Including a live band, Joshua could hear the music from where he stood. Again he heard footsteps, this time coming up the stair well. Once more he backed into a doorway and into the darkness, hoping that the footsteps weren't going in his direction. They weren't, instead they stopped at the very last door. He could hear a key turn in a lock and then Dante's voice. "Eden my dear, I have a surprise for you." He entered and closed the door behind him. Now at last Joshua knew where she was. He waited and waited, and finally the door opened and Dante came out locking the door behind him. As he made his way down the corridor he paused and turned around to look in the opposite direction. Dante had an intuition about something in the hall. He began to walk down the corridor, looking in all the doorways, when one of his guards came running up the stairs in a fury. "Sir, there is trouble outside." The guard said. "What kind of trouble?" Dante asked calmly. "There are people around the property and their reciting something." The guard replied. "Well let's go have a look shall we?" Dante instructed. Joshua heard them go down the stairs quickly. He knew that this was his only chance to get to Eden.

Quickly, ducking into each doorway, he finally got to the one Eden was behind. Joshua felt around with his hand to see what kind of a lock it was. It was one of the old turnkey locks. He was familiar with locks because his dad was a locksmith and he grew up knowing about locks. He took a file from his back pocket and jimmied it into the lock, twisting and turning until finally it popped. Slowly opening the door he saw her.

She stood before him, dressed in a long white gown, with a wreath of blood red colored roses on her head. He ran to her taking her in his arms and Eden clung to him. "Oh Joshua!" Eden exclaimed in a hushed voice. She wrapped her arms around him and he kissed her tenderly and she kissed him back. "Why are you in this dress?" he asked. "I am to become Dante's bride tonight." Eden replied. "No you're not." Joshua told her. "He has my parents, I won't let anything happen to them." Taking her face in his hands he kissed her forehead. "Eden your parents are outside with hundreds of Christians praying for you . . . he doesn't have them." He led her by the hand, keeping her behind him and approached the door. "Wait." He whispered. Peering out he looked up and down the corridor. "Follow me." He said quietly as they walked down the narrow path and then suddenly heard footsteps. Quickly Joshua pushed Eden into one of the doorways. Stupidly they had left the door to Eden's room open. The guard realized Eden had escaped, as he came running down the corridor, Joshua tripped him and then jumped on top of him, stabbing him in the neck with his file, killing him almost instantly. "Forgive me Daniel, I saw no other way." He whispered, dragging the dead guard back to the room and closing the door.

Quietly, he made his way back to Eden. "Joshua how do we get out of here?" Eden asked whispering in his ear." I only know of one way, but there is another set of stairs . . . I'm just not sure where it leads." He answered whispering in her ear. "Let's take the way that you know." Eden suggested. "That will lead us to the ballroom . . . where all the nuts are." He responded under his breath. He started walking keeping his body close to the wall, he had Eden's hand in his, and she followed close behind. Stopping she tugged at his hand and he stopped. "I can make myself invisible Joshua." She said keeping her voice low. "Do it," he replied mouthing the words, "and follow me." Wow he thought to himself, Daniel was right. When had she tried that? When had she realized she could do it? What else could she do?

Slowly, they made their way down the stairs leading to the ballroom. Joshua pulled the mask, around to the front of his face and put it back on. Downstairs, as people where still milling around, he drifted back in to the crowd seemingly unrecognized. However he had no idea where Eden was. Things were really rolling as he looked around, as guests were eating, talking and some were dancing. The adjoining room had a band playing eighty's music. Joshua made his way into the room where the band was, which led to the front door. Now he could only hope Eden was behind him. Suddenly as he approached the exit, someone tapped him on the shoulder.

The music had stopped and in seconds he was surrounded by guards. "Hello Joshua." The voice said. Joshua turned and saw Dante standing in front of him. "Well, I see you like crashing parties." Dante said smiling. "This isn't a party, it's an execution!" Joshua replied seething. "Well, I think that depends on where you stand, and this is my house, these are my guests and you have no right being here." Dante said in his controlled and charismatic way. "I am sent here from the almighty." Joshua shouted. Dante started to laugh, and as he laughed, others joined him. "Oh Joshua you are so naive." Dante replied. "But you know I like your spirit, I really do." Dante taunted him. Then turning to his guests, Dante asked, "would you all like to see a little trick? . . . I know you like playing with fire, Joshua." The guests and the guards moved away from Joshua, who now stood encircled by everyone.

Dante stood back and said. "Watch and learn." Dante snapped his fingers and set Joshua on fire. However, although he was on fire, he felt no pain, something was keeping the fire from burning him, it was as if he had a protective layer keeping the flames away from his skin. Dante snapped his fingers again and the flames stopped, the guests were in awe of what they had just witnessed. "Hmmm," Dante hummed. "Quite interesting . . . I have to say I underestimated Daniel." He said as he walked around Joshua thinking. "I guess I'm really going to have to play rough." Dante concluded. Suddenly, Joshua felt his throat being squeezed and his air supply being cut off. Joshua pulled at his throat as if trying to remove something that was choking him. Dante held his hand out in front of him closing his fingers and slowly making a fist. Dante did this through sheer force of will as he hadn't actually put his hands on Joshua. Joshua collapsed on to the floor.

"Well you see now, I guess Daniel just didn't cover all his bases." Dante stood above Joshua's lifeless body. "Take him downstairs and cuff him to the wall." He ordered his guards. "I'm growing bored with all this drama." Dante commented walking away.

Many of the quests looked on in terror, as they now realized that this wasn't just some bizarre sex show they were invited to, but someone being put to death. Slowly and as inconspicuously as possible some of the guests left the mansion. Others were intrigued and wanted to see more. These were the people Dante was interested in. Dante saw the world as everyone being good or evil, weak or strong, there was no middle ground for Dante. He built his legion on the ones he could easily control and eventually destroy, or the ones who were strong and would willingly choose evil as their lifestyle. Dante expected a certain number of his guests to leave after the show. Those that left would wake up tomorrow not remembering anything of what happened. However, they would be plagued by nightmares the rest of their natural days. That would be his little thank you gift. The ones who stayed would prove their allegiance to him, or die. With Dante you disappeared from family, friends and loved ones. He became your master, and lord and you did as he commanded or you would be found dead somewhere, someplace. A missing person, with no leads, like Sienna. It was all a part of Dante's global plan. Dante was a sadist, enjoying the pain of others.

However, down, deep in the recesses of his soul, there was something else. A very uncomfortable reminder that he was partly human. Always knowing it was there he fought hard within himself to destroy it. He must destroy it, as it was his safety, his resilience against the rest of the world. He had grudges, lots of grudges against his parents, especially. He had his own internal demons, but he would conquer them now as in the past. Inside of him was an internal struggle, which left him weak at times. Being raised by

Dominic Marchette he had trained himself to rise above the weakness by being tortured himself. As a small child Dominic would allow no small sign of empathy or kindness. As he did with his other sons and daughter, he did with Dante. Dominic created evil monsters, and trained them through various means of punishment to enjoy giving pain. There was one small problem with Dante's scheme of things. Although he had sought her out, and thought he knew what he was up against with Eden, he really had no idea what he would be in for . . . not really. Much like Dante, Eden had no idea that within a few hours, she would be fighting to save Dante's soul.

"Love has no other desire but to fulfill itself."

Kahlil Gibran

Immortal Desire
Chapter Six

Mortamion was losing his men. His guards began seeking employment in other parts of the organization. This was to be expected, as he was no longer part of The Council. Although he could afford to pay them, there was dissention among them due to the fact that they were all immortal and Mortamion and Lillianna were mortal. Most of his guards were no longer under direct orders from The Council to aid Mortamion and Lillianna. As free agents they were able to leave his employment without any ramifications from The Council. Slowly, each guard left, finding other avenues of employment, and Mortamion and Lillianna found themselves alone, with the exception of Louis and Talus who had stayed on. Talus was awaiting his new post which would be in a whole new country, America. Louis had been with Mortamion since Mortamion became a captain for The Council. Mortamion had worked his way up from a soldier. He was an expert marksman with a pistol, but sword fighting was his specialty. Throughout his career, he'd won many battles over the soldiers of The Dominion.

Lillianna was in another world both mentally and emotionally. Thinking of her pregnancy, and upcoming motherhood. Mortamion did his best to support her, but he had serious concerns about their well being. Now with just Louis and Talus, they were unprotected. Trips into town to find servants who would work in the castle had proved unsuccessful. The castle had the reputation of death and evil since the time of Dominic Marchette. Still Louis did what he could, to keep the castle running. Mortamion knew that he had enough funds to keep them both well established in to their old age. However, his intuition caused him concern about their safety. He decided that although he owned the castle out right, after the baby was born, they would move away from the village of San Michelene, back to the estate of his parents in Paris. In the mean time, Mortamion planed a trip to buy Lillianna a Franklin stove, and enough provisions to get them through several months. As winter would be fast approaching and the mountain road would be too dangerous to attempt. He took the large carriage and set off with Louis on a week's journey.

Trusting Talus whom he thought of as a brother, to take care of Lillianna in his absence he felt secure in leaving Lillianna behind. The road over the mountain could be rough and dangerous. So, even though Lillianna wanted to go, Mortamion thought it best that she be comfortable, as they knew not yet if she had conceived. The morning was damp and misty and the temperature still cold, as the sun had not yet risen, when she kissed him goodbye and he set forth with Louis on their journey. Wrapped in her hooded long pink satin cape, that was beautifully lined in white ermine she stood outside, watching as they left the main gate. She watched until the carriage disappeared into the forest and the rocky terrain, and she could no longer see them.

Talus was seated in the drawing room when Lillianna entered the house. He called to her to sit with him a while. He was seated on the settee, laying back casually facing her as she entered. She sat herself down on one of the winged chairs, her long cape splitting open at her knees revealing her pink silken nightgown. Quietly she stared into the fire, remembering weeks ago, when she and Mortamion had sat in front of the fire drinking wine and toasting to their future together. "Are you lost in thought?" Talus asked. Coming back to the moment, she looked at him. "Yes, he is gone but moments and already I miss him." She answered him turning her gaze back to the fire light. "How does that happen?" Talus asked her. She didn't understand him, what did he mean? "I love him." Lillianna replied, turning to look at Talus, her tone quite serious and slightly annoyed. "There is that word again . . . love." He stated as if he were seeking the definition and clarity of it. "I don't think love exists, rather it is lust." He concluded. "No, there is a difference, I know that now . . . now that I am mortal." Talus laughed and Lillianna sensed that he was baiting her. Lillianna rose to leave but Talus stopped her by grabbing her hand.

"Please." Talus said standing. "I'd like you to show me the difference." Lillianna pushed him away from her but Talus pulled her towards him. "If this great love changes everything, show me!" He demanded, forcing his kiss on her. She pulled away from him and ran for the door, but he was too fast for her.

He lifted her up in his arms and carried her up the stairs, as she punched him and fought him to get away. Talus took her to her bedroom throwing her on the bed, the same bed she shared with Mortamion. He pinned her down, underneath him. "I want to see this great love you speak of, Lillianna." His voice was low as he kissed her hard on the mouth. "Talus, please don't do this . . . you will regret it always." Lillianna gasped, struggling against him. "I am immortal Lillianna, remember I don't feel theses emotions you so easily speak of." Talus told her as he desperately tried to kiss her, she shook her head from side to side, trying to escape his lips on hers. Pushing him with her arms, she struggled desperately to get him off her, but it was no use, as he out matched her in size and strength. "I want you Lillianna, and I will have you." He told her.

Talus was insatiable and completely immersed in Lillianna's infinite beauty and sexuality. He had wanted Lillianna since she had first come to the castle. Now, having her once was not enough. He wanted her completely, he wanted her to want him. When morning came he left the room to retire to his own bed. Lillianna knew there was no point in running, there was no place to run to. Besides that Talus would find her. As a Council member he had fast, sharp instincts. He would find her easily. He was immortal and that was his strength over her. Lillianna's only choice was to stay until he was tired of her and Mortamion returned. However, if Mortamion knew about this he would seek revenge from Talus, . . . and would lose. Talus also knew this as well. He knew Mortamion was no longer any match for him. Lying in his bed, Talus thought the same thoughts as Lillianna. He knew Lillianna would be silent, rather than risk the life of the man she loved. He felt no remorse for his actions, for he understood nothing of her being mortal. This was a game to him, a foolish game, which did not deserve his respect. Love? . . . there was no such emotion familiar to him.

He had lost respect for Mortamion as well when he followed Lillianna into this travesty of becoming mortal. As far as Talus was concerned his actions were that of any man who lived by the laws of instinct alone.

He had not hurt her physically, and that was all that really mattered, to him. Talus justified his actions by Mortamion's neglect in leaving Lillianna behind. After all Mortamion should have known there was a possibility this could happen. Mortamion was aware of Council member's intense sexual desires. Talus also understood Lillianna's strong sensual desire and womanly needs, mortal or immortal, she was a woman to be desired. There were times, during the night when he truly believed she had enjoyed his sexual expertise. Lillianna had given in to Talus, because she knew she didn't have a choice. She resented him for his actions, and yet there was a part of her that also understood them, as she had once been without a soul as well. He had hurt her heart deeply, but he didn't comprehend it.

When she was immortal the thought of Talus as a lover had crossed her mind, as she was sure that Mortamion had thoughts of other women also. Yet to her knowledge he had remained faithful to her and her to him. For in themselves, they found a solace and understanding that had brought them to this place and time. Now their feelings for each other were tenfold. This is what Talus could not grasp. The truth was that Talus was a passionate and giving lover, but she longed only for Mortamion now. His body, his heart, his soul. Talus was every woman's dream with his strong features, and long blond hair. He carried an air of strong sophistication, bordering on arrogance, which women were drawn to. Talus had also been created with a special gift that few other Council members contained, his ability to read thoughts. He knew what Lillianna was thinking as she thought it. This gave him extraordinary insight and control over most situations.

In her mind Lillianna could be analytical about what had happened, because she had been immortal herself. But, that didn't stop the tears that soaked her pillow. Her cries were for Mortamion, not herself. The love she felt for him was all encompassing and being taken by Talus left her feeling tainted for the man she loved. It would be her resolve to never let Mortamion know the truth about these days while he was away and what had happened to her. She would never let him suspect anything . . . now she needed to somehow convince Talus to do the same thing. She knew he would want her again and she could give him what he so desperately desired . . . her lust for him in return. She would do whatever she had to do, to protect Mortamion from ever knowing, for it would destroy him.

Although Lillianna had the avenue to tell The Council about the infraction, which would be detrimental for Talus, Mortamion would eventually find out and it would break his heart and that, was something Lillianna could not withstand . . . for it would break her heart as well.

Talus understood everything from a Council member's perspective. He also did not let empathy or sentiment stand in his way. He wasn't created to have feelings, but exist on instinct. Talus simply took what he wanted if given the opportunity. However, he went out of his way not to be involved with mortals, Lillianna was the exception to the rule. Talus only dated women who were Council members and thought as he did. Love was not something he remembered, understood or could feel. Now however, he lusted for Lillianna and was not sure how easily he could give her up. He had a week to enjoy the pleasures of her body, but then it could become a problem as she could seek The Council's intervention. Talus had crossed some serious barriers, as it was against Council law to take a mortal woman against her will, especially a married mortal woman. To continue this trend could put him in danger of expulsion. It all depended on whether Lillianna would press the issue, there by letting Mortamion know what had happened. It was a gamble Talus would choose to take.

When he came back to her room, he had washed and dressed. Not to his surprise she was not there. He knew she was in the house as he had heard her earlier. Making his way downstairs, he found her sitting by the hearth in the kitchen, she was washing herself, covered only by a bed sheet. Water droplets trickled down her neck as she ran the cloth along her skin. Her blond hair piled up high on her head, the beauty of her shoulders exposed. The fire cast a golden glow on her skin as she sat there in his full view. He walked over to her and removed his jacket, laying it on the table. Talus pulled one of the wooden stools over to the hearth and sitting next to her he held out his hand. Lillianna handed him the wash cloth. She was all too aware of his physical needs. Talus rolled up his sleeve and put the cloth in the kettle that sat above the fire, the water was warm.

Gently he passed the cloth along Lillianna's back, watching the water fall from the cloth and cascade down her back. "Why do you have such disdain for me Talus?" she asked him quietly. He put the cloth in the water again, and wrung it out only slightly, so that he could once more watch as the water glided gently on her skin. "I don't have disdain for you Lillianna, on the contrary, I have a fondness for you." He answered. "How is it you can say that . . . when you took me against my will?" she searched for his eyes, but he was concentrating on the way the water made her skin glisten against the fire light. Finally, he stopped and looked at her. "Perhaps, you think it was against your will, but my loins convince me otherwise." He answered her. Lillianna put her hands to her face as tears filled her eyes. Talus pulled her hands away from her face holding them in his own. "Look here." He began. "I know you are human now and you have this great love for Mortamion now, but I am also a man in my own right, and have needs . . . and those needs include you." He could see her tremble. "Are you trembling from fear of me?" he asked, both surprised and concerned. She did not answer. "Or are you cold?" he asked leaning toward her kissing her bare shoulders. "Both." She whispered. Talus took the sheet and wrapped her up in it and then put his jacket over her shoulders. "You and I were one and the same once." He said quietly.

"No Talus . . . I have always belonged to Mortamion." She insisted. "Woman you continue to defy me and test my patience!" He shouted and standing he turned away from her resting his fists on the long wooden table, which stood nearby. Exhaling deeply, he faced her again. She sat there by the fire wrapped in his blue jacket with its shiny brass buttons attached to it. They reflected the glow from the firelight and shimmered like gold. Her hair was like delicate strands of silk falling in ringlets about her shoulders. He was entranced with her beauty and grace. Although he had known her as Sophia Basset and her personality was the same, her beauty and sensuality were very different as a mortal. The truth was she was the most beautiful woman he had ever seen. She was incandescent and magnetic. The animal instinct in him could not walk away from her.

Talus knew what he was doing was wrong . . . not based on human moral code, but by The Council's code, yet he was willing to risk his future on this woman who he could never completely have. This thought mystified him and intrigued him all at the same time. In all his years both mortal and immortal, he had never had to take a woman by force, women chased him, on a constant basis, to the point of annoyance. Yet, this woman now wanted nothing to do with him. A part of him just could not comprehend this, because it had not happened to him before. This is where his arrogance came into play. He had given her everything he had to give as far as sexual pleasure last night and yet here she was rebuking him. What fascinated him was that Lillianna exuded a childlike innocence mixed with a woman's sexuality. Talus did not know this now, but a hundred years in his future, in another time and place he would meet another woman child, who would also test his patience.

Talus sat back down on the stool next to Lillianna. "I do not understand or feel this love you speak of." He tried to explain. "Yet I do know wanting and lust for a woman, and I want and lust for you, more than I have for any woman, past or present." He told her. Talus was being completely honest and Lillianna knew it. "As I am . . . I would fight all three dimensions, if they were to keep you from me and if that's what you ask . . . you ask too much." Talus said. "I will give you everything you ask of me . . . all that I am Talus . . . if you will promise me and give me your word as a Council member, that you will leave me before Mortamion's return . . . for this would break his heart." She pleaded. Once again Talus lost his temper. "Woman what do I care of love and hearts, I know only of want and need!" He shouted, standing up. "I can take you by force." He reminded her. "Yes, I know you can and will." Lillianna whispered. Pulling her up, she turned away from him. "Look at me!" He commanded. Lillianna looked up at him. "I don't want you that way, I want you to want me." He insisted. "Give me your word Talus." Lillianna implored. Talus lifted her up in his arms and cradled her close to him as he felt her body shiver. He kissed her and carried her up the long staircase, to her bed and placing her on it he spoke the words she needed to hear. "I give you my word, I will leave before your husband's return, and of this he will not hear from my lips."

Lillianna was true to her word and surpassed his expectations, for he had never known such a lover as she. Her lust and passion far exceeded anything he had experienced. In truth Lillianna wanted to run to Mortamion and tell him all her sorrows, but those were imaginary conversations she had with herself. As she fulfilled Talus' dreams she thought it as part of her penance for wanting to be mortal. Talus kept his word and left before dawn the day of Mortmain's expected return, while Lillianna slept. On her bed he left a note, which read simply; "I can love you never, yet there will always be a part of me that will belong to you, and only you, T." Lillianna burnt the note for fear that it might be discovered and she could not risk that. With open arms of love and longing she ran to Mortamion upon his arrival. Never speaking of her week with Talus. Mortamion expressed disappointment that Talus had left her alone, and had not waited for him and Louis to get back before leaving. "He received word of his new post and left yesterday." Lillianna replied lightly. "Where will he be going?" inquired Mortamion. "My sweet, I have been so anxious for your return, that I forgot to ask him." She answered hugging him. In her heart it didn't matter that she had slept with Talus. Mortamion was her truest love and she embraced her time with him as never before. She wanted only for his safety and happiness and to have his child. She prayed that it would be his child she would bring forth in to the world.

Talus was not completely unmoved by Lillianna's feelings. He just could not give in to them. He viewed all situations from an unemotional and logical perspective. She was a beautiful and sensual woman. He wanted her and there was no one to stand in his way, from having her. He also resented her change to mortality. A part of him wanted to bring her back to the realization of who she had been and claimed to no longer be. Talus was confident in his abilities to please a woman. He had taken great pains to not hurt her, which had been difficult the first hour of their union, as she continually fought him. Then, as he had suspected she ceased to struggle against him, and he believed she might very well have enjoyed some of what happened. He was not without his understanding that she was loyal to Mortamion.

For Talus, he was fulfilling a physical need, his need at the time, and if she had needed him, he would willingly have granted her, himself. Members of The Council often did this, as long as it was sanctioned by the other partner, if there was another partner. In truth, longevity in relationships was not common between Council members. As she and Mortamion were no longer Council members, he knew of course, Mortamion would never sanction his approval for Lillianna to be with him now. Knowing Mortamion, he probably would not have sanctioned it in the past either, but perhaps she would have. It was difficult to say because they were now so emotionally tied to each other.

Talus had never been intrigued by Lillianna before her becoming mortal. It was as if she sparkled with an internal light, which he craved to get close to. She was radiant and luscious to him and he wanted her. Talus didn't comprehend the idea of hearts or loves. He understood he had hurt her pride and disrespected Mortamion, which Talus felt Mortamion deserved. Talus lost respect for Mortamion when he made the transition from immortality to mortality. He also felt Mortamion had been careless and foolish in leaving Lillianna behind and at risk. It had not been his intention to take Lillianna away from Mortamion, but rather to borrow her. His masculinity was drawn to Lillianna's sensuality and he chose to ignore that she was now mortal.

Talus rode his horse hard and fast once he got down the mountain. He wanted to get as far away from Lillianna as possible, or he just might have to stay and fight Mortamion for her and that would be the ruination of everyone, himself included. He didn't completely understand his own thinking. She had this hold on him that he had not experienced before and it was haunting him. Talus knew he had to light a fire under The Council Tribunal to hurry them up and assign him a new post. He didn't care where they sent him, as long as it was far away from Lillianna and Mortamion. As he rode across the open field, he saw a carriage in the distance, his keen supernatural eyesight recognized Mortamion, and he quickly detoured and directed his horse into the surrounding forest. It would lengthen the distance he had to travel, but Mortamion was the last person he wanted to see.

Alestasis came in to the world nine months later, February 6th 1893. A robust violet eyed baby boy. Weighing close to nine pounds. There were moments of terror for Mortamion during Lillianna's labor, had it not been for Louis who kept a level head, Mortamion would have lost his mind, seeing and hearing Lillianna in such pain. Mortamion had been both doctor and mid wife, with Louis at his side, wiping Mortmain's brow. The labor had been long, lasting two days. Lillianna though happy at seeing her new son, was exhausted and fell into a deep sleep. Mortamion had never imagined such a feeling of joy, as he felt guiding his son out of his mother's womb into this new world. These feelings that mortals experienced were so powerful, he thought as he lay next to Lillianna and Alestasis. Here was true happiness and joy in the world. In all the years he had been on this earth nothing could compare to what he now felt, nothing ever would. In the days that followed Mortamion never left their side, spoon feeding Lillianna soup that Louis had made. He took care of her and Alestasis as a nurse maid, tending to their every need.

Mortamion was in a complete state of bliss, having now created a human life. When Lillianna regained her strength, she tended to her son, breast feeding him and placing him in the crib that Mortamion had brought back with him. It was a crib suited for a prince of gilded white and gold scrolled iron. Along with other provisions he surprised Lillianna with a small Franklin stove, which Louis was making good use of, as now he was much more than a man servant. Louis had become a cook virtually overnight, although he personally had no use for food, his employers were always ravished with hunger and extremely tired, as baby Alestasis was always hungry and enjoyed the warmth and security of his parent's bed. Louis wondered why the infant needed a crib after all. This was now the life of the small family, as they prepared to enjoy their future together, as mortals do.

The winter had proved to be colder than expected and the small family nestled quietly in the comfort and safety of Lillianna's bed. Mortamion busied himself, chopping wood for fire and hunting for pheasant when the weather allowed it. He was proficient at both, having served in the military in his past life, Mortamion would now be using the skills that his memory afforded him. Fortunately Louis did not desert them, although he could have, had he chose to. Receiving telepathic communications from The Council Tribunal Louis was a free agent to continue working for a Council Captain somewhere else, or to stay with Mortamion and Lillianna. Servants did not have to follow the same rules as captains, soldiers, negotiators, or administrators. Servants were in a different class of responsibilities and it was not crucial for them to only work for Council members.

There were many Council servants in the employ of mortals. The unemotional effectiveness of their job made them an excellent fit for mortals that could afford them. By most accounts they usually ran the whole entire household, by simply putting reason, logic and necessity before emotion and their masters adored them for it. Louis chose to stay simply because he was intrigued and curious about their mortal life. Louis had grown bored over the past one hundred years, this new way of life suited him for the time being. When the small family became too emotional or baby

Alestasis cried endlessly, Louis would retire to his room on the other side of the castle. Both Mortamion and Lillianna understood Louis and trusted him.

Mortmain's anxiety had ebbed for the winter, he knew that the mountain passes would be much too treacherous to climb during the winter months. He brought back lumber with him, the week he was gone and he and Louis had sealed off all the windows and doors, except for one in the back of the house which had direct access to the root cellar and carriage house. Beyond that stood the back gate of the castle and beyond that the forest. Mortamion did his best hunting there, twice bringing home a turkey that Louis roasted on the open hearth as it was much too big for the stove.

Lillianna had some worries of her own. Past memories which awakened her from a deep sleep at times. She worried about Mortamion and his safety. Her dreams haunted her about her week with Talus. Being a woman she worried about her looks, since she had given birth her tiny waist had grown considerably. She would look in the mirror daily and frown, Mortamion would take her in his arms and comfort her doubts. "Lillianna, never could I love anyone but you, not in this world or any other. You are as beautiful to me and as irresistible as you have always been, even more so now since you became a mother." He knew her insecurities and tried to quell them. "So you still think I am pretty?" she would ask pouting, her tone begging for reassurance. Mortamion would smile at her and sit her on his lap. "Well you are a trifle heavier." He'd say seriously. Then after kissing her deeply he would reply. "You are perfect everyday . . .you are perfect and I would want no other." It was a game they played daily and one of which they did not tire of.

"Love seeketh not itself to please, nor for itself hath any care; but for another gives it's ease and builds a Heaven in Hell's despair."
William Blake

Paradise Lost
Chapter Seven

The winter passed without incident and baby Alestasis was now sleeping in his own crib as spring approached. Slowly, Mortamion and Louis began to remove some of the wood which closed off the doors and windows to the castle. Lillianna missed having the sun light in her favorite room which faced the garden. She would often take Alestasis through the French doors which led to the garden, telling him stories about baby rabbits as she carried him in her arms. Spring was still chilly up in the mountain air, so it was the end of June when finally the garden was in full bloom. Lillianna spent her whole days outside on the grassy knoll behind the castle with Alestasis on her lap, Mortamion joining her for lunch that Louis had prepared. Mortamion held her in his arms as she nursed baby Alestasis. For Lillianna this was everything she had ever wanted and she was filled with joy and promise of days to come. For Mortamion he saw dark clouds on the horizon and beckoned they go inside as a storm was surely approaching.

"No my darling, the sky is clear." Lillianna said kissing his lips. "There is a chill I feel, tomorrow is another day for now it is time to end the day and begin the night." Mortamion replied. As they walked inside, Mortamion looked out again at the sky, the wind had picked up and it surrounded him with a momentary feeling of emptiness. Once inside he closed the doors, locked them and followed Lillianna upstairs. As she laid Alestasis in his crib she realized that his small wooden rattle had been left outside on the grass, she called downstairs for Louis to retrieve it for her, which he did.

George and Carlotta learned to live without Lillianna in their lives, but it had a major effect on the closeness they once shared. Carlotta withdrew more and more away from George and George didn't know how to deal with it. Naturally he had lost a daughter as well, but he was fortunate that he had two others. Elise had recently given them a granddaughter who she named Lilli and Margot had recently been married, so now it was just the two of them. Early one morning George took his carriage into town. He was shopping for provisions and while he was there he saw Inspector Laurent shopping with his wife.

He discreetly pulled George aside, giving him a valuable bit of information. "It seems all of Delmont's employees have left him, including his brother." Laurent told George quietly. "Why?" asked George. "I don't know but several months ago he came into town, trying to find people to work for him." He continued, "however no one would go up to there." Laurent nodded in the direction of the shop keeper. "He mentioned it to me, just a few moments ago." Laurent explained. George hastened to go to the shopkeeper to question him, but Laurent stopped him. "Why don't we go and see if we . . . you and I can gain entrance?" Laurent whispered. "When?" asked George. "Tomorrow morning . . . ? asked Laurent, fidgeting with his moustache.

The men made a plan to meet at the base of the mountain and climb up to the castle at dawn.

When George arrived home, he told Carlotta about his conversation with Inspector Laurent. She surprised him with her response, she shook her head. She felt that he should let this pass. George asked her why, she responded that she had a bad premonition about it and the events that might happen. George assured her that both he and the inspector were going armed. They ate dinner in silence. George was confused about his wife's reaction to his trying to gain access to the castle. He knew she had suffered terribly from the loss, but so had he. Now he had a second chance. After all, Lillianna hadn't disappeared into thin air. He had felt certain from the beginning that she was there. He had seen it in the eyes of Mortamion, who had tried to lie to him a year ago, but had not succeeded.

Before she went to bed Carlotta kissed George on the cheek and whispered to him. "Do not go to the castle tomorrow, if she is there, perhaps she belongs there." He sat at the kitchen table stunned. George asked her again, "why?" but she did not respond. She went to her bed silently. George stayed up till right before dawn and road his horse to the edge of the clearing, tying her up to some branches he lit the lantern and made his way to the base of the mountain. There he found the inspector holding a snifter containing brandy. "Nervous are we Inspector?" asked George. "It takes the chill off the morning air." The inspector replied. He offered George the snifter but he declined. He didn't want anything blurring his vision or his judgment.

The mountain was rocky and steep, taking them a several hours to climb up and then there was about a half mile walk to the perimeter of the gate. The gate was tall and encircled the property completely, but due to the ground not being fully level, there were areas where it was shorter.

The inspector and George found such a spot and hoisted themselves over the gate. The air was thick, still heavy with morning fog, walking along the inside of the gate they followed it to the side of the castle. They made their way through the shrubs that lined the side and front. There looking through the side window of the French doors, George saw expensive furniture that few people could afford, and it had a feminine quality that indicated to him a woman lived there. The inspector agreed, quietly. "That furniture is something a woman would have, not a house filled with only men." Assuming the front door was locked they tried entering by the French doors and it worked as they were unlocked.

George and the inspector readied their pistols and continued through the room where Lillianna and Mortamion enjoyed the fire, toasting and professing their love for one another, close to a year ago. Now they were at the base of the stairs. So far it seemed as though the house was empty, they made their way up the stairs as quietly as possible. Holding their breath when they heard the slightest creak from one of the steps. The inspector cursed below his breath that there were forty five steps, eleven more to go he thought.

It was on that very step, that Mortamion heard something. Lillianna sleeping soundly next to him, heard nothing. He got out of the bed, still dressed in his pants, as the baby had kept them up all through the night. Lillianna had been exhausted, so Mortamion cradled his infant son until he fell asleep. He had just placed Alestasis in his crib in the next room, closing the door and then quietly slipping into bed next to Lillianna. On the stairs, below both the inspector and George hastened their bodies against the wall. Mortamion's instinct told him something was not as it should be. Louis was on the other side of the castle. Mortamion fully opened the door and walking into the hallway, called for Louis . . . who did not answer. Suddenly he saw movement running across the landing. "Louis!" He called out. There was very little light, but Mortamion could see two shadows approaching him. Finally, recognizing George he yelled for Lillianna.

Lillianna bolted up grabbing the sheet and wrapping it around herself; she often did not wear night gowns or dress until she was fully up for the day, as she was usually breast feeding Alestasis. She ran into the hallway where she saw Mortamion slowly walking backwards. Both the inspector and George had their pistols aimed at him. She came up behind Mortamion. "George . . . please let us explain the situation." Mortamion began. Lillianna held Mortamion by the waist. Now they were back in the bedroom in front of the bed. Mortamion in just his pants and Lillianna wrapped in only a sheet. As the early morning sun rose streaming light into the room, George looked at Lillianna with shock. Realizing she was not here against her will, he screamed. "Is this how your mother and I raised you?" tears welled up in his eyes. "Get some clothes on girl, you defile yourself." George spoke through his tears.

The inspector glanced around the room, spotting a pistol on a dresser that stood next to the large oval mirror. Mortamion, tried to diffuse the situation by saying, "Lillianna is my wife." But the very sound of his voice enraged George. "Speak you not to me, liar!" George shouted. Mortamion continued slowly, as Lillianna held onto his waist. "We are married, . . and our son sleeps in the adjoining room." Mortamion spoke slowly. "Lillianna get dressed I am taking you home." George ordered her. "This is my home and this is my husband." Lillianna replied. "Your home is with your mother and me!" George shouted and began to lose all control, tears streaming down his face, the gun shaking in his hand. "Do you have any idea what your mother has been through? What I and your sisters have been through?" George was filled with anguish and despair, the inspector realizing this interjected, hoping to calm the situation. "Perhaps you could go now with your father, for a short visit . . . Lillianna?" suggested the inspector as he was also trying to quell George's temper. "Perhaps I will, with my husband and son, but not now." She replied her tone serious and direct, as she still held onto Mortamion. "I am taking you back with me now!" George yelled. "Your mother has suffered enough!" He lashed out.

Suddenly, Louis appeared in the doorway, causing the inspector and George instinctively to turn. At that moment Mortamion leapt for the pistol, fearing they would force Lillianna to go with them. His thought was to keep her with him, and perhaps they could visit George and Carlotta with the baby, as a family. When the shot was fired no one was sure who had fired the gun or if it had hit anyone. It was not until Mortamion held his chest and staggered towards Lillianna, his blood pouring out from the wound, that George realized he had pulled the trigger. Everyone stood for what seemed moments, shocked to see Mortamion fall to his knees, his pistol still on the dresser as George had shot before he was able to reach it.

Alestasis' cries were drowned out by Lillianna's screams, as she held Mortamion in her arms. Her screams filled the castle walls and reverberated in George's ears, sending shock waves through his body. Lillianna cradled Mortamion's upper body rocking back and forth, leaning over him kissing his lips, his face, covering the wound with the sheet, exposing her body. George staggered out of the room, as he covered his ears, he could not stand her screams, and he could not look at the sight of Mortamion dying. His daughter was unclothed and hysterical as the inspector followed George into the hallway. Louis ran to Mortamion, covering him with his coat. Trying to stop the bleeding he pressed down on the wound. "No!" Shouted Lillianna, "That will only cause him more pain." Lillianna knew she had only moments left with the man she had loved for two hundred years.

Mortamion, gasping for breath looked into her eyes and smiled faintly as he asked her. "What has been your happiest moment?" Her long blond hair surrounded his body, her face inches from his. "Every moment with you, has been my happiest." She replied through her tears. As his body went limp, he spoke his last words, "I will wait for you." Lillianna screamed out like a wounded animal. Her cries did not sound human to George or the inspector. Mortamion's body began to slowly turn into dust as George and the inspector came back into the room, Lillianna lay with her hands empty, with no sign of blood, as Mortamion had disintegrated. The inspector and George were only now beginning to understand and yet it seemed impossible.

However their shock was just beginning as Lillianna stood up, and slowly pulled the sheet up, covering herself with it. The sheet that had been covered with blood, was now covered in Mortamion's dust. She slowly walked to the French doors, which led to the balcony. As if in a trance Lillianna opened the doors and at that moment a gust of wind entered the room. She knew it was Mortamion's spirit essence coming for her. George ran to her but she was quicker than he. Looking over the balcony he saw her body, lying on the stone below. The inspector ran down the steps and out the front door, but as he approached her he could see that her neck was broken. She had most likely died instantly upon hitting the ground.

By the time George got to her, Lillianna's body had begun to fall away like translucent powder, sparkling in the cool morning wind. All that was left was the sheet she had been wrapped in. George took the sheet in his hands and cried uncontrollably. "She was not of this world, he was not of this world." He sobbed. "What a horrible course of events has led to this tragedy." Said Inspector Laurent, sighing with complete shock, at what he had just witnessed. The inspector put his arms around George and said, "Perhaps the child is." Slowly they climbed up the large staircase. George with hope of bringing something of Lillianna back to his wife.

As George and the inspector reached the top of the stairs, they both looked at each other. Why was it so quiet? There were no cries from Alestasis. The house was now cool from the wind that had blown through it. It was also unnaturally still. Entering the baby's room, they approached the crib. The crib was empty, all that was left behind was the small wooden rattle. Nothing remained, nothing except the sound of Lillianna's voice in the distance. Both George and the inspector could hear it as if in a far off place. "We are sorry for the pain we have caused you." George fell to his knees next to the crib. He was beyond understanding and filled with guilt and regret.

The sun was setting as they made their way back down the mountain, after having searched the whole castle for Lillianna's son Alestasis, to no avail. They knew that Louis had taken the baby and left the castle, but where had he taken him? George was not going to search for him. He was done searching. His search had ended today with Lillianna's death. His spirit was shattered and he now knew why Carlotta had insisted he forget Lillianna.

She saw something in her premonitions after all. He somehow did not feel remorse for Mortamion, being her husband he should have been honest with him in the beginning. George tried to rationalize his feelings. Perhaps Mortamion didn't say anything because of how he had behaved, trying to strangle Mortamion over a year ago, or because Lillianna didn't want him to. He was certain of one thing and that is they were not of this world. What he had experienced in that castle would go to his grave with him, as both he and the inspector knew that they would both be declared insane if they spoke of it. Once on the bottom of the mountain, they made a pledge to never disclose what they had seen with their own eyes.

Somehow he would manage to tell Carlotta that he searched the whole castle and found nothing, nothing except the sheet he carried back with him . . . the sheet that carried the very essence of Lillianna's soul, and part of Mortamion's. How would he sleep? He knew he would be haunted by this to the end of his days. Haunted as Carlotta had been after Lilianna's disappearance. His mind raced as he road back on his horse to the dairy farm. George arrived back at the farm in the darkness of night, carrying his lantern as he walked from the barn to the house. Carlotta was waiting for him. Sitting in the kitchen with her, he described the day and how he and the inspector had found nothing. The castle had been left abandoned and empty. All he had found was a pink silken sheet with the initial L embroidered in script at the top of the sheet. Carlotta held it to her face and smelled it. She told George she knew Lillianna had died wrapped in this sheet. George was taken aback by her instinct and intuition, but said nothing of what truly had happened. He could not, for although he knew Carlotta would believe him, he also knew it would kill her. He held her in his arms as they slept and told her he loved her, more than life it's self.

Carlotta had been the true love of his life and that is why he wanted to bring Lillianna home to her, to bring her happiness back. Thinking over all that had happened, George realized Lillianna was not the same person he and

Carlotta had brought into the world, and raised . . . or perhaps she had never been of this world. He knew that she had somehow changed into another being. Eventually George gave in to the sleep he so badly needed, not waking till well past dawn, opening his eyes, he wondered where Carlotta was. Why hadn't she wakened him?

His first thought was that she had gone to the grotto in the mission to pray. One of the friars had sculpted a statue of a young girl, dressed in a peasant dress, with long hair. She stood barefooted, holding a small bird in her hand. A year after Lillianna's disappearance, the friars unveiled the statue and dedicated it to Lillianna's memory. In summer the statue was surrounded by hundreds of flowers. Often Carlotta could be found there, as she found solace for her loss being near the statue, for it was an exact likeness to Lillianna as a child.

George got up slowly, in nineteen years of marriage never once had he awakened to a house so still, so quiet? Even when Carlotta was in shock after Lillianna's disappearance, Margot and the friar were still there, but now the house was eerily quiet. He dressed as fast as he could, and went into the kitchen. Carlotta was not there. Then he proceeded to look in the three bedrooms that had once belonged to his daughters, everything was in its place as if they still lived in the house. This farm house that had held a quaint, country charm for him, now suddenly felt large, cold and unfamiliar. He began calling her name through the rooms, as he walked almost aimlessly, panic began to set in. His mind began racing, as it had yesterday when he saw Lillianna. His mind took him back to the moment Lillianna threw herself off the balcony-as if by some twisted circumstance, he knew where Carlotta was.

George ran from the house across the meadow to the barn, already knowing what he would find. Carlotta's lifeless body hung, from a rope she had tied to the rafters up in the hayloft. George stood, staring at the way the profusion of gravity moved her body ever so slightly in a circular motion. Oddly, he was not surprised and quickly climbed the ladder up to the hayloft. He gently pulled her body up, lifting her up by putting his arms under hers. He felt the heaviness of death surround him. Then he laid her down on the hayloft. He removed the rope from her head and held her in his arms, holding her until the inevitable stiffness of rigor mortis set in. It was sunset before he walked to the mission and enlisted the friar's help in getting Carlotta down from the hayloft.

Elise and Margot made all the preparations for the service and burial. Their husbands, helping them maintain their emotional stability and running the farm temporarily. George did not speak for weeks. He did not eat or wash himself. He was dead inside and could not deal with the reality of his life. Elise went to see Inspector Laurent and asked him to come and speak with her father. The inspector had been to the service at the mission and had paid his respects to George, but it was as if George was not aware of where he was or who he was. Elise implored the inspector to come and see her father, for the doctor had said there was no medicine that could help her father . . . nothing except time would cure George.

George had sustained a major shock and it could be months or even years before he would come out of it. The inspector entered George's bedroom. Walking around to the front of the bed he observed George, who sat upright and facing forward. Clutched in his hands were Carlotta's bed clothes, held tightly to his chest. His face covered in a grey beard, his eyes glazed over. Inspector Laurent pulled up a chair and put his hand on George's hand. Talking of anything, his family, idol bits of gossip, went to no avail.

Inspector Laurent tried to get some response, but George had no reaction to his even being in the room. The inspector game every day to visit and talk to George, he would sit for an hour and then leave, just shaking his head.

As days turned into weeks, it was decided that George would do better in a sanatorium just outside of Paris. The doctor recommended this because George was wasting away and suffering from malnutrition . . . if left in this condition he would surely die, physically. It was clear he had died emotionally, mentally and spiritually.

Elise and Margot were now living there with their husbands and baby Lilli, who was now six months old and making quite a bit of noise, as she would gurgle and coo, as infants do. One sunny afternoon, while she was seated at the kitchen table on her mother's lap, George made his way, unsteadily into the kitchen as he was weak and frail. Sitting down he held his arms out in a gesture to hold Lilli. Elise placed her on his lap. In a scratchy and hoarse voice he asked her, "Who is this young lady making all the noise?" Lilli, being naturally out going and friendly, playfully tugged at his beard.

This was the turning point for George; finally he came back to the living. Finally he found a reason to live, a reason to go on, a reason to leave the past behind. Lilli was the catalyst that George needed to regain some small fraction of hope. Every day he was able to speak a little more. He began to eat and bath and shave his own beard, but it had taken months to find his sanity. A year after Carlotta's death George decided to sell the farm. He had offered it to Elise and Margot, but their husbands had professions that were lucrative and sustained them sufficiently. For George, it was time to go home.

It was not long before a large French dairy company made him a respectable offer and George accepted it. He arrived in London on a rainy day on October 1895. Having written to the Stevens family about his arrival that would be his first stop. Mr. Stevens had long retired from the printing business. George was now forty-eight years old and a part of him felt that he had lived too long. His presence was very well received by the Steven's who were not alone in their reception.

At their home George met his future wife. Claire Taylor, a fairly young widow, with the most endearing mannerism. She took to George immediately. He was touched by her but; the loss of Carlotta still clung to him. However Claire was of strong British stock and with that came the tenacity of an English terrier. She knew she wanted George and with the nurturing of the Steven's family, she became his wife. After a very lengthy courtship, George and Claire were married in the spring of 1900. Sometimes having the companionship of a loving partner who understands your needs is all one requires to have a happy marriage. This was the case of George and Claire Taylor Evanharth. There was a bond that they shared, both having lost the great loves of their lives, they understood each other. So without much trouble they both settled into a loving partnership, filled with understanding, trust and affection.

Claire Taylor was a bricklayer's daughter who had been raised in a Christian household in the outskirts of London, her values and morals were similar to George. They both attended mass every Sunday and quickly became part of their church community. Claire had been married to a minister for twelve years and had lived in South Africa. After his death from malaria, Claire came back to London and her roots. She had definite ideas on how a husband should be taken care of. Her duty was to George, who was second only to God and her faith. Claire led the choir at church, as she read music and played the piano well enough to earn a little extra money teaching children of their parish. She did not have the sensual and ardent beauty of Carlotta, but she was quick witted, well spoken and kept a clean orderly household. More than that she took care of George, giving him back his self confidence as a husband and member of society.

For in this new world he was not so isolated, as he had been in San Michelene, where the center of his universe had been only his close family. Here his house was filled with children, coming and going, as mothers and fathers came to drop off and pick up their children. For the first time music became a very important part of his life, and he loved it. During the holiday's Claire played all the Christmas Carols he remembered from childhood and it brightened his heart, and he eventually would thank God for giving him a second chance at happiness.

In 1906 Claire gave birth to a baby girl who they named Rebecca. Her full name on her certificate of birth was Rebecca Lillian (derived from Lillianna) Evanharth. She was eleven pounds at birth, with white hair and bright blue eyes. Becca as she was called, was the apple of George's eyes who was now fifty nine years old. Claire had a difficult labor as she was now forty three and Rebecca was her first child. Claire raised Rebecca from her early years to become a strong advocate for a group that was born from their church. A group of people who believed they were needed to protect all mortal souls, from the eager and unrelenting force of Satan. In fact Claire's great grandfather was one of the original founding fathers of The Path, a very religious sect that had exceptional strength against the forces of evil. In South Africa she honed her skills in exorcism, practicing along side of the wise men of the tribes. She was able to cast out the demons that take procession of a human soul.

Although The Path was not recognized by every parish, there were those that kept the members close at hand, in an underground connection. Some of the ministers sanctioned it while others turned a blind eye. Rebecca being Claire's only child was exposed to its functions at a very young age, and it was said by members of The Path that she possessed supernatural abilities. George had little to say about this as his confidence in Claire was unshakeable.

Rebecca thrived in all areas in school and religious training. She being as logical and sensible as her mother, and showed great promise for teaching. She was sixteen when she met Jacob Linden, a Barrister, who belonged to the same parish. They were immediately smitten with each other. He was twenty-four and had just graduated with his law degree. Claire and George thought Rebecca was too young to make any such commitment to a proposal. They insisted that she finish school and then if they felt the same about each other George and Claire would pay for the wedding and supply a nice dowry. Jacob and Rebecca agreed that this was a reasonable request. In 1924 with the blessing of her parents she and Jacob married in the parish they both attended. Jacob was twenty-six and Rebecca eighteen. As was not unusual for the time, Rebecca kept her maiden name. She was now Rebecca Lillian Linden Evanharth.

Shortly after Rebecca's marriage, George passed away from pneumonia; Claire of course was devastated as now she had buried two husbands. Elise and Margot had visited London many times throughout the years, bringing along their husbands and children. Although Claire was very different from their mother Carlotta, she made their father happy and that's all that mattered to them. They were all greatly saddened and stayed several months to help Claire adjust to her life without George. Claire began to succumb to various ailments over the next few years and at age sixty-six she died of heart complications.

Rebecca was now twenty three years old and was called upon to take over where her mother left off in the matters of The Path. At first she declined, but Jacob convinced her to reconsider. Jacob believed strongly in The Path and thought Rebecca's work was crucial to its continued longevity. Prayer was the foundation of its core but, meditation and visualization played a strong supporting role. However, being a member was not for the faint hearted. In truth sometimes it was hard to separate true procession of the soul, from mental illness.

At times it took days to cast out demons and Path members had to be replaced because of exhaustion. The true test was when the devil himself had to be battled in his own form. On these occasions, The Path would send their Warriors of God to face Satan. These were members who had been born with supernatural abilities, and were chosen at conception through The Highest Realm. Rebecca was one of these warriors. In these cases which were becoming more frequent, angels from The Highest Realm would actually take human form and help the warriors to save the soul of the intended victim.

One of these angels was Daniel, who had come to the aid of Claire many times and would prove to be invaluable to Rebecca as well. Daniel was the most powerful angel in The Highest Realm and was head of The Path in the spirit world. Rebecca would become one of the very few mortals who would lead The Path on earth.

Rebecca and Jacob left London, at the end of the Second World War. She was now thirty eight and Jacob forty six. They settled in Boston where Jacob had relatives and a brand new law practice with his uncle who had a well established clientele, as Jacob's practice had suffered during the war years. The other reason was also a good one; the new parish in America needed members of The Path Legion and this was a perfect opportunity. The Hadleyville Fellowship Church was fairly new to Hadleyville Massachusetts, having been erected in 1940; the church needed a strong leader to continue The Path in New England. Rebecca was the one, with Jacob at her side. Taking after her mother Claire, Rebecca gave birth to Thomas later in life at age forty one, Thomas was unplanned and a complete surprise. Like her mother before her, Rebecca was smart, tidy, a good cook and responsible. Jacob's law practice was doing well and the family was both financially and spiritually sound.

Rebecca quickly became an important member of the parish, devoting much of her time developing a strong foundation in the community helping others. The parish was her full time job as she was the secretary and treasurer. Thomas would later let it be known that he resented her time and devotion to the parish, and the time it took away from him. He remembers his mom being preoccupied, with church work, and his missing her. Rebecca would say that he was a good son if very needy, by nature. She having literally been raised within The Path had a strong belief of its foundation in her work and responsibility to it.

It was by Rebecca's continued involvement with the parish through the next two decade, that Thomas met Rachel, who would become his wife. The Path was not only committed to the safety and welfare of its followers from the lure of Satan, but was involved in issues of domestic violence and poverty. Rachel was a young woman who Rebecca found on the steps of the parish hall, early one morning. She came seeking work, as her father had died the previous year. Rachel's mother was struggling as a seamstress hardly making ends meet. Rebecca was touched by her delicate and well raised manner. Within a few weeks Rachel was working in the parish office as a receptionist and Rachel's mother was making all the choir robes. Even though the current robes were in good condition, Rebecca thought new red ones would be nice for the holidays. It wasn't long before Thomas was smitten with the petite strawberry blond with the large green eyes. He would make all sorts of excuses to stop by on his way home from class, to say hello to his mom and have a chat with Rachel.

Thomas was now twenty three and in law school following in his father's footsteps. He had gone out with a few girls in high school and college but nothing ever developed. In his first year in law school his concentration had been on his grades, for his father Jacob's expectations were high. It came as no surprise to Rebecca when Thomas asked Rachel out on a date and she accepted. A year later Thomas proposed to Rachel, presenting her with his grandmother Claire's diamond ring, which Rebecca had inherited. Two years later they were married in The Hadleyville Fellowship Church. Rebecca and Jacob held the reception in their back yard. Living in a small flat near Hyde Park was all the newlyweds could afford as Thomas had one more year of school to finish, before he could take the bar exam.

The day he took the exam, Rachel presented Thomas with a small gift . . . she was expecting. Nine months later Baby Eden was born, named after The Garden of Eden. She was a beautiful baby with large blue eyes and a full head of blond curls the color of pale wheat. Eden was a happy even tempered baby, with delicate features, and a soft completion.

Thomas joined his father's law firm and gained a healthy income. Rachel had fallen in love with a house on Sparrow lane, in Hadleyville, not far from Rebecca and Jacob's house. Thomas took his wife to see the house and complained the whole way there. Once inside he complained that doorknobs were not tight and needed to be replaced, the windows were old and drafty. The furnace was old and a new one would have to be purchased. Rachel was saddened but told Thomas that if he wasn't happy, neither would she be happy. Kissing him on the cheek, Rachel prepared to leave. Carrying baby Eden in her arms, she turned to Thomas and said that he was more important to her than a house. That's when Thomas took the keys from his pocket and gave them to Rachel saying "Welcome home sweetheart." That's how Thomas was . . . a bit on the needy side.

"I am only one, but still I am one. I cannot do everything, but still I can do something."

Edward Everett Hale

Warrior of God
Chapter Eight

Eden was the center of everyone's attention as she was a happy active baby and found her place in Rebecca's heart immediately. Rebecca was getting older now and had hoped that Thomas would help her in the work of The Path, strictly as an assistant. Helping with the countless hours of prayer that it sometimes took, to expel Satan from someone's soul. But, Thomas was completely against it. He had viewed one exorcism when he was fifteen and vowed to himself never to get involved in The Path. It had frightened him to see it, but it also frightened him to see his mother perform it, with his father at her side, she would literally transform herself into someone else. Rebecca's voice became powerful and deep she would go into a trance like state with her eyes rolling back in her head. The power of her faith was so strong that she could levitate herself off her feet and verbally do battle with the evil spirit, conjuring him out of the body and soul he had taken over. In the background were Jacob, Father Clemmens and Father Odell, loudly reciting scripture. Thomas wanted nothing to do with any of it. This was a part of his lineage he could not accept. A big part of him believed it to be uncivilized, and when he told his mother this, she replied, "Satan is uncivilized." A person needs a certain fortitude and belief to attempt anything like that, he thought and Thomas knew he wasn't cut out for it. Rebecca had been born with it, as she believed Eden had. When Eden was two years old, her baby brother entered the world.

Thomas and Rachel named him Benjamin after Rachel's deceased father. He was adorable as most babies. Benjamin resembled his sister, except that his eyes were green like Rachel's. When Benjamin was two, he contracted Scarlett Fever and had to be hospitalized. His fever was so high it caused him to have convulsions. The doctors tried every available antibiotic but nothing seemed to work as it was a viral infection. Rebecca was sure it was something else, something was pulling him into the deep dark hollows of death. She pleaded to Thomas to allow her and Jacob to sit by Benjamin's hospital crib and spiritually cleanse his soul, but Thomas became outraged, yelling. "He's a baby his soul is clean!" Adding. "He was Christened or isn't that good enough anymore?!" Rachel sided with Thomas telling Rebecca, "We know you mean well, but we prefer to leave this to the medical professionals."

From there on Rebecca interfered no more, as she had no choice but to respect their beliefs. Baby Benjamin died a week later of a severe lung infection. Rachel was inconsolable and was put on tranquilizers, unable to even attend the funeral. Thomas could barely speak, his heart was so broken. The only reason the family survived was that Eden was there, and with time she reminded her parents there was a reason to go on. As Eden grew she became more and more the center of her parent's world, and Rebecca's world as well. Rebecca saw something unique in Eden, she knew it was a special gift from God but, she would never speak openly of it. Thomas and Rachel had made it perfectly clear where they stood as far as her leanings in the religious sect of The Path, she would not go against their will . . . at least not until it was absolutely necessary.

Rebecca was a believer in mystic abilities. She felt the universe was infinite and therefore had many different life forms. Although, her primary faith was Christianity, she knew that there were other dimensions, because she herself had experienced them. Communicating with spirits had proven that to her. Angels existed and could be contacted, just as Satan could be conjured up from hell. Satan often made appearances' without an invitation. As well as Council members who were of the middle dimension, and were able to exist on all three spiritual plains. The ability to communicate was directly connected to each individual's acceptance and open mindedness. The balance of good and evil was how the universe functioned, as each life form was a combination of both positive and negative energy. This was the main principal of The Path. The Path members believed in possibilities, and the ability to connect to the past by communicating with spirits. However they only accepted God as their creator and believed in his son Jesus Christ as the Messiah. For Rebecca the balance of good and evil was a constant work in progress. She was of the mind that even the most righteous humans had the choice to do good or bad, it depended on the human and the situation that was put before them. Sometimes that in itself is a difficult concept, because as humans we are not perfect and just like the universe, we have both positive and negative energy, at times one more than the other.

To keep peace in her own family, she kept The Path to herself and Jacob. Jacob had seen Rebecca cast out many a demon and believed in her powers, but he followed her lead when it came to Thomas. Jacob was aware of his son's feelings and knew that he did not have the passion to be part of The Path. The parish now consisted of at least two thousand true followers and out of that two thousand, one hundred were devoted members to The Path, in their congregation. A small number to fight the continuous aggression of Satan. However there was more than just this parish, still the numbers were small, because the responsibility was great. It was a hard job, and those who were dedicated understood it from the start. It took a special breed of humans to be a part of it, and they knew who they were practically from birth.

Eden had the special gift, but it had to be nurtured and it was up to Rebecca to be as creative as possible to make sure Eden developed the foundation she needed when she came to the fork in the road. Ultimately it would be her choice to make, but at least she would have some skills to fall back on. Rebecca could not, and from her own word, would not go against Thomas, but there was nothing wrong in playing little games that sharpened the mind. At an early age Rebecca taught Eden how to meditate and focus on her intuitions. She counseled her often on The Creed of The Path, which was the hallmark of principals that brought out the best in all Path members. As far as Father Odell and Father Clemmons knew Eden was an outsider and Rebecca did not discuss her as a possible follower of The Path. That would be something Eden would have to decide on in adulthood, as it would be her decision to make.

Eden grew to adore Rebecca. Rebecca also adored Eden who stopped by at the church every day after school to visit with her. Eden showed a tremendous interest in the church at a very young age. Her sensibilities well out did her years and that was a confirmation that Rebecca had not been wrong in her assessment of Eden. Eden followed her grandmother's advice on all things, for in her were the same fundamental ideals as Rebecca and her great grandmother

Claire. The connection was one of birth, but also the clarity of thought and reason and supreme sensibility. One could say to believe in the devil was not sensible, and to believe in other dimension's was, without just reason. But to the members of The Path these were the traits that were essential to their survival. These were the traits that made a Warrior of God, fighting the battles against The Dominion, the underworld and followers of Satan.

In all things Eden counted on her grandmother's advice alongside of her mothers. Her father was far removed from many of her concerns, as these were her formative years in becoming a young woman. She had outgrown being daddy's little girl at an early age. Thomas would come to her aid in other things but that was still a long way off. As Eden grew older she relied more and more on her relationship with her grandmother and took more interest in the church, never missing a service and becoming a member of the choir. Having grown up in a small traditional town, Eden had many acquaintances, but was selective in her friendships. This came with time and experience. She understood where her priorities were. To Eden her church and family were the rock of her foundation, and her education was her next priority. This coming from a young girl who could easily be called, the most beautiful girl in school was unusual to say the least.

Eden was an Evanharth, as was Lillianna and Eden resembled Lillianna, in both her looks and mannerisms. The boys all wanted to be around her and the girls all resented her. Within Eden was a self confidence that prevented her peers from knocking her down, it was not arrogance or self-centeredness that she was better than everyone else, but rather the understanding that she was different. Eden knew that one day she would go where others could not follow . . . but these thoughts were now to remain on a subconscious level. Still she had an uncanny instinct about people and their nature and followed those instincts. This gift would prove to be essential later on. She was not alone as there were other young mortals who were part of The Path. Due to her father's insistence that she not be educated in The Path principals and ideas, she did not know them. However, the time would come when she would not only know them but they would come to her aid.

While Thomas was working on a case, he indiscreetly got involved with his client. The affair lasted only a few months, but during this time his actions proved detrimental to the case, causing a counter suit against the law firm in which he was partners with his father, Jacob. It was amazing that he was not disbarred because of his irresponsible actions. The law firm was cited by the judge and fined 40,000 dollars. To make matters worse the young woman with whom he had the affair was with his child. She threatened to sue Thomas for child support, but suffered a miscarriage. Thomas paid for her medical bills and gave her 15,000.00 dollars in punitive damages.

Rachel was first shocked, than angry, then betrayed and finally guilty for not being a good enough wife. She resigned herself to the fact that he didn't love her. Which Rebecca disputed, she knew her son. Thomas did love her but . . . he allowed himself to be tempted in another direction away from true love and devotion. Instead he chose the way of lust for desire and attention sake. Jacob was more than disappointed in his son, he couldn't understand his actions. However Rebecca did, and hastened to Rachel's side. Thomas had always been a "bit needy," and Rachel was caring for two small children, when the affair began. Thomas was lured by the thrill of someone thinking only of him and longing only for his attention. Given the weak nature of his character it was no surprise to Rebecca and

Jacob when little Benjamin became ill and eventually died. Their son's actions had destroyed the life of a young woman and had also taken the life of her unborn child.

The Council felt justified in their decision, to favor on the side of The Dominion. Rebecca and Jacob believed in a very old saying, that a person reaps what he sows. Daniel fought for baby Benjamin against The Council's decision to allow baby Benjamin's soul to return to the side of The Dominion. The Council resolved the case believing their decision was fair and substantiated. The sins of the father would fall upon the son. The Council told Daniel that Benjamin would live again and his joy or sorrow would depend on his strength of character. Talus Rand being lead Council negotiator delivered the message.

The Dominion would have free rain over him. What he chose was up to him, good or evil, The Dominion would continue to lure him as they saw fit. His new name, as his soul entered the earth a second time was Joshua Pendleton. The Council did not pick favorites; it was their duty to be fair to the positive and negative forces of the universe. However, Daniel would never lose hope that one day in the future Benjamin would walk on the side of The Path. Indeed that day would come but not for a long time. Benjamin would pay the price of Thomas' transgressions. It was just to The Council and they were the deciding factor, within the laws of human nature.

Souls were eternal, unless the limits of The Council were tested, and then your soul would be expelled. If The Council deemed a soul to have certain qualities that were useful, an offer would be made and the soul had a choice to come back to earth as Talus had, immortal to fight on the side of The Council.

Born to the parents of a locksmith and a city worker. Joshua was the oldest, with a younger sister born ten years after him. Given the circumstances of his predetermined family and where they lived, temptation was a way of life for Joshua. He was tempted at a very early age into the drug culture. Joshua began experimenting with drugs at age twelve and he began selling drugs at fourteen. His parents were hard working people who had fallen on hard times, constantly having money problems.

He wanted desperately to fit in and have the lifestyle that many of his peers had. So, he simply found a way, a short-cut to give him the material things he wanted. That was not all Joshua wanted, he craved for the security, that his parents could not afford to give him.

Often his father was out of work, struggling between jobs, as he was an independent contractor and had to hustle for work, which was often taken up by men who owned their own shops. That had been a dream of Jack Pendleton for a long time. Or as Joshua would say, it was a pipe dream.

His mother had to support the family, and her earnings were not enough to shoulder the burden. Unemployment checks were often stolen in the mail, causing everyone in the family more grief. However, his mother and father loved each other and stood side by side on most things, including how they felt about the direction in which Joshua was headed.

Fighting became a way of life for Joshua and his parents, who tried every avenue to keep him away from the environment that kept him in the drug business. They often resorted to throwing him out of the house on occasion, when they found he had taken money from them. He would pay them back but it would often take weeks, setting them back on the rest of their debts. As handsome and charming as he could be and frequently was, he could also be cunning and manipulative. In truth, there was a part of Joshua who wanted to be different and break away from the drugs. He just didn't know how, as it had become a way of life for him.

Sometimes he hated himself for who he had become, but he felt trapped in a vicious cycle where there was no exit.

If life was hard at home, Joshua was liked and sought after in school and in the neighborhood. However things were changing in the drug business in general. News of a new king pin had been generating. Pushers, sellers and runners were worried, about their jobs and their future within the business. Rumor had it that a new sect was moving in who had the capabilities of changing the whole drug network. The organization was from Europe and was taking over the entire East Coast. Slowly, but predictably changes were happening and new faces were knocking on doors. One of the first doors to be visited was Joshua's. Fortunately he was driving his mother to work. However, the door had a business card left inside the door jam, which Joshua found when he returned home. It read . . . Peris Donahue with a phone number. Joshua was not sure who had left the card, but thinking it was a debt collector or lawyer, he promptly threw it away. It's funny how things happen in life as in death. Now as he was chained to a wall in the lower level of Dante's mansion in Claremont.

Joshua thought about this as he was chained to the wall. How his life had taken a drastic turn for him. Joshua remembered the night Peris, Dante's number one man had come looking for him. Either way he would have faced death, eventually. Now he was truly glad he had done it on his own terms instead of someone else's, especially Dante and his goons. Joshua didn't care about his future anymore, one way or another. Daniel would make it right, and he knew that. All that mattered to him was Eden. She was the one that needed protection and now he was chained to a wall. This hadn't been part of the plan, things had gone terribly wrong and he had no idea how he was going to fix the situation.

Perhaps somehow Eden had escaped, and then he hoped death would come swiftly for him. Knowing Dante he already knew that would not be the case. Perhaps Daniel would show up and storm the place. It's funny how he had hope. He actually had never lost hope, not once . . . even when life seemed horribly miserable, there was always hope. Hope, the eternal sanctuary of human existence and mankind. Dante had hope too, hope that Eden would come back to save Joshua. Actually it was more than hope it was completely predictable and he was enjoying all the drama. This had become a three ring circus and he was the ring master. He was aware of the religious ritual outside and was impressed by the outcome, it added to the overall embellishment.

He instructed Peris to turn on the water hoses and saturate the members of The Path, he didn't want to kill anyone yet . . . there was plenty of time for that. When Dante took someone's life it was on a much more insidious and personal level. He had his own faith that the strength of the water hoses would send them all scurrying like rats. He started to laugh, louder and louder, above the guests and the music that was making its way down to the lower level where Joshua was.

From where he was chained Joshua could see that the corridor led to a very large room. He stretched his body out as far as he could and saw what looked like a bed, draped in black. It sent shudders through his body, as he knew what it meant. Eden was going to be raped on that bed, in front of hundreds of Dante's followers. Suddenly, he heard a thunder of footsteps coming down the stairs. The guests passing him in large groups and staring at him, like he was an amusement. They laughed at him, as they held their champagne glasses. Following behind the crowd was Eden walking alongside Dante. She was still in the white gown and she had the wreath of red roses on her head. He closed his eyes, thinking he must be hallucinating. But, then he heard Dante's voice. "No Joshua, this isn't a hallucination from one of your drug intakes, this is real." Dante said.

Joshua opened his eyes and spit in Dante's face recoiling with disgust. Dante took the sleeve of Eden's dress and wiped his face with it. "Let him go." Eden demanded. Dante stepped back, "No I think not." He replied. "Dante keep your word that was our agreement!" She shouted. This can't be happening, thought Joshua as he looked at Eden. "Yes, it is happening Joshua, Eden exchanged her life for yours . . . what love! What sacrifice!" Dante boasted. "Eden set yourself free . . . go, get out of here!" Joshua implored. "Please! Eden save yourself!" Joshua yelled, as now his light of hope was dimming. Dante leaned against the wall, observing the two of them. "No, Joshua I won't abandon you." Eden told him, holding his face in her hands. "Isn't she something, she simply could not leave you behind, Josh . . . I'm really impressed." Taunted Dante.

As quickly as he spoke, he removed a knife from his cloak and stabbed Joshua in the stomach. He twisted the knife and pushed it in, whispering in his ear. "You think you burned the first time, you haven't begun to burn." Joshua's head fell onto his chest as Dante grabbed Eden and sent her flying across the crowded room. Dante followed, addressing the crowd. "Here she is folks, the future mother of my child!" The room broke out in applause, as Eden's body was hurled across the marble floor. Now Eden came at Dante and punched him in the face, sending him flying across the room. She ripped the bottom of the dress off and revealed black pants and boots, which held tiny golden daggers strapped on the sides. With speed and precision of an expert she threw them at Dante catching him in the arm and leg. But, it did nothing except excite him more.

He came at her lifting himself up and spinning, he tried kicking her on the side of her head, but her instincts were quick and she bent down, coming up and thrusting a dagger in his side. Some of the guests were intrigued and others uncomfortable, but Dante had all exists closed off and guarded. Many of the guests thought this was part of the show, until they realized it was actual blood pouring out from Joshua's shirt. Eden ran over to Joshua, covering his wound with some of the fabric from her dress. She held his head up and his eyes opened slightly. He whispered "I love you Eden, and I always will." Then he gasped once and died.

Eden kissed him and his head fell forward, as life left his body. Now Eden's hatred grew as she glared at Dante, she wanted to destroy him. Anger filled her veins as she looked at him. Dante was now on the floor as the dagger was lodged up in his rib. He groaned and cursed and mayhem began to break out, amongst the guests. Dante pulled the dagger out with one violent tug and stood up. With undeniable swiftness, he sent a candle pillar flying across the room, toward Eden. She caught it mid air. "Come on then, let's see what you've got." Demanded Dante.

Eden walked toward Dante and with stealth accuracy sent the pillar through the air smacking him in the chest with it. It knocked him down, but he was up again with determined aggression. Now the room was a mass of people screaming and pushing each other to get through the exits, which were barricaded by Dante's guards. Dante began flinging anything he could levitate. Outside a battle commenced as well. Thomas, Uncle Eli, and the Father's along with Nia and Leah had overthrown many of the guards, dragging them through the mud into the forest, tying them to trees and gagging them. Nia and Leah used their arrows to disable them. The tips of their arrows were coated with an elixir to put the victim into temporary sleep.

Eden had indeed escaped from Dante, but she told her parents that she must go back in to save Joshua. They tried to discourage her, but realized that she had already made her decision to become a Warrior of God. It was then, that Nia gave her the daggers as protection. "These to do not have a sleep elixir, but are sharp and can do damage." Nia advised Eden. The mansion was encircled with members of The Path who were reciting scripture out loud. Some guests began escaping as they begun to over throw Dante's men and some were falling down and getting hurt. Dante was in his glory now, realizing that this would be a fight to the finish-which he would win. In an instant he lit one of the black candles and placed it on the bed. The black fabric quickly created an inferno. Now complete hysteria began and bodies were catching on fire.

As Eden tried to avoid the flames she threw one of her daggers catching Dante in the shoulder. "Close, but not close enough." Snapped Dante grinning at her. Eden took her last three daggers from her boot as he was coming at her. She threw all three daggers in succession, hitting his chest, his forehead and shoulder, causing him to fall on the marble floor harder than he expected.

Suddenly the fire ceased, the doors opened and all of the remaining guests went running out of the mansion. In the middle of the floor stood Daniel in human form. Eden was standing beside Dante, who was now getting up.

"Well . . . well . . . well, this just gets better and better." Exclaimed Dante limping over to a tall black velvet chair which stood on a platform. "Come over to our side Alestasis." Said Daniel. Eden stood next to Daniel now. She knew it was Daniel, by his speech and although he was in human form, his body glowed. Dressed all in white,

Daniel had long white hair and penetrating blue eyes. His face serene and tranquil, but Eden knew his power from his presence. Dante rubbed the blood off his face with his cloak. "Who is Alestasis?" he asked disinterested. "You know the answer to that question, why not give him a chance." Daniel persisted. "Oh you mean the son of that whore!" Dante shouted. Suddenly, Talus walked into the room. Eden was immediately taken with him. "She was not a whore, she was a lady I was the whore as I took her against her will." Talus answered him. "So what? . . . I don't care, I have but one family." Dante sneered. "Oh sit there and shut up." Scolded Talus losing his patience. Talus walked over to Daniel. "Do with him what you will . . . The Council sides on the side of The Path." He told Daniel. "Alestasis . . . that is as you were born, show us just cause why you should not be destroyed and we will consider saving your soul." Daniel's voice was calm, but direct as he spoke. Dante in rage and arrogance stood up. "Just cause? Old man you have it in reverse . . . give me a reason not to destroy you!" He shouted to Daniel and Talus. "My father is greater than both of you put together!" He screamed.

Then Dominic Marchette appeared and walked over to Dante. Dante was filled with pride and confidence, not expecting the words he was about to hear. "You are not the son of my loins and you have not handled this well, Dante, you have caused unnecessary attention to The Dominion." Said Dominic. "We have no battle in this." Dominic told Talus as he left, he knew he was out matched with Daniel and Talus, this was not the time to start a war . . . Dante would have to be sacrificed, at least for the time being. "Well, it would seem that you have been abandoned by all Alestasis." Spoke Daniel, looking over at Talus. "Yes, as you know he is my son, but I am incapable of empathy for him, do as you will Daniel." Said Talus, his voice was not sad, just indifferent. Eden was shocked by his response. Daniel looked at Eden and then at Talus. "Destroy him." Daniel said simply. Talus looked at Dante who began almost immediately to fall to his knees and writhe with pain. Black shadows in the shape of rats encased his body. Dante tried pulling away from them, but they pulled him back, eating the flesh off his bones. His powers were frozen by Talus who had all the control. Eden looked away, she could not watch as he was eaten alive and his body mutilated.

Daniel led Eden over to Joshua's body. She fell down at his feet, tears filling her eyes. Daniel put his hand on Joshua's head and rested it there. Slowly Joshua's soul began to turn into spirit essence and left his body, floating above it. Eden felt the warmth of his glow touch her face as she looked up at him. The light sparkled and was so bright it was hard to look at it, but she forced herself. Eden reached out her hand to him but he began to fade into the atmosphere. "Eden, do not cry . . . he is at peace now. Joshua was your baby brother Benjamin two lifetimes ago." Daniel explained. "Is he an angel now?" she asked. "He always was, but it is official now." Replied Daniel. "He sacrificed his life for mine, Daniel." Eden said her voice still shaken. "Yes I know, I sent him to you." Daniel answered. "Why did he have to suffer, didn't he suffer enough in his other lives?" asked Eden. "There is much you must learn about the dimensions as well as the spirit world Eden and with time you will." Daniel replied.

As Daniel and Eden walked back into the large room, Talus was sitting on Dante's chair watching his son suffer mortal anguish, without emotion or interest. "How can he be like that?" she asked Daniel. "Who is he?" Eden persisted. "He is lead Council negotiator for The Council Eden, they are the ones who balance our universe." Answered Daniel. Eden questioned Daniel with her eyes, but before Daniel could continue and answer her, Talus did. He walked over to her. "It seems you are truly a novice." He said. Eden took exception to his tone. "In some things." Eden responded. "In most." Talus replied as if he knew everything about her. Eden thought him extremely arrogant, but captivating and handsome. "Thank you for the compliment but, I am not arrogant, I just know my job." He answered her thoughts. Eden was embarrassed that he had read her. "Did your grandmother tell you about the dimensions and the laws of the universe?" he asked her. "No, not entirely." Eden replied softly. "Do not be ashamed, you have been very brave here today." Talus said looking at his watch. Dante was still suffering the torture of his soul being purged from his body. What amazed Eden was how unmoved Talus was toward Dante and the torture he was suffering.

Eden thought about Talus and how he looked, it was obvious that he was very concerned about his appearance. She thought his suit and shoes to be quite expensive. His hair was long and blond and pulled straight back and fastened. No man could wear his hair that long, without having a great amount of self confidence. He stood over six feet and his eyes were deep brown and mesmerizing. Talus did not need to read Eden's thoughts to know from her energy that she was physically attracted to him . . . most women were, so he was use to it. What she didn't have any way of knowing, as she could not read thoughts yet, was that he was captivated by her as well.

Her resemblance to Lillianna had taken him aback when he first saw her. She looked over at Dante, "When will his torture end?" she asked out loud. "When The Council Tribunal tells me they have his soul." Talus answered. He spoke with an air of self confidence and control. "Can his soul be saved?" Eden questioned. "Yes." replied Daniel, without hesitation. "Why would you want to?" Talus asked both surprised and irritated. "Aren't we in the business of saving souls?" asked Eden with true measure of her innocence surfacing. Daniel replied first. "Yes, Eden, that is what we do . . . but." Talus cut him off. "Excuse me, if I am a bit agitated Miss Evanharth, why would you want to save this monsters soul? . . . he almost killed you!" Talus was controlling his annoyance because of her inexperience . . . but Daniel was grateful he had her on board. Eden looked at Dante who was completely ravaged and in insurmountable pain. "I sense there is good in him, my heart feels his pain and internal struggle." She said surprising even herself this time. "This is what makes me crazy with you mortals, you let your emotions rule you intellect!" Talus said raising his voice. He walked over to the chair and sat down shaking his head. "Silly girl," he said under his breath, "just like Lillianna."

The words took him back in time, when he went to the castle on the mountain, after Lillianna's death. He rode up to the front gate on his horse, dismounting, he tied the reins to the side of the entrance. The gravel on the walkway was now over run by weeds. Remembering the week he spent with her, he looked up at the balcony. He tried to imagine her falling off the balcony, but he stopped himself, he couldn't even imagine such a horrific sight. He forced himself to come back to the castle to sort out his thoughts. He needed to pay respect to her death, to her grave . . . why he didn't know. It was just not possible for him to feel anything, he didn't have a soul, so then why was he here?

As he thought of Lillianna he looked at Eden, she could be a reincarnation of Lillianna. It had now been close to a hundred years since her death and still he thought of her. After Mortamion and Lillianna died, Louis escaped with Alestasis, auctioning him off to the highest bidder, with The Council's permission. Talus had put in a bid, but lost to Dominic Marchette. Talus in good conscience could not fight the bid as he probably would not have made a good father. Upon adopting Alestasis Dominic changed the baby's name to Dante. However, in retrospect, Talus realized he would have been a thousand times better a father than Dominic Marchette.

Dante continued to suffer the anguish of death as Daniel educated Eden on her lineage and The Path. Talus sat on Dante's chair and went far back in his memory again, to the day he visited the castle in San Michelene. He entered the front door of the castle that had been abandoned and empty. Most of the windows were broken and shattered glass was everywhere having been carried by the wind. He walked up the long staircase and down the hall to her bedroom. The once elegant boudoir was now, ravaged by times past and the elements. Memories filled his senses. The French doors leading to the balcony were weather worn and the strength of the wind had caused them to open and close repeatedly, shattering all the glass panels and splitting the wood.

Her headboard, once rose pink satin was now grey and torn. Talus stopped at the bed and picked up the sheet, covered in dust and debris, remembering how he had carnal knowledge of her on this bed, on this sheet. Letting the sheet fall from his fingers small partials of dust fell onto his boots. He noticed that the dust sparkled and instead of wiping it off he let it remain there. As he walked towards the balcony he caught sight of his reflection in a large oval brass mirror to his right, he glanced at it, believing it to be himself. It was Lillianna looking back at him, wrapped in her pink sheet, with his blue jacket on her shoulders, the shiny brass buttons shining through. Her arm stretched out to him, reaching through the reflection. He ran over to it and pressed his face and body against it, as the image faded . . . and it was now just his image he saw looking back at him. He remembered all of it, her beauty mostly and how she had fought him at first. Stepping away from the mirror, he was coated in dust. He walked out onto the balcony and shouted her name over and over again. "Lillianna, Lillianna, Lillianna!"

He ran out of the castle with all its haunting memories and mounted his horse, and as he did a whirlwind blew around him . . . he knew it was her spirit essence. Somehow, somewhere, in some lifetime, he would make it right. When and how he had no idea, but to save his sanity he would have to. Why he had these thoughts truly eluded him. It was beyond his understanding. He was immortal; he wasn't supposed to feel anything. All these years the memory of her had plagued him and now standing a few feet away was a reproduction of her in Eden.

Dawn was breaking and many of the volunteers of the congregation had dispersed. The prayer vigil had lasted through the night and early dawn. Daniel's angel warriors had since risen back to The Highest Realm, as their light and energy had immediately put a stop to all the fighting. Only humans with the purest of souls could look upon them. All of Dante's men ran from the mansion and the guests did the same, having no ability to remember what had occurred as they ran.

Dante was being eaten alive slowly and painfully, as Talus sat patiently waiting for his complete demise. It was his job, his responsibility; he couldn't leave until the job was done. If Talus felt anything it was a loss of Lillianna and the pain he had caused her. The fact that Dante who was really Alestasis, was part of him, was immaterial to Talus. There stood Eden watching Dante go through the process of losing his soul while still living. Daniel had stated to her that Dante's soul could be saved. She asked him "By whom?" Daniel looked deep into her eyes. "By you." Daniel answered her. She was silent. Talus looked up and showed his disapproval at Daniel's suggestion.

"Isn't every soul worth saving Talus?" asked Daniel. "No." Talus answered looking down at the floor. "What about Lillianna's soul?" Daniel asked. Talus looked up at Daniel. "She chose mortality . . . and with that comes great pain . . . and death." Replied Talus. "That's not what I asked." Said Daniel. "Should Lillianna's soul be saved?" Daniel repeated. "Yes, yes it should." Replied Talus. "Why?" asked Daniel. Talus ignored the question. "Tell me why, it should be saved." Daniel repeated, contained and without emotion. Talus got up off the chair and went to Daniel. "Where are you going with this?" Talus asked him. "I would just like an answer to my question." Daniel responded. Talus stood there staring at Daniel, considering whether or not he would give him the answer he was seeking from him. The words were there but stuck in his throat, finally he spoke, in a hushed voice Talus replied. "Because . . . she was loved, by many." Then he walked back to the chair, and resting his chin on his hand became lost in his thoughts. "What say you about Alestasis, there is still time Eden." Daniel reiterated. Eden looked at Dante, powerless, falling in and out of consciousness. "You are the only one who can save him Eden." Daniel said encouragingly. "I can't do it alone." Eden replied, genuinely surprised that Daniel would really believe she had the ability, never mind the motivation. "You won't have to." Daniel assured her with stoic enthusiasm.

Talus looked up at Eden and Daniel clearly not in approval of this venture, "Before you do anything, the process must continue and end." Talus reminded them. "Can't we stop it?" asked Eden. "No," said Daniel. "He made his choice as Dante, and must die as Dante . . . we will bring him back as Alestasis." Daniel assured her. Talus came over to them. "The Council Tribunal does not agree." Talus told them as he was receiving messages telepathically. "What can we do then?" implored Eden. "He has raped, tortured, killed and defiled mortals for close to a hundred years, and you feel his soul should be saved?" Talus asked shaking his head in disbelief.

"You sir, by your own admission, took his mother against her will and defiled her!" Eden shouted. Talus came back at her, his long blond hair flying about him, as he had unclipped it. He was inches from her face. "I miss, am not mortal and I do not have a soul, I live by The Council's code not mortal code." He told her irritated, but controlled. "But his mother was mortal and had a soul and suffered and died!" Eden spoke back, tears welling up in her eyes as she spoke. Daniel watched them both and already knew the root of their discourse and it had nothing to do with Dante or Lillianna. In the back of the hall Eden heard her name called it was her mother, running to her. "No, please stay back," Daniel put his hand up. Thomas stopped Rachel and embraced her. "She's ok, she's still alive." Thomas assured her.

"I don't believe you." Eden challenged Talus. He ignored her statement. "I believe you feel remorse and regret and pain . . . and his mother was loved . . . by you." Eden shot back at Talus. Talus turned and slowly walked up to her, took her in his arms and kissed her. Daniel did not interfere as he knew she could handle herself. Eden allowed the kiss, she did not struggle against him. Stepping away from her, he said simply, "I feel lust and want and need, I exist on my basic instincts, but I do not feel these other emotions, I have just proved it to you." Talus contested her analysis. "You have proved the opposite, as I know you are attracted to me because I resemble her." Eden replied with confidence. "You more than just resemble her, but you are certainly no comparison to her beauty, her femininity, or her . . . sensuality." Talus replied with heightened sarcasm.

Talus went to the chair and sat down, and Eden walked up to him, considering another form of negotiation, she knew that she might have a chance with him, if she backed down slightly. "If you felt all that you have felt for his mother, can you not save the soul of her only son, who is also your son?" her voice was strong and assertive, but respectful in its tone. Talus looked up at her his brown eyes seeing through her. There was no mistaking what was going on here, this was a force of will, as they both were completely physically drawn to each other and neither knew how to handle it very well. "Daniel can you kindly restrain your protégé, this woman child." Talus insisted. "Talus I feel my protégé, as you call her, is within her legal rights, by definition of The Council Tribunal, woman child that she may be, she is within legal age by our laws to speak and be heard." Daniel protested in Eden's defense. "Do what you may, but The Tribunal requires a hearing and sponsors on her behalf." Talus responded. Daniel rested his hands on his chest and closing his eyes, called in the legions.

Lillianna was the first to arrive in spirit essence. She was a vision surrounded by white light, cascading downward and hovering above the floor. She was the Lillianna who Talus had held in his arms and still longed for. He knew she could not be touched and she could only communicate with Daniel. Slowly other spirits descended, showing their support for Eden's request to save Dante's soul. Rebecca and her husband Jacob, Eden's grandparents. George and Claire Evanharth, Rebecca's parents and Nora Kincaid (George's mother) and Daniel who stood at their side. Seven spirits in all stood in defense of Eden's request to save the soul of Alestasis, who was near the end of his mortal suffering. The grey shadows began to recede into the stone floor and finally, Dante breathed his last mortal breath.

There was nothing left of him but skeletal remains. Talus stated the rules of the hearing. "Daniel as you hold high council I will direct all my questions and statements to you." Eden stood fast next to Daniel as her parents watched in amazement at the proceedings. "Daniel, please ask each spirit, beginning with Lillianna, why this soul should be saved." Instructed Talus. Daniel turned to Lillianna who faced him. "Please tell the hearing why you would save his soul." She answered Daniel in strange high pitched sounds with musical overtones that were understood to say, "Because he is my son and I love him." Talus would communicate the response back to The Tribunal who would communicate their responses back to Talus telepathically. Each soul responded independently. All were behind Eden and her request to save Alestasis' soul. "What exchange do you offer on behalf of The Dominion?" asked Talus.

"We plead with The Council, that this gesture is in good faith and we ask for leanency, but we offer no exchange." Daniel replied. Talus communicated Daniel's response to The Tribunal. "There must be an offering or exchange." Talus insisted. Eden turned to Daniel, "What do they mean?" she asked. "They want another soul or a contribution, some sort of payment or sacrifice on behalf of The Dominion." Daniel explained. "But the representative from The Dominion, was here, he did not defend Dante . . . I don't understand?" Eden interjected. "Eden, The Council sets the law, whether we agree or abandon our rights is irrelevant to them." Daniel was quiet in his response, allowing Eden to stretch her mental abilities, Daniel waited for her to come up with a suggestion, or plausible solution. He knew that she had the thought process and intuition to initiate the next step, he would give her the opportunity. "Then why don't you ask the legion members represented what they think we should do?" Eden offered. Daniel closed his eyes and put his hands to his chest, slowly asking each spirit telepathically, what they would consider fair.

This took several minutes as Eden and Talus waited patiently, so did Eden's parents who were now frozen in reverence of what they were witnessing. Then after long anticipation Daniel had a response, but Talus interjected as he had received a new message from The Tribunal. "The Tribunal seeks a merger, between the soul of Alestasis and Miss Evanharth." Rebecca Evanharth made it known, that was not acceptable to her, by a resounding thunder that shook the structure. "That is not within reasonable limits." Daniel stated assertively. "That is their only consideration." Talus answered his tone professional and direct. "We are at a standoff situation." Daniel told Eden, "as there is only one spirit that would suggest this compromise." Eden slowly walked over to Lillianna, though she could not touch her, she could feel her love and her pain.

As a spirit essence, Lillianna was breathtaking, in life it was no wonder to Eden that she had invoked such passion in Talus . . . or anyone else for that matter. Her hair was like waves of white soft silk falling almost to her feet, her eyes clear blue. Her face soft and delicate like the day she died. Eden saw her ancestry and now was aware of her resemblance, not just to Lillianna but to Nora Kincaid. Eden spoke directly to Talus. "What would be required of me?" she asked him. "Please ask her to stay within protocol." Talus directed his response to Daniel. "Eden, it is I that must communicate with The Council." He admonished her. "I am sorry . . . I apologize for my lack of experience." Eden told Daniel.

However, now Rebecca and Jacob were shouting their disapproval of any such union, thunder and lightning crashed against the structure. The noise was so great Eden's parents covered their heads with their hands, fearing damage to the mansion. "Daniel, take control of your legions or this hearing will come to an end." Talus shouted. "Daniel, I will do as they ask." Eden said out loud. Eden's parents came running up to her but Talus came and stood between them. "No! No! Please we have already lost one child . . . don't do this please, whoever you are!" Rachel cried out. "Madam, she is of legal age, seek your argument elsewhere." Talus responded quietly but sternly. "May I speak to them, for just a few moments . . . please?" Eden asked Talus, but Daniel replied nodding his head. Eden then took them aside. "This is who I am, this is my place in the world, you must respect that I know what I am doing, and trust that I have had a great teacher . . . she will always protect me." Eden kissed and hugged them both. Rachel began crying uncontrollably and Thomas searched his daughter's eyes with his, to provoke some amount of hesitation in her, but Eden eyes held a determination and strength behind them that was clearly unbreakable. "You must both go now, and I will communicate with you when I can." Eden turned back to face the hearing. "Eden! Eden!" Rachel called out, but Eden turned to her mother and father and shouted "Go!" They now both saw in Eden a mighty strength and a strong conviction, and were without recourse. Quietly and sadly they left the mansion. She was no longer Eden their daughter, overnight she had become Eden, Warrior of God.

"There are more things in Heaven and earth Horatio than are dreamt of in your philosophy."

William Shakespeare's Hamlet

Woman Child

Chapter Nine

During the time when Eden was in conversation with her parents, Talus asked Daniel permission if he could confer with Lillianna. Being immortal and a Council member, Talus had the right to approach Lillianna, but proper etiquette delineated that he ask permission of Daniel first, as she was in his dimension. Daniel gave his permission if Lillianna approved. To no one's surprise she did. Talus stood before her spirit essence. She smiled at him and he smiled back. Then they communicated telepathically. He asked for her forgiveness and she gave it to him. He asked for Mortamion, she replied that he had been sent to earth, for his soul was so pure in nature that he was wanted again as a mortal, but she knew not where he was. Why had she not gone with him? Talus asked her. Lillianna's face expressed great sadness. She had taken her own life, and in the process had abandoned a child; she could never be mortal again. The legions of The Path had struggled to keep her, but her time was tenuous as she was a floater, as Joshua had been.

A floater was a spirit who did not have a permanent home. These decisions were based primarily on your actions as a mortal and how they affected other people. Why had Mortamion left her to live on earth again? He asked her. Lillianna smiled at Talus, a soft demure smile, raising her hand, she pointed it in the direction of Alestasis. Of course, he realized…Mortamion had learned that the baby Lillianna gave birth to was not his. It didn't matter that she took her own life to follow him into death, Mortamion had felt lied to and betrayed. Talus saw the situation from Mortamion's eyes. He was justified, but the true culprit was he; himself, Talus. He knew that then and he knew it now. How terribly wrong everything had gone, and what a complicated mess. Talus ended the conversation, wishing her well, he knew at some point he would have to resolve this issue for himself. Even in her spirit essence her beauty was incomprehensible, her skin was like porcelain and her hair incandescent.

Hours had passed and no clarification or resolve had been reached. Dante's soul would die, with his body and that was fine with Talus, that's how it should be. It didn't matter if that was his son or not. There was no debate or question here. Dante had forced the balance of nature too far. Eden felt differently. She knew that Dante had suffered enough all through his life and thought he should have a second chance. his parents had been taken from him, and he had been raised by a monster . . . yet she felt that he was not a monster. Lillianna could not have given birth to evil. Eden conveyed her feelings to the spirits and asked them to show mercy for Alestasis, who had lived and died as Dante, through no fault of his own. Talus was receiving more information from The Tribunal and called for everyone's attention.

"In order for The Council to honor what The Path wants, a merger, must take place to cement both parties together, as

I previously mentioned." He continued, "This union must be in the presence of all who are here and must be sealed with matrimony." There were a few gasps, but nothing too loud. "If this soul is to be saved, it can be . . . by marriage to Eden Evanharth." Talus explained. Daniel communicated to the spirits that as set by Council law Eden was free make her own choices as a Warrior of God. If this was what Eden wanted, the choice was hers and hers alone to make.

Talus spoke wisely and clearly and there was no confusing what he said. If this soul was to be saved Eden would have to marry him. She needed to think, to clear her mind which was racing with thoughts.

She thought about Talus, he had a wonderful command of the English language, though he spoke with an accent, for his soul had only lived once before his unfortunate death. His roots were German but, he did not remember any specifics, of time and place. Talus tried his best to help Eden with her decision, without being partial, so he offered more information. "Before any separation can take place in the future, a mutual agreement by The Path and The Council members would need to address the circumstances, however a separation could take place given the appropriate circumstances." Talus added, "The Council requires an answer in ten minutes, passed that point Dante's soul will no longer exist." Talus walked to the chair and sat down and looked at his watch, and waited. Eden turned to Daniel, "What is an appropriate circumstance?" she asked. Daniel put his hand up, calling for a stop to the clock to answer Eden's question.

Talus walked over to her and Daniel. "A couple of examples would be spousal abuse or infidelity." He explained. "What if I just don't like him . . . or get along with him?" Eden asked. Talus closed his eyes and exhaled, with frustration. "Don't like him? You don't even know him and you're the one who wants to save him." He stated walking back to his chair. Mortals frustrated him in general, but so far Eden held the record. Talus knew that it was partly due to the fact that he was so attracted to her. Not that anything could come of it, just the same he had not been this attracted to a woman since Lillianna. There was also a part of him that respected her, as what she had initiated took courage and determination. However, she was a Warrior of God after all.

Daniel smiled over to Eden. "He will belong to you, you will make it right Eden." Daniel assured her. All the spirits indicated it was too much of a risk for Eden, except for one, Lillianna. Eden wanted to be of service, but could she at this age, make such a commitment? "Daniel read her mind. "It is a monumental commitment, that would not take place over night . . . but eventually it would." Daniel explained. "As a warrior for The Path it does become our life's work." He told her. "The question now becomes . . . how far will you go Eden, to save a soul?" Daniel rested on those words. There it was. The ball was in her court, she could walk away, and never be part of this world and live a normal life or could she? She had already given her word of allegiance upstairs, hours ago, when she was Dante's prisoner. Was her word only as good as it suited her? Or was she a true Warrior of God? Talus read her thoughts and believed her to be brave but too emotional. Daniel read her as well . . . he already knew what her answer would be.

Eden's parents were now home on Sparrow Lane. If they had not seen it with their own eyes they would never believe it. Aunt Ro and Uncle Eli sat shocked and mesmerized as Rachel and Thomas told them of everything they had seen. If inside the castle had been a nightmare the outside hadn't been easy. Dante's men had sprayed them with long water hoses and fights had ensued with many of the church members being hurt, which included Father Odell and Father Clemmons. As the war had raged inside, outside the battle had been long and furious. Then someone shouted that Dante had been stabbed, and many of the guards ran away fearing the police. Many of Dante's recruits were gang members and knew all too well how to street fight. Most of them already had prison records of some sort. Leah and Nia had brought down many with their arrows, the tips carrying a sedative. By dawns light, the sedative wore off and the puncture wound was no more than a surface scratch on the side of the neck. The arrows had disintegrated into the dirt. Uncle Eli and Thomas as well as the two Fathers, were forever grateful to Nia and Leah who were experts at their craft, without them it would have gone far worse.

Thomas rebuked himself for all the years he denied his mother and The Path. As they sat at the kitchen table they wondered what Eden would do. It's true she had Rebecca on her side, but Rebecca was a spirit, Eden would have to live and sleep with this person Alestasis. They had known her for eighteen years and now she was a stranger to them. Would they ever see her again? If not who could they go to? No one would believe this story. Rachel cried for the son she lost and the daughter she might lose. Would his soul be good or evil? How would Eden know? Then Uncle Eli spoke out loud. "Let's all hold hands and pray that Eden chooses wisely and it all works out." Rachel began to speak and then stopped herself as she took hold of Thomas' hand and kissed it, gently Thomas caressed her cheek. "You are a good man, don't ever think you are not." She whispered to him. "I'm grateful to you Rachel, for being the most loving and caring wife a man could have." Thomas was grateful indeed and remorseful, for many things that he had and hadn't done. Now all they could do was wait, and pray, that Eden would have the strength and fortitude to withstand whatever it was that she had to face.

Having Rebecca on her side was wonderful, but was it enough. Thomas and Rachel knew the form they saw dressed in white was the angel Daniel. Would he and Rebecca be enough to save her if she needed them? It was Uncle Eli that spoke words of wisdom, in a question he asked, seeking the truth. "Who saved Eden tonight?" They all looked at each other and then Rachel answered, "Maybe she saved herself." Uncle Eli, looked at his wife, and then at Rachel and Thomas. "Sister who do you truly believe saved Eden?" he asked Rachel. Rachel thought for a moment and then answered her brother. "Blessed be the name of God from age to age, for wisdom and power are his. He changes times and seasons, deposes Kings and sets up Kings; he gives wisdom to the wise and knowledge to those who have understanding." She replied, quoting The Bible, Daniel 2.19. "Yes." Added aunt Rowena. "It was the angel Daniel who saved Eden."

Daniel explained to Eden that it could go several different ways . . . Alestasis could come back into the world and be good and pure, with no lingering trace of Dante attached to him or . . . Dante's soul could emerge similar to what he was before, in which case an all out cleansing would be needed. These soul reversals could be quite delicate. Anyway one looked at it, it was a definite risk. Daniel conferred with the other spirits who waited for the conclusion. All but Lillianna, thought it too much of a risk . . . but if one considers the source, Lillianna was a risk taker. Eden searched the answer from inside herself. If Alestasis came back and was like Dante, did she have what it would take to break his spirit and bring him over to the side of The Path? So much had happened in twenty four hours, Eden felt that she had aged twenty four years. Now she stood next to her grandmother's spirit essence and she hadn't even had the funeral yet. Joshua was gone . . . safe but gone. Somehow and she didn't know how, she was still able to handle everything that had happened.

Visions of sending her parents away from her came into her mind. How did she do that? What would Alestasis look like? This body that lay savagely torn apart in front of her would not be "useable," as Daniel phrased it. It was only the soul that would be saved. It didn't really matter what he looked like, she thought after all that's not what is important, Eden decided. Talus called out a five minute warning. Eden thought Talus was pretty good at his job if, socially lacking. She thought about her parents, she needed to tell them about baby Benjamin, who had come back as Joshua and helped to save her, from Dante . . . who was really Alestasis, whom she was going to marry. It was completely . . . out of this world, from another dimension and few mortals would believe it, or comprehend it. Where would they find a body? Daniel said it would take several days, so although the answer was needed now, the marriage would have to wait for The Highest Realm to find Alestasis a mortal body that his soul could enter. Time would also be needed to form a union.

Daniel assured her that The Highest Realm would make a good and wise decision on the selection. Talus called a two minute warning. Eden came out of her deep thoughts to the reality of her life. She turned to Daniel, "I am ready with my answer." She said. Daniel called the stop. Talus looked up, got off the chair that he had made his own and planned to take with him. He walked over to Eden and opened a small leather book from which he read, "Before you give your answer, I must ask you, Eden Evanharth, by rules of The Tribunal that heads The Council, is the answer that you provide true and correct by your own will?" Talus asked looking directly in to her eyes. "Yes." Eden responded, her heart pounding in her chest. "Have you in any way, been coerced to go against your own will?" he asked. "No I have not." Eden replied firmly. "With that being said, do you fully understand that to go back on your word, can cause The Council Tribunal to take your own very soul?" Talus said that without reading it, looking at her he studied her features and how much she looked like Lillianna. "Yes, I understand." Eden responded feeling light headed. Then turning his body to face the spirits and Daniel, and in front of Dante's skeleton, he continued reading from the book. "In front of these witnesses who represent The Path, and I who represent The Council, what is your answer?" For the first time Eden felt unbalanced and her knees weak, Talus instinctively took her hands in his to help steady her.

Talus asked Eden again, "What say you?" he demanded. Eden breathed in deeply and exhaled, and then she replied, "Yes, I will save the soul of Alestasis." Eden replied. "And?" Talus demanded a full response. "I will marry him and be his wife." The words finally spilling from her lips. Talus addressed everyone openly. "This hearing is over and everyone is now free to go until further notice." One by one Eden could hear the spirits say goodbye in that high pitched musical tone, and then evaporate into air. Now it was just her, Daniel and Talus. "What happens now?" she asked openly. Talus answered her. "We all go home, our days work is done." He said lightly. Then he realized that she needed more information. "Go home, in less than a week you will receive a visitor that will be Alestasis." Talus replied. "Daniel?" she turned to him, clearly seeking confirmation. "Do as Talus has stated, when I have more information, I will contact you, there is a clearing near Glen Cove . . . Nia and Leah will take you there, they will know when." Daniel walked over to the mutilated body of Dante and touched it and slowly it turned into powder and evaporated.

Talus was on the platform measuring the chair, "I wonder if it will fit into my truck?" he thought out loud. Eden prepared to leave the castle. "Wait," she said, remembering she was very far away from Hadleyville. "I can't walk all the way home." Daniel was already gone, he had evaporated into the atmosphere as well. Talus looked over at her. "You needn't be concerned, I'll give you a lift." He offered. As it turned out the chair was too big to fit into the back of his Mercedes SUV, so he left it at the bottom of the steps outside. On the way home, they rode much of the way in silence. Except for Eden mentioning what a nice car he had. He corrected her that it was an SUV, not a car. Talus asked her if she was comfortable, she replied that she was, but in truth she was anything but comfortable. She had not eaten, not slept and she had butterflies in her stomach, from a man who probably disliked her.

Eden all the while trying to quell the strong attraction she felt towards Talus, and he reading it in her. Talus knew she had the ability to also read thoughts but, not the practice or the experience. That was just fine with him, for he knew if she could read his thoughts, they would both be facing a dilemma, as he wanted her as well. Halfway between Claremont and Hadleyville Talus stopped for gas and asked Eden if she wanted anything from inside the convenience store, she asked for a coke if he wouldn't mind. Getting back inside the truck, Talus handed her a bottle of water. "Soda is not healthy, water is better." He said as he handed it to her. Eden smiled and thanked him. Quietly she drank the water, offering him a drink at one point. "No, I am very rarely thirsty, but thank you." He responded. His demeanor was quiet, restrained and professional during the rest of the ride.

Finally Eden spoke. "Will he say his name is Alestasis?" she asked. "No, he will have a different name, it's up to The Highest Realm and who they choose . . . Daniel will let you know . . . do not be concerned as The Highest Realm will protect you, as will Daniel." Talus explained pulling up alongside the curb at Sparrow Lane. "How did you know where I live?" she asked. "I know a lot of things." Talus answered her. "Will you also protect me?" Eden didn't know where she was going with this, but Talus did. "Yes, I did today." He responded sternly with strong arrogance, correcting her as if her memory of the events had somehow escaped her. "Where do you come from?" she asked wanting to know more about him, her curiosity getting the better of her. "I have been alive for more than one hundred and fifty years." He turned to look at her, as he spoke, amused by her question. "I mean . . . where are you from, before you belonged to The Council?" she asked slowly. "I was born in Germany to German parents, other than that I don't know, as a member of The Council, it does not concern me."

He went on, as he knew she was just learning the meaning of the dimensions. "When you transfer dimensions, into The Council, you are not supposed to remember . . . if you choose to be immortal The Council keeps your soul and erases your memory, it's easier that way." He said simply. "And are you happy being immortal?" she asked him. "I think it's better than being mortal . . . look at all the trouble you people cause." He said with slight laughter, which made her laugh. Then he changed, and his voice took on a serious tone. "To be immortal, is much less complicated, there are no emotions and feelings of love and hearts, and it is more about needs and wants."

"It is how this generation phrases it, we have a lot less hang ups." He was indeed trying to dissuade her from her attraction to him. She didn't know it, but he was fighting for her virtue. There was also a part of him that did not want to embarrass her as she would be working alongside him and Daniel in the future. Talus was taking all this into consideration. "Actually I think that phrase is from the seventies, or the eighties." Eden replied. "Well, it does not matter I am using it as an example." Talus responded with slight annoyance. Several moments of silence passed. "There is no happy or unhappy for us Eden, we are motivated by our instincts." He said, his voice deep and low as he ran his hand over the steering wheel feeling the embossed leather. And then Eden spoke, trying to break the awkwardness they both felt. "You can be charming, when you want to be." She said smiling. Talus put both his hands back on the steering wheel, grabbing it tightly and turned away from her. This was going down the wrong road. The physical attraction he felt was too strong and he needed to end this now.

Talus had been completely honest with Eden. He was motivated and highly in tune with his basic instinct of his nature, and right now those instincts were igniting inside of him. His professionalism would have to win the battle in this case. He knew better than to get directly involved with a mortal. Especially Eden, who was vital to The Path and had her destiny planned out in front of her. The fact that she was mortal was enough to keep him from her, but being Eden was the biggest reason. Talus did not have a lot of experience with mortal woman, only with one in fact. Yet he knew from that experience, mortal woman thrived on love. Protecting it and nurturing it, at the cost of their own mortal lives. That was something he could not offer anyone. At least when he dated other Council members, both sides knew what to expect, they had an understanding between themselves. They could not conceive or fall ill with disease, as they were protected by The Council Tribunal.

In the silence Talus waited for Eden to open the door and go into her house, where her parents would be relieved to see she was still alive. Eden was waiting for something to happen. She felt the same magnetism and didn't completely understand it, how could she? After all she had never felt such a strong sensual pull towards anyone before. Even her connection to Joshua, felt different. As she waited for Talus to speak, she already knew that she wanted him, physically. Logically, it didn't make sense to her, but right now her mind was being ruled by her instincts as well. Somehow Eden needed to reach out to him and she knew she would have to make the first gesture. There was a part of her that was seeking something from Talus and she was going to get it. She had come to believe it was necessary for her own survival. Eden had felt this when she had first set eyes on him last night and it had only intensified through the night into the dawn. He had something she needed, and now her instincts prevented her from opening the door of the truck.

"I think you should go now, I am sure your parents are longing to see you." He said facing forward. "Yes, you are right. Thank you, for bringing me home." Eden reached over and gave him a kiss on the cheek. As her hair brushed against his face, he turned and pulled her close to him, taking her in his arms. He kissed her deeply, fervently and sensually. Differently than the kiss he had given her at the hearing, and she kissed him back, grabbing him and putting her arms inside his jacket to be closer to him, she wanted to feel him all around her. This was not like Joshua's kiss, this was a kiss of life after death, and internal desperation. Suddenly Talus pushed her away from him. "No . . . No this cannot happen." He said holding her at arm's length. Eden shrunk back, as she felt shame fill her and yet the intensity she felt kept her from leaving.

Talus was annoyed with himself, what he was doing with this woman child who was going to marry Alestasis? He could see that she didn't expect that reaction. "Eden, you have been through so much in the past twenty four hours and I can understand that you are overwhelmed with many different sensations, but . . . you cannot seek something from me that is not within my power to give you." He spoke slowly, choosing his words carefully. "What is within your power to give me?" Eden asked. "There is nothing I can give you that you could not find with a mortal man, like Alestasis who can also give you love and his heart." He answered her. "What if I don't want his love or his heart?" she asked, somewhat defiantly. "You are a mortal woman, and I know from experience, a mortal woman needs both, as she needs food and water." He explained, clearly upset that his physical needs had gotten the best of him. "I am not Lillianna." She said indignantly. He paused to look at her. "You are a mortal and a Warrior of God by your own oath, you are also betrothed to Alestasis . . . not to mention you are a woman child!" Talus was fighting hard to control his patience as she tested him well.

She could not argue, for he made perfect sense. He knew her . . . and he clearly knew himself. "I'm sorry, I am surprised at my behavior." Eden responded quietly. "I am not surprised, you and I have just experienced something extraordinary together, something I do all the time and I'm use to it." He paused and then continued. "But for you, today has been monumental and you have fear rising inside you . . . this is not an easy transition, for mortals." Talus still waited for her to go into the house. Realizing she needed help, he got out of the truck and went around to the passenger's side and opened the door for her.

Eden stayed silent, but she agreed with everything he was saying. She was afraid and needed his strength. Slowly she took hold of his out stretched hand. "When will I see you again?" she asked looking into his large brown eyes that could see everything she was feeling. Talus smiled, "Soon, we will be working together." He got back into the truck and started the engine. As he sped down the street, Eden's hair blew wildly in the early morning wind. Talus looked in his rearview mirror, watching her as she watched him drive down the street and turn the corner. That was a close call he thought to himself. He had his own moral code which he had crossed with Lillianna. He wasn't about to do it again, if he could help it. Especially not with Eden. He had recognized strength and conviction in Eden, and knew that in her own way she could be a force to be reckoned with. Talus had dealt with enough forces today.

This was history repeating itself, Talus thought as he drove away from Eden, but in the reverse. Talus knew that his attraction to Eden was that she had a close resemblance to Lillianna and that was enough to get him and her into serious trouble. The Council Tribunal would look unfavorably on it because, he was immortal and Eden was mortal. Not, to mention that the recent events had now promised her future to the soul of Alestasis. Talus was a ladies' man, although he had been on the earth for a hundred and fifty years, he was still a twenty year old physically and always in the height of his sexual inclinations, but extremely selective. He had his choice of women, but was not promiscuous. Women were attracted to him because Talus had a cool reserved air about him, in a strong sensual charismatic way. This is what had drawn Eden to him. As, reserved and abrasive as he had been, she had found his masculinity and sensuality calling her to him.

In her, Talus had seen a reserved strength of will that he admired and a well hidden passionate soul, bursting with sensual fire. Eden and Talus both followed their instincts and analytical sides more than their emotional side, but with Eden, time would show that of the Seven Creeds, controlling her emotions was where she was weakest. Talus had trouble controlling his lust, when he found someone that attracted him, which was very rare. He had stopped dating years ago as Council women had grown boring to him. Talus was well versed in most things, having been on earth for so long and not a novice, but Eden was just beginning to realize all her potentials and that was dangerous.

Rain had begun to fall heavily as Talus made his way on to interstate 95 headed toward New Hampshire. He had purchased a parcel of land, eighty years ago way up in the mountains, secluded and protected from nosey humans. Until tonight he hadn't realized what had attracted him to live there, but now he understood it reminded him of his youth in Germany. The house he had built was more of a huge lodge, completely made of wood and stone, similar to his parent's home. Thinking about it he wasn't sure if he was happy about remembering. What good was remembering it only took one out of the present moment? That's all anyone has, is the here and now, he thought as he parked his truck in the circular driveway in front of the house.

Once at home he lit a fire in the stone fireplace, and opened a bottle of wine, though he did not need sustenance, he enjoyed the flavor and color of red wine. Overall today had gone well, he reflected as he looked at the flames of the fire increase. He had the chance to apologize to Lillianna and that made it possible for him to move forward. Sitting quietly he heard a knock at the door. Talus was cautious by nature and instinctively went on guard, as no one knew where he lived, except Daniel and The Council Tribunal. It was almost impossible to find him, unless he had been followed. He quietly opened the back door and came around to the front of the house. He relaxed his Council powers when he saw that standing in the pouring rain at the front door stood, Eden. Hearing him walk up to her she turned to him. "Eden what are you doing here?" he asked her. It was as if she couldn't speak. He tried to read her, but her thoughts were confusing. "Did you drive yourself, is that your car?" he asked her, searching her eyes for a response. "Yes." She replied finally. Talus put his arm around her. "Come into the house you silly girl." Once inside he took her jacket off and led her over to the fire place. "I'll be right back." He told her and went to get some towels.

"Eden why are you here?" he asked sitting down next to her. "I had to see you, I just needed to." She answered him, her voice filled with longing and emotion. As he dried her off, he focused on the right words to tell her. "I know you and I are both very physically attracted to each other, I should not have kissed you earlier . . . I was wrong to do that, please accept my apology." He explained as he gently dried her hair with the towel. "I can help you in the ways of The Path and with negotiations between the dimensions, but you must understand that we both have commitments that we must keep." He looked directly into her eyes to make sure she understood him. "Eden, you are a beautiful young woman, who has exceptional powers and is about to marry a man she wants to save . . . where can I fit in that?" he asked her. "Of course I know that . . . my mind tells me that, but my heart says something else." She replied sadly. "I think it is your physical needs that have swept you away, not your heart." Talus replied.

Putting the towel around her shoulders, he offered her his glass of wine, but she refused it. "How could I forget, Warriors of God don't drink." He replied smiling. Eden sat motionless, staring into the fire light. Talus tried to appeal to her sense of reason, "It would never work, even if you had not taken the oath . . . you are human and I am not, I could never make you happy and The Council Tribunal would frown on such a union as well as Daniel." He told her quietly, completely understanding her needs. "You have been through a lot in the past two days, this is understandable." Eden rested her head on his shoulder. "I think I'm in love with you." She said, in a whisper. "No, I think you confuse love with lust." He contested. She looked up at him. "You loved or still love Lillianna and she was human?" she questioned him. "No," he replied. "I was very physically attracted to her, but it's because Lillianna was one of us for many, many, years . . . that I didn't take her mortality seriously, but I should have." Talus clarified as he took a drink from his wine. "I do not love Lillianna, I am not capable of that emotion." He responded. "So, you could not love me?" Eden asked him. "I could want you and lust for you . . . and I do, but love you, no . . . not being who and what I am." He answered in his straightforward manner, a characteristic Eden both liked and disliked about him.

"Then want me now, lust for me now!" Eden implored. "No, it would be wrong for us." He chastised her. "Why?" she asked him, tears forming in her eyes. "I know you want me, I can feel it." Eden replied firmly, her eyes seeing through him. Talus paused and then gently smoothed the hair away from her face. "Because I will not take from you, that which can only be given once." He answered her in a tone that was direct and serious but gentle. "I don't understand what you mean?" Eden questioned him, perplexed by his comment. "Your purity, your virginity, I'm not the man to take it from you." His voice becoming elevated. "Now you are presuming I am a virgin!" She said angrily and completely losing control. More than that she knew she was being immature and not worthy of the Evanharth name. "I am not presuming anything I know that for a fact, and it is very admirable, but I am not the man to take it from you."

Talus knew her to the core of her being, it was foolish to continue. Containing herself Eden stood up and put her jacket on, "I am sorry that I burst in on you . . . and threw myself at you, I won't do it again." She told him quietly, as she walked over to the door. Talus followed her, putting his hand over hers as she grasped the doorknob. Her head was down, as he rested his hands on her shoulders and turned her to face him. Lifting her chin up with his index finger, he asked her, "What is it you truly seek of me?" Her eyes gave him his answer before she spoke. "You . . . only you." Eden whispered.

"Never, ever lower your head to anyone, Eden." He told her. "Talus, I am lowering it to myself for my gross misconduct and immaturity." Tears' filling her eyes, her voice was hushed as she continued. "Talus when you kissed me I felt something I have never felt before . . . you're right, this is all wrong, but as much as I know that . . . it doesn't matter because I still want you and I know you want me too." She told him as she grabbed the door knob and pulled at it, but it was locked. "You should wait till morning, it's raining so hard and the road down the mountain can be slippery." He said as he took her jacket off, and placed on the back of one of the kitchen chairs. Eden looked at him. "For eighteen years I have followed the principals of The Creed," she said pausing. Talus leaned against one of the wooden beams near the entrance. "Eighteen years?" he asked, his implication was that eighteen years is not a very long time. Eden shot back, "Alright maybe I haven't been here for hundreds of years like you, but it's still eighteen years and their mine!" Eden exclaimed her eyebrows furrowed. Talus watching her smiled and responded. "Touché, indeed and they have been eighteen mortal years." He agreed. "I have listened to my church, my grandmother, who I cherished and my parents who I love . . . but now, right now I'm listening to myself." He read her, but did not speak, this was her moment, she needed to think it, to say it, and to own it. Eden still had on the top of the wedding gown and her black pants, "I feel wet and dirty." She said with a familiar pout, he recognized. Eden knew her next step would be the deciding factor, if she took her jacket and put it on, he would let her leave. Talus knew that she didn't want to.

Finally he made the decision for both of them. He took hold of her hand and led her to his bedroom where he undressed her and himself. He then took her into the large stone shower stall. Turning on the water, he adjusted the temperature. As the water fell on the cold stone, steam rose up and encircled their bodies. Kissing her neck and then her shoulders, he pressed her body against his. "I guess you win, just be prepared for the consequences of your emotions." He said holding her in his arms, as the water and steam covered them. "I am." She answered. Eden was prepared for the consequences of her emotions and feelings, or so she thought. Talus took care of the rest. He did not want what happened to Lilliannna, to happen to Eden or anyone else for that matter. The effects could be devastating on both sides and their world as they knew it would be destroyed. Being mortal, she could become pregnant with his child, which was one of the reasons, it was so much simpler to be with someone immortal like himself. Talus wanted Eden as much as she wanted him, but he also knew he had to be the adult in the situation. Knowing how mortals behave, and living as long as he had, he knew that Eden was also being directed by her sexual instincts and not by her logic right now. He had to protect them both.

Wrapping her in towel Talus dried her off, than he took her face in his hands. "Eden, there is still time, to change your mind." He told her. You can sleep here in my bed and I will sleep in the other room . . ." He suggested gallantly, uncharacteristically for a Council member.

He was right, although it was clear to Eden by the change in his anatomy, that he was aroused, nothing had happened in the shower, except kissing and heavy breathing. Although he wanted her, a part of Talus wished she had not followed him home. He knew that eventually she would want from him the three things mortal women value more than anything else, the love, heart and commitment of the man they love. However, they both knew that her sleeping in his bed without him was not even remotely possible. She was so slender in his arms, he lifted her easily and carried her to his bed. Lying down next to her, she rolled her body into his, and Talus drew her close to him, holding her. They both realized there was no turning back now. "Where does this desire you feel for me come from Eden?" he questioned her. "I felt it from the moment I saw you . . . and then when you kissed me . . . both times." She answered softly, as she caressed his chest with her fingers. "It is instinctual, something I don't have complete control over." She continued, "I have never felt this way before, for anyone Talus." He nodded and then replied, "Yes, I know and I understand how instincts work . . . it is the way I live my life." He responded.

"What does your instinct tell you about me? She asked him, playfully. He pulled her body under his, kissing her deeply. Her eyes were closed and her long eyelashes clung to her dampened skin. She waited for his kiss again, but Talus looked at her until she opened her eyes. "It tells me that I want you Eden . . . I want you . . . and I always follow my instincts."

Talus held Eden close to him. His long hair usually tied in back, was now loose about him and still damp from the shower, it mixed with Eden's hair as their bodies wrapped around each other. Talus releasing his strong sexual urges and Eden leaving innocence behind. His lean muscular body gave Eden a sense of security. "What if I need to talk to you, how can I reach you?" her lips touched the side of his neck as she spoke. He gave her a soft squeeze. "Just use your mind, to talk to me." He answered in a whisper. "I have that power?" she asked her breath entering his ear as she spoke, sending goose bumps down his leg. "Yes." He replied holding in a giggle, "and many others." He told her, his voice trailing off, as he began to fall asleep. Eden ran her fingers lightly along his side and he awoke. "What are the parameters?" she asked. Talus closed his eyes but spoke clearly, keeping his voice low. "We cannot date . . . but we can be friends, however we must always be professional when we work together."

He reached down and pulled the large white comforter up to his chin covering them both. "Were you professional yesterday when you kissed me during the hearing?" she taunted him. "No, I was not. I wanted you from the first moment I saw you." He answered sleepily. Then he rolled over on his side, forcing her to roll on to her side, her back facing him. Talus cradled her with his body as she finally let her eyes close and began to let her body and mind relax. She felt like a woman, and now the sheer excitement was hard to control. Eden glorified in the moment, she wanted it to last as she knew not when she would ever feel this way again. Being mortal she should be exhausted, but it seemed to be the other way around, with Talus now being sound asleep. She gently ran her fingers through the tiny blond hairs on his arms.

As content as she was, she also realized it would be short lived. There was no way for Talus and Eden to have a man and woman relationship, given who they were. Even though there was a part of her that longed for that possibility, it was only natural . . . she was mortal and this was her first sexual experience and she had instigated it. Talus had warned her and given her three opportunities to walk away, but yet in the depths of her soul, she felt that he was the man to bring her to womanhood, Talus had accomplished that. What would happen when she married Alestasis? Who would he be? What would her life be like? Suddenly she felt Talus kiss the back of her neck. "Don't think about these things now." He whispered, tenderly nibbling her small delicate shoulder, arousing her with new passion. He kissed her earlobe and she turned in his arms to face him. "How will I leave in the morning?" she asked him. "With strength, determination, and knowledge." He replied, kissing her lips. "It will be hard." She said simply. "Few things in life Eden, are not hard for mortals." He spoke from experience.

"How do you know, I have all this strength, knowledge and determination?" Eden asked him as she ran her fingers through his hair. Talus caressed her face. "My dear, determination you have a lot of, obviously. The strength is within you, as you fought Dante today, you saw some of it surface and more is still dormant but Daniel and I will help you to seize and harness it, and knowledge well, one receives knowledge every day, whether one chooses to recognize it, that's a different issue." Talus closed his eyes and pulled her in close to him. "How are you so sure of all this?" Eden asked sleepily. "I have seen the dimensions and how they coexist for many, many years and I know who you are, and who you will become." He said, with a certainty that was unquestionable. In Talus she had found much more than a lover, he was becoming her mentor and his commitment to her would become his own salvation.

"Who is wise? One who learns from all." The Talmud

The Master and the Pupil
Chapter Ten

Eden slept within his arms, cradled and secure. The rain heavy and then soft at times, creating a kind mystical sound, that would lull her to sleep and then wake her up suddenly. Talus slept soundly holding her in his arms, even as he slept, his extra sensory perceptions felt her next to him. She savored every moment of his being, his breath, his skin. Eden knew this would happen only once, once in her lifetime she would experience this kind of passion, longing, and fulfillment. Her instincts had guided her to this moment, which needed to happen. Talus had led her to a new stage in her life and now she could move forward-now she was capable of doing anything and withstanding anything.

As the rain began to subside Eden fell into a deep sleep. Dreaming that she was a small child again, playing outside her parent's home, she was running across the yard. The day was sunny and and the sky was clear, she looked up to see her mother and father smiling down at her. Her baby brother Benjamin crawling on the grass, trying to keep up with her. Then she turned to see Joshua standing before her, next to him her grandmother Rebecca.

Slowly her mind drifted back to consciousness, and her senses returned as she heard sounds around her. Now she smelled food cooking, she was in that in between state of being asleep and awake. Was she home upstairs in her room? As her eyes opened they began to focus and she saw the wooden beams across the ceiling and realized she was with Talus, who was gone from the bed. Getting up, she wrapped herself in the bed sheet making her way into the kitchen, she found him busily, making breakfast. "Good morning." She said. Talus turned away from the stove, and was momentarily taken aback. Standing there with only the sheet wrapped around her, she was like a reincarnation of Lillianna. The way her blue eyes looked at him, the way her hair fell over her shoulders, the contour of her face, were Lillianna. The difference was that Eden was slightly taller in stature. Lillianna stood a mere 5 feet 2 inches, Eden had three inches on her. Coming up close to him, she put her arm around his waist. "What are you up to?" she asked already knowing, but being playful. "A long time ago I saw two people who were madly, insane over each other eating breakfast together, I thought I would do the same for you . . . you must be hungry, are you?" he asked, as he flipped the eggs over. His mood was light and casual, Eden wondered if it was the sex or how he was, when he distracted himself from his work. "Yes I am thank you. I didn't know you knew of such things." Eden replied. "I do live in the world, you know." Talus teased, patting her lightly on the bottom.

They sat quietly as Eden ate her eggs and toast, and Talus drank his coffee. Even though Talus had no real need of food, he enjoyed the taste of certain things like wine, coffee and apple strudel. As Eden finished her breakfast, she felt the beginning sensation of loss and separation. Talus read it in her, as he reached out his hand to her, she grasped it with her two hands, as his hands were very large and hers were small by comparison.

Eden wanted nothing more than to be with him. She was young, inexperienced and in love. She had been from the moment she saw him. His masculinity and good looks had turned her upside down. Now through her own force of will she was here with him. "How was I as a lover?" she asked innocently. "Isn't that usually a question mortal men ask mortal women?" he responded smiling and a bit shocked. "I don't know Talus, I've never been through this before . . . tell me I want to know." Her innocence, poking through. He caressed her hands, with his and thought about his response. "You are sweet and gentle, sensual and a little bit clumsy, which was wonderfully refreshing for someone like me." He replied honestly in his straight forward manner. Eden took a drink from his coffee mug and made a face indicating she didn't like the taste. Talus laughed and said, "You would like it better with milk and sugar."

"I want to be everything for you." Eden told him. "Eden that's impossible, no one person can be everything for another." Talus let go of her hands and took a drink from his coffee cup. "You say that because you are not human." She sighed. "No, I say that because I have been on the earth for one hundred fifty years, more or less and I know the nature of humans." He spoke without looking at her. "How old are you really?" Eden asked.

"Council members do not age Eden, they are as old as they were at death . . . twenty-one or twenty-two . . . maybe twenty, I don't really know for sure." He answered her matter of factly. "It doesn't matter; I love you the way that you are, one hundred and fifty or twenty-two." She replied, her eyes searching his. "Eden, what happened here last night cannot be repeated, Daniel already expressed his sentiments and they were very unfavorable." Talus said sternly and looked annoyed. "You told him? . . . did you tell him I threw myself at you too?!" She was shocked and clearly upset, feeling as though he betrayed a secret. "No, I said you came seeking advice and my instincts took over." He explained. "You told him you forced yourself on me then?" she asked. "No! Eden why would I lie? I spoke the truth to him, he knows it was consensual, I respect our working relationship too much to tell him otherwise . . . besides that, as a Council member it is impossible for me to knowingly lie, especially to a leader of one of the dimensions."

Talus was losing his patience, but did not want this to get out of hand. "Did you also tell him that you take my breath away?" Eden asked, her voice soft and low. "Do I?" asked Talus. "Yes." Eden answered, "you always will." She told him. "He knows how I am, how all Council members are, we react to our natural basic instincts . . . nothing more, nothing less." His voice took on an almost harsh tone. Eden calmed herself down. "Did you tell him anything else?" she asked quietly. "He asked me if I had hurt you in anyway, I told him I didn't think so, aside from the obvious." He replied. "It didn't hurt as much as I thought it would." She replied looking down at the table. "That's good, Council members sometimes don't know their own strength." Talus replied after a few moments, changing his mood. "I was gentler with you, then I've ever been with any other woman." Talus responded sounding pleased. They were both silent for a few minutes, Eden contemplating all that was said. Talus, fighting the urge to have her again. "I know I ask a lot of questions and it annoys you, but I feel like I'm taking a test that I haven't studied for." She explained. "Eden, this is not a test. You are a Warrior of God and that happened the day you were conceived . . . you have chosen, by your own free will to take up the staff, and with that comes challenges and sacrifices."

He watched her, waiting for her response. "I am trying so hard to rise to your level." She replied. "Then you deem your worthiness too low, for you are already there, with me and Daniel." Talus insisted. "You have our support and respect, we both know you're potential and also, your inexperience."

Inside she was testing his patience on a much more organic level. "Do you also respect The Dominion as you respect The Path and Daniel." She asked, pulling her feet up on the chair and wrapping her arms around her knees, causing the sheet to loosen about her. He stayed focused on the question. "Yes, of course." He answered abruptly. "But how can you, they are evil?" she asked with disbelief. "Eden, one cannot exist without the other, it is the balance of nature as all souls can be good and bad and always are a combination of both . . . even in your short life you have seen this evidence." He said with certainty. "Look at Sienna, was she all good? No. Was she all evil? No." He stated definitively. Eden interjected. "You know about Sienna?" Eden was amazed at his reference. "Yes, of course, I know everything about you, I wouldn't be very good at my job if I failed to do my research . . . Daniel and your grandmother intervened on her behalf while she was still alive . . . but I am not going to elaborate on it, I am using it as an example to illustrate my point, look here at your own life, some might see you being with me as bad or evil." He looked at her and she recognized the intensity behind his large brown eyes. "It would help me a great deal if you were to put some clothes on." He suggested. Eden put her legs down and her feet on the floor and pulled the sheet up above her breasts as it was slipping down. She looked into his eyes, which were on her, taking her all in. "I want you too Talus, but I will not throw myself at you again, especially now as you think me bad." She said coyly, with a raised brow. He knew she was playing, but he wasn't. "Don't try to manipulate me Eden, you know what I think, and how I think." Talus corrected her.

Though she was just beginning to understand the sexual nature of men and woman, Eden knew her next gesture would bring him to her. She knew it as well as she knew her own name. As she stood and walked away from the table, she paused and turned her head to look back at him, her long silken hair descending down the small of her back, the sheet falling trailing behind her. Talus came up behind her and tugged at the sheet. He lifted her up in his arms and took her to the bedroom. This time Eden was a little less clumsy and a lot more sensual. It wasn't manipulation, it was instinct . . . Eden's instinct.

The afternoon sun made its way into the room and its beams fell over their bodies, its warmth reminding Talus and Eden it was time to return to their separate lives. "I see the pupil has learned quickly from the master." He said smiling. "Are you my master?" She asked resting her head on his shoulder. He pulled her closer to him. "No Eden, your master is The Devine One who lives in The Highest Realm and who speaks directly through Daniel." He sighed, bending his head down and kissing her. "You must learn to communicate with Daniel as he is your direct contact." He told her, as he nibbled her bottom lip and gave her a pat on the bottom. That was Talus talk for it's time to get up. Getting up he went to shower. "Come on you laziest of warriors!" He called out to her. She had begun her love with him in the shower and was ending their love in the same place. "Talus?" She asked. But he already read her mind. "No more questions." He replied. Then as he washed his chest he saw the look in her eyes, she is childlike in so many ways he thought to himself, struggling to be a woman.

"Alright just one more, only one so make it a good one." He teased, but he was serious just the same. "How are mortal women different from Council women when they make love?" She asked washing his back. He turned and put his arms around her, "This is your last question?" he asked smiling at her. "Yes, it's a very important one . . . to me." Her brows furrowed, her eyes intently waiting for the answer, she hung on his every word.

"Mortal women are nurturers, so full of emotions and life flows through them, this is how they make love, as if their next breath depended on it. A mortal woman would die for her love. Council women do not have these emotions or capabilities, and do not feel love . . . and so the experience is a different one, we also refer to it as having carnal knowledge of each other, rather than making love." He explained.

He turned the water off as they stepped out of the shower, and handed her a towel. "Perhaps one day in the future I will ask you the same question Eden, when you have someone to compare me to." He said as she dried off, it was a punch she was not expecting. "That was mean Talus and hurtful." She responded, wrapping the towel around herself and promptly leaving the room. "It was not meant to hurt you, but to remind you." He followed her into the kitchen, where she sat herself down at the table holding her face in her hands. Talus had the towel wrapped around his waist and bent down next to her, he pulled her hands away from her face, forcing her to look at him. "Eden, look at me . . . you have given me a wonderful gift of yourself and it is something I will never forget, as long as I exist, but your future as a woman is not with me . . . . have I lied to you? Did I misrepresent myself to you?" He waited for her answer, it didn't come. "I told you I could not love you, but now, that is what you seek from me." His voice was as usual, controlled and direct. "When I asked you last night if you were prepared for the consequences . . .

this is what I was referring to." He said standing up, looking at her. "So I am asking you a question, one that you need not answer, but think about instead." Talus paused, choosing his words. "Last night you came here as a child and today you are leaving as a woman . . . was it worth it?" His truth rang out in her ears. She took the blows because he was right in everything he said. "It's hard to argue with the truth Talus." She replied softly. "The mortality in you, will be reciprocated in all the ways you desire, from a mortal man, he will also take your breath away." He said trying to comfort her with his words, but Talus was always painfully honest.

"I know I have hurt many, many humans throughout these years, men and women alike. Mostly for how my decisions effected the consequences of their actions, rather than directly. I had hoped, Eden not to make you one of them." He explained in his own defense pulling up a chair, as he sat down he faced her. "You have not hurt me Talus, you in fact have given me what I came seeking." She replied composed. "What is it that I gave you, which you could not have gotten from any other man?" Eden stood up and sat herself on his lap. "You have given me knowledge and strength . . . and my womanhood." She told him adding, "Yes, I could have gotten my womanhood from someone else, but not the knowledge and strength that I need from you." She kissed him tenderly on the lips and then walked into the bedroom to get dressed. Her clothes were revoltingly filthy and she cringed putting them on. Eden knew she had to get home, she had taken Uncle Eli's car. From past experience she knew he always kept a spare key under the driver's side floor mat. By now she was sure it was reported missing.

Talus came into the bedroom. "Don't put those on, I have some clothes you can use." In his room stood a large oak dresser. He opened one of the drawers and removed a pair of tan corduroy pants and a brown turtle neck shirt.

He handed them to her. "Who do they belong to?" Eden asked surprised. "A woman I use to date, a long time ago." He replied. She took them and proceeded to put them on, at least they were clean. "They're a little big, but will serve the purpose." Talus told her nodding. "I'll wash them when I get home, and return them to you." Eden assured him. "No, I don't need them, actually I forgot I had them or I would have thrown them out a long time ago." He replied simply.

"Come on, put your boots on, we will go out in back of the house for a while." He told her as he got dressed. As Eden slipped her boots on, she watched him. Obviously his two favorite colors were, black and grey, the clothes in his closet reflected it. He wore a pair a black jeans and a grey crew neck sweater, which accentuated his muscular chest. He went into the bathroom and brushed his hair out and she followed him. "Talus my hair is still damp, do you have a blow dryer?" she asked looking in the bathroom cabinet. "No, it will dry in the air and sun, you don't need a dyer, and it's bad for your hair." He replied indignantly. Then he handed her the brush, with a hair elastic. "Here put your hair up, it will be easier." He suggested, putting his hair in one as well. "Why? . . . what will we be doing?" she asked with intense curiosity. "You'll see." He replied and walked to the back door of the house.

As they stepped outside, Eden saw how extensive the property was, and the forest beyond it. "Do you own all this?" she asked. "Yes." He answered with a degree of satisfaction. "Let us walk for a bit." He said taking hold of her hand as they walked toward the forest. "Talus, what is the difference between your spirit and your soul?" Eden asked as they walked along. Talus didn't answer for a few moments. Finally he replied. "Although they are both somewhat connected . . . they can be separate, especially in Council members." He pulled her in closer to him as they walked, his arm around her shoulder, her arm around his waist. "Your spirit is more like your personality, your personal energy and your soul is your loves, your hates, your emotions and the truest nature of who you are. Someone can have a very youthful spirit and yet be a very old soul." He explained thinking of Lillianna. Eden didn't reply, he read her thoughts, she needed more information. "When I do battle in the middle dimension it is with my spirit as I do not have a soul, because I do not have a soul, I do not feel things like a mortal does." He clarified using an example. "And Daniel and The Dominion?" she asked.

"Unfortunately they bring both, so it makes it harder." Talus answered her shaking his head, with a little laugh. "Who usually wins?" Eden asked, resting her head on the side of his chest. "Eden The Council always wins . . . it is our job to control the war between the entities." He assured her. "Do the warriors get hurt?" Eden stopped to look at him, her face showing concern and sadness as she asked. "Yes, of course they do . . . Council members too." He answered indicating by his tone that he had been hurt many times.

"We'll head back now." He said as she stood still, her mind was still concentrating on all this information. He gave her a tug. "Eden, the history of the world shows us that war is a part of humanity . . . and no you cannot go to the middle dimension, because you are completely mortal." He said answering her thoughts. "All your battles will be fought on earth."

"But . . ." She began. Talus interrupted her. "Eden, if there was no evil in the world, how would mankind know he has to rise above it?" he asked, not wanting an answer. "Are there wars in the spirit world?" Eden asked. "Yes sometimes, now on to more important topics." Talus told her, closing the subject, but reading her he knew another question was rising to the surface.

They were back now just at the edge of the forest. "No more questions." Talus answered her thoughts and was all business again as he spoke to her. "Move that rock over there." He dictated. "Which one?" she asked, walking toward it. "Get back here next to me." He scolded. "Talus, what do you mean?" Eden questioned him and his attitude. He put his hands on her shoulders as he stood behind her. "Focus on what I am saying." He ordered her. "Mentally . . . move that rock, the one with the white stripes going through it, bring it toward you." He instructed. "There are so many rocks, which one?" She was becoming emotional, he could read it in her. He stepped away to give her room.

Talus looked at her, indicating this was not a game. "Alright I see it now." She said, sighing deeply. Eden was staring at it but nothing was happening. "Eden you're not concentrating!" Talus raised his voice. She wanted to cry, as he was being mean with the sound of his voice, but she controlled it. He came up behind her. "Don't think about whether you like my voice or not, think about the rock." He whispered in her ear. Eden looked at the rock and focused on it, but nothing happened. "Watch, like this." He said, as he mentally lifted the rock and brought it toward her and it floated in front of her face in mid air and then he let it drop. "Talus, I can't do that!" She argued, losing control. She turned to walk toward the house. "No, we are not done Eden." He said, taking hold of her arm. "Try again." He commanded. He knew she was using this tactic because they had been intimate with each other and Eden was allowing her emotions to overrule her concentration. Exhaling deeply she gave him an annoyed glance and then picked out a funny shaped rock about the size of a small egg. She focused on it, she thought about lifting it but nothing happened. "I can't do it." She said bluntly.

"Yes, you can!" Talus insisted his voice loud but in control. "Stop it, take hold of your emotions, this is within your capabilities . . . you can and will do this." He reprimanded her. "Maybe The Highest Realm made a mistake." She replied, her tone sarcastic. Talus was not going to give into her. "Eden you were born with these abilities and you will learn to do this or it is going to be a very long day." He replied in his unemotional way. Eden bent down picked up a rock with her hand, held it out in front of him and then dropped it. In a fit, of emotional immaturity, she turned and proceeded to walk back to the house. Suddenly, it was as if an invisible strap was pulling her backwards. She struggled against it, but it was too powerful. It swung her around so now she was facing Talus and the forest behind him. Eden kept pushing against his mental force to bring her toward him. Digging her feet into the ground, she continued to fight against him, losing her balance and falling down. Getting up she still fought against his energy force, as it pulled her towards him.

Finally his force of will dragged her all the way back to where he stood. She now faced him, completely shocked, and embarrassed. "Are you done playing now?" he asked her. "Yes." She replied in awe of his supernatural abilities. "Now, let's try this again shall we? Like adults." He said standing in back of her, his hands on her shoulders at first and then he touched her forehead with his open palm. "Close your eyes." He said softly, and Eden closed her eyes. "This is your mental energy and sensory perception." Then he put his hand on her solar plexus. "This is the center of your physical energy and will help you to influence your mental abilities . . . combine both together." He explained, as he stood behind her, his eyes closed as well. "Combine your mental energy with your physical energy, make them one now." He whispered. "Eden, bring me a rock . . . any rock."

He told her. Eden opened her eyes and concentrated on the rocks in front of her. She focused all her physical and mental energy on the rocks and cleared her mind of all other random thoughts. All of a sudden hundreds of tiny rocks began to rise about two feet off the ground.

She closed her eyes again and focused on moving them until they rose higher in the air. Now hundreds of small rocks and pebbles were hovering high above the ground. Talus remained silent. He wanted her to experiment as much as possible. "Eden bring me one, just one." He spoke quietly. Suddenly all the rocks and pebbles came flying toward them. Eden ducted down, but Talus stopped them in mid flight and they fell to the ground. "I did it! I did it!" Eden jumped up and down. "I can do it! Talus you saw that I can do it!" She squealed with delight. She wrapped her arms around him, smiling and giggling, like a woman child.

Eden looked at him as he appeared pensive and far off, his thoughts far away. "Are you not pleased?" there was that little pout again, he thought. "Yes, that was good, but you need more practice . . . try again, with only one rock." He told her. Eden looked around and found one about the size of a baseball. Talus thought she was over compensating, but he refrained from comment. Eden managed to move it slightly, but not off the ground. "It's not working." She said losing confidence. "Why not try a smaller one?" he suggested. Talus walked out in front of her about ten feet and picked one up putting it in the middle of his palm. "Here, take this off my hand." He called to her, this time she was within in range of her experience. She focused all her energy on it and him. "No cheating." He called out. "Stop thinking about my naked body and think about the rock." He said smiling.

Slowly the rock began to rise off his palm as Eden willed it towards her, where it found her open palm and rested there. Talus began clapping his hands as he walked towards her. She wrapped her arms around his neck and he picked her up by her waist and swung her around, in a circle, her feet off the ground. Then stopping he kissed her. "You must practice this daily and above all else, you must practice emotional restraint." He stated, as they walked back to the house.

Once inside the house, she saw her jacket sitting on the back of one of the kitchen chairs. The day was coming to an end and she knew she needed to leave. Being a mortal and having emotions, Talus knew that it would be hard for Eden to leave. In truth, he enjoyed her being here with him. She was young and innocent and fun, something he hadn't realized was missing in his life. He also knew that when she left, he could do easily without her. Just as he had in the past, when he experienced anything remotely to a feeling of loss, he was able to separate himself from the emotion quickly and effectively. All Council members had that strength and composure. Although they rarely needed to bring it to the surface. This was the second time in his life Talus would need to rely on his internal strength to detach himself from his feelings for a woman. However, as detached as he believed himself to be, this woman child would begin to draw him in, just as Lillianna had in the past. Talus would find himself wondering how much longer he could be immortal. The question would be one that he would ask himself more than once, the longer he came to know Eden.

"I am really going to miss you, Talus." Eden said, as she put her jacket on. Talus looked at her and smiled. "Think of me as your closest ally, second to Daniel, for that I shall always be." He replied. "Always?" she asked. "Yes, nothing can change that, not even time or space." Talus responded knowing her next question. "Will I see you again?" she asked, a little afraid of the answer. "Yes, of course as we will be working together." He replied, guiding her towards him and hugging her. She rested her head on his chest. "That is not your question though is it?" he asked her. "No." She whispered, her voice reflecting her sadness. "We have different paths to follow, it would not be wise or responsible for the two of us to get any more involved." Talus spoke caressing her hair.

Eden stepped away from him and took off her purity ring. She handed it to him and he accepted it. "Do you know what it represents?" she asked. "Yes, I do." He responded. "Are you sure you want me to have it?" he asked her, his brow raised, as he studied the details and inscription on the inside. "Yes, I would like you to have it." She replied softly. "Well then, I will wear it always." Talus smiled and pushed it on to his left hand pinkie finger. He walked to the door and opened it. Eden smiled and kissed him on the cheek. "Eden?" he asked with a certain level of ambivalence which was odd given who he was. "Yes?" she replied, with questioned aspiration. "Thank you for giving me that which, can only be given once." He replied.

As she started the engine of uncle Eli's car, Talus bent down and kissed her lips. "If you ever need anything . . . you know, with The Council or . . ." He was trying to find the right words to speak. "I know Talus, I know you are here for me . . . I will always know." She replied. He watched her as she made her way down the long, winding dirt road until her car was no longer visible.

Father Odell read the eulogy at Rebecca Evanharth's gravesite. It was a truly beautiful and touching tribute to a woman who had, sacrificed more than her personal life for the privilege of service to others. He spoke about her generosity of spirit. Mentioning how she lead the choir and the countless hours of charity work, she had done over her lifetime. Father Clemmons came in at the end and spoke a few words about how she had meant so much to so many families in Hadleyville and the surrounding towns, through her good will and contributions to the need of others. Always putting herself last. Many cried, friends and loved ones alike. Eden did not cry, not one tear, not once. She was, as Rebecca would have insisted she be . . . stoic and reserved.

Not once did either of the Fathers allude to who Rebecca really was. Eden thought about an old saying, that Rebecca often said when she was in doubt, "seeing is believing." Eden remembered when she was small, a vacuum cleaner salesman came to the door, dressed in a suit and tie. He seemed to think, Eden's grandmother would be an easy sale. Was he ever mistaken. She did buy the vacuum cleaner, after he vacuumed the whole house, including the base boards and drapes. Then she did the white glove test. It was a good thing it was a pretty good vacuum cleaner or she would have thrown him out on his ear. She could be stubborn and hardnosed, and she was nobody's fool. Finally Eden got up to speak. There was easily over three hundred people at the cemetery. More had filled the church that morning.

She looked out at all the faces, there were so many that had no idea who Rebecca Evanharth really was. Clearing her throat she began. "Thank you Father Odell and Father Clemmons for those very kind words, I would like to tell you about Rebecca Evanharth from a granddaughter's perspective." Father Odell and Father Clemmons both seemed more than overly attentive. "She was a tender voice in the night, when I had a bad dream. She was a world of hugs and kisses. She was tireless when it came to anything she believed in, . . including me. My grandmother was the voice of sensibility and reason, always, teaching me the importance of staying true to my responsibilities and commitments, within the church, my family and in the community." Eden paused, controlling her emotions and then continued. "Rebecca Evanharth was strong and fearless in the face of evil or wrong doing . . . she was the grandmother every child should have, and I am so glad I did. She was many, wonderful things and above all else, she was a salvation to many more than I can know or count. If I can be half the woman she was, I will have accomplished a great deal in my life. My grandmother was and always will be my champion. Thank you for being here Nana, and for all the knowledge and love you bestowed on me." Eden bent down and kissed the top of the coffin.

She walked over to her parents, friends and family members who were all hugging and many were tearing up over Eden's eulogy and gesture. As she looked out among the crowd she saw Talus, then she lost sight of him. Eden saw him again as he was getting into his truck. His show of respect meant a lot to Eden. It was more than professional courtesy and she knew it, because she felt it. His gesture was one that she would never forget. She wanted to run to him and be held in his arms, but she couldn't and controlled the emotion. Besides she needed him too much to risk losing his respect. Of course she wanted to feel his skin upon her own, to kiss his lips, to look deeply into his eyes. That was all true, but even more than that, she needed his skill and guidance into The Path. She needed Daniel too. That was a given, but Talus was instrumental because all decisions concerning The Path and The Dominion went through him first.

As much as her body and emotions wanted him, her intellect told her he was much more valuable and necessary as a friend and colleague. She knew by his visit to the gravesite, that he was completely on her side and that he would be there when she needed him . . . professionally.

He was holding true to his word and she was grateful and appreciative.

A large gathering of friends and family came back to the Evanharth house following the gravesite eulogy. Fortunately, many had brought food to the house previously and practically no one entered the Evanharth residence empty handed. Aunt Rowena and Eden's mother Rachel had prepared food and Uncle Eli and Thomas had rented tables and chairs, as they had a good sense of how many people would come back to their home. Mostly everyone had parked in the school parking lot and walked over to Sparrow Lane. Uncle Eli had contacted the school superintendent Mr. Matheson for permission to use the school lot. He was there today with his wife. A good friend of Eden's grandmother, Mrs. Matheson was part of the same charity groups that Rebecca was affiliated with. As it turned out the afternoon was sunny and pleasant, an easy day for walking.

Eden was exhausted by the time five o'clock rolled around and there were still at least fifty visitors left. All chatting about the old days and telling stories about Rebecca. Excusing herself, she went upstairs to kick off her shoes and take off her stockings. She had worn a black sleeveless dress with a black jacket to the wake and funeral, along with black hose and black high heels. She had all intentions of changing into her black sweats and a black tee shirt. It was the custom in her church family to wear black for three months while mourning an immediate family member. Her mom had mentioned that it was an ancient custom and she didn't need to follow it, but she wanted to.

She opened the door and fell back against the wall, when she saw Rebecca standing before her. "Don't be alarmed dear." She told Eden. Eden caught her breath and stepping inside her room closed the door behind her. Eden looked at her strangely. "I am only here for a few minutes, Daniel has given me permission just this once to take human form." Eden went to her and Rebecca held her as they both sat down on Eden's bed. "I did expect to see you at some point, but only in spirit essence." Eden replied. "I wanted to see you again as I was." Rebecca told her. "I want to tell you how proud I am of you, watching you the other day become a Warrior of God . . . dearest Eden, you must now more than ever follow The Creed, let it be the foundation of how you make your decisions and your choices." Rebecca said. "Nana, you are speaking of Talus, I know that . . . but that won't happen again." Eden answered. "When I became a Warrior of God I had your grandfather and he was a wonderful support for me, perhaps you will find that support with Alestasis." Rebecca replied, holding Eden's hand. "Don't misunderstand what I am saying, Talus is a good man, a fair minded man, but you need a mortal man." Her grandmother explained. "I know all that you are saying to be true, Nana." Eden said softly. "Stay close to the cause and your mother and father, let there be strength behind your convictions and above all else honor The Path and Daniel." Rebecca stood up and kissed Eden on the cheek. Eden knew their time was ending. "I must go now dear . . . I will always be with you." Rebecca said as her vision began to fade. "Nana, please tell me what are my powers?" Eden called out to her. "Anything you will yourself to do, you can do . . ." she replied to Eden, her vision completely gone.

As Eden sat on her bed, there was a tap on her bedroom door. "Eden?" It was her dad. She stood up and opened the door. "Uncle Eli and Aunt Ro are leaving . . ." He said his voice sounding sad. "Oh, well let me come down and say goodnight." Eden said closing the door behind her. They were all standing in front of the door downstairs, waiting for Eden. Hugging both of them at the same time Eden said, "You both mean so much to me and mom and dad, we are so lucky to have all of you!" Eden exclaimed tearing up, and looking down at Samuel and Caleb, who were holding on to the hem of Aunt Ro's dress. Uncle Eli kissed Eden on the cheek. "We're here for you guys whenever you need us . . . and my car too." He said, his eyes filling up. Eden and her parents watched them get into their car, the one she had taken to see Talus, and drive away.

Eden helped her mom clean up and then kissing both her parents goodnight, she went to bed. She knew it was hard for them as well. Tomorrow she would sit down with them and have a long talk. But tonight she needed rest, sleep and the security of Talus lying beside her, but he was not a possibility so rest and sleep would have to do. As she closed her eyes she heard something, an interruption of her thoughts, but she was too tired to concentrate and let sleep take her to her subconscious mind.

"It is characteristic of wisdom not to do desperate things."
Henry David Thoreau

Impetuous One
CHAPTER ELEVEN

Eden rose early as she had originally planned, dressed and headed downstairs for breakfast. To her surprise, her parents weren't up yet. She went back upstairs and knocked on their bedroom door. Her father opened it slightly still in his bathrobe. "Hey, dad is everything alright?" Eden asked. She couldn't remember the last time they had slept in. "Yeah, your mom and I are just tired, I took a few days off from the office, we're just tired honey, that's all." Her dad sounded convincing but something was off. "Dad can I come in and see mom for a second?" Eden moved the door slightly and felt her dad's resistance. "Dad I'm sorry but I have to come in!" She pushed the door open and saw three men, one had a gun to her dad's back and one had a knife to her mother's throat. "They broke in when we were downstairs . . ." her dad managed to tell her before the man with the gun whacked him in the back of the head. "Who are you?" asked Eden oddly calm. She somehow knew her dad would come to in an hour or so. Her mom cried out. "Eden!" "Mom calm down, you'll be ok, it's me they want." There was one sitting on the rocking chair, in front of the large picture window. He finally spoke. "You're right about that, it's you we want." He said. Eden recognized him from the battle; he was one of Dante's hench men. Eden came farther into the room, "Well here I am." She said.

Then she went for the man who had the knife to her mom's throat, by jumping in the air, spinning and kicking him in the head so hard that his neck snapped. Her speed and strength were supernatural. When she turned, both of the men had guns aimed at her. She remembered her grandmother's words "You can do anything you will yourself to do." Remembering how she became invisible when she was locked up as Dante's prisoner, she fell down on the floor and willed herself to become invisible again. Then coming up behind the one who hit her father first, she pushed him into the man who had been sitting in the rocker with such force they both went crashing through her mother's picture window, landing on the front lawn, wrapped up in lace curtains and part of the window frame. She saw that a black limo was waiting for them outside. Shades of Dante, being repeated. Eden went over to her mom who was on the floor, she was hysterical and scared, but not physically hurt. She checked her dad and knew he would be alright, but he was out cold. Then she called 911 and told the dispatcher what had happened. Her mother was hysterically trying to wake her father up when the police arrived.

Eden explained the situation as best she could. Three men broke into the house and she and her parents fought them off. Two got away and one broke his neck in the scuffle. The paramedics were able to revive her father who had a slight concussion, but refused to go to the hospital. Eden had been clear to her mom, before the police came. "Let me do the explaining mom." She insisted, which worked out fine because, every time her mom tried to speak, she started crying uncontrollably. Eden knew who had sent them, Dominic Marchette, of course. She went outside while the detectives took finger prints. She could hear her dad in the living room, "You'll have to ask my daughter, because they hit me and knocked me out and I can't remember anything." Eden was not worried about the outcome for her family. Her parents were well known in the community and she had heard one of the detectives say that he knew the dead one. "Yeah, this one's got a rap sheet a mile long." He told one of the police officers. Eden needed to communicate this to Daniel and Talus. Using the same focus Talus had taught her to use to move the rocks; she sent them both telepathic messages. She closed her eyes and tested her abilities, and then she waited for a response.

Eden felt someone tap her on the shoulder, and she opened her eyes. It was one of the detectives. "I know you've had a pretty rough morning, I asked your parents to come down to the station and we can fill out an official statement . . . it doesn't have to be today. We'll need one from you too." He said blandly. "Will tomorrow be ok then?" she asked. "Sure, no problem." He started to walk away. "Can I ask you something?" Eden called out, catching up to him. "Do we need legal counsel, my dad's a lawyer, but do we need our own lawyer tomorrow?" The detective looked at her. "No, your dad asked me that . . . these guys that broke in, and the one that's dead upstairs, go way back with us. I wouldn't worry about it Miss Evanharth . . . the statement is routine." He handed her his card, got in his car and drove away. By this time several neighbors had approached the house, but yellow tape encircled the perimeter of the house. Two police officers stood in front of the house, telling everyone that they should go back into their own homes.

Eden walked back into the house, while they were bringing the dead man's body downstairs. Her mom and dad were both still emotionally upset, especially her mom. "Eden we are all going to stay with Uncle Eli and Aunt Ro, your mother is beside herself." Her dad said. Eden put her arms around her mom. "It's ok mom, I think I should stay at Nana Becca's house for awhile. "No Edie, they'll hurt you, you should not be alone." Her mom said tearfully. Then the realization of who Eden was and how she displayed her powers came back to her. "I guess you know best Edie dear, we know you can handle yourself . . . but I'm still your mother." Her mom said tearfully, trying to put on a brave face. " . . . and I'm your dad, and I worry about you too, we both do." Her dad replied in a tone that indicated that he was resigned to her new life. "I know this is hard for you guys, it's hard for me too, but I know I'll be safe at Nana's." Uncle Eli came to pick up her parents and after he boarded up the window in her parents' bedroom, and her mother packed, they locked up the house and left. Uncle Eli dropped Eden off at her grandmother's house and then drove off with her parents to his house.

It was strange walking into Nana Becca's house without her being there to greet her and give her a big hug. After putting her things down and locking the door, she instinctively went to the back of the house and opened the sliding glass door, which led to the garden. As Eden had suspected, Daniel was there, in human form. The glow from his body intensified under the night sky. "Hello Eden, I received your message and thought it best that we meet here." He said. "Yes, it is very appropriate." Eden replied. "What happened today is an isolated incident, Talus spoke with Dominic Marchette this afternoon." He assured her. Eden wasn't so sure. "How can that be Daniel . . . I mean Sir?" Eden asked, correcting herself. After all, Daniel was the lead angel for The Highest Realm. "Eden, Talus can read thoughts and he was convinced that it was not initiated by The Dominion." Daniel's tone was definite.

Eden sat down on the stone bench that faced Lillianna's statue. Obviously Daniel had as much faith in Talus as she did. "I have known Talus since he first became lead negotiator for The Council. I may not always agree with his decisions but, it is evident that he has great interest and concern for your safety . . . and Dominic Marchette fears him." Eden looked at Daniel who began to fade into spirit essence, she had no comeback. Even if she had, Daniel was finished with the conversation.

She had to trust Daniels words and she had to trust Talus. She did trust them, but she didn't trust Dominic Marchette and The Dominion. Her faith was being tested in more ways then she could imagine. Eden knew one thing and that was that, she could not allow her family to be at risk. What happened today could not be allowed to be repeated. As she unpacked the clothes she had brought from home, she made a decision to make a journey to the Marchette Mansion tomorrow, and alone she would face Dominic Marchette and throw down the gauntlet. Too much had happened to her this past week and she knew that this was one of those moments in life when you have to take a stand and fight single handedly.

The Marchette's were bully's and she had to stand up to all of them. First she'd pay a visit to Nia and Leah and see what else they had in their arsenal. Eden was aware of the fact that she was stepping out of rank and this could mean some sort of punishment, or expulsion from The Path, but she was willing to risk it, because she would not allow her family to be hurt. If Dominic wanted her he was going to get her, but now she'd come prepared.

Daniel arrived at the clearing in Glen Cove just as Talus was getting out of his truck. "Our girl has a mind of her own." Daniel told him, as they walked deeper into the forest. "My concern is that she is too impetuous." Talus replied. Both men stopped and looked up at the moon. "Do you . . . feel something for her Talus?" Daniel asked hesitantly. "Nothing more than friendship." He replied picking a leaf off a branch as they walked. Daniel stopped and looked Talus in the eye. He waited until Talus spoke. "Who better then you Daniel, knows that I am incapable of that kind of emotion." Talus replied. "She's in love with you, you must know that." Daniel stating the obvious, as they continued their walk. "She is young yet, and will forget me as soon as Alestasis appears." Talus replied belittling the sentiment.

Daniel stopped walking and watched Talus. Talus came back to him, knowing an apology was in order. "Daniel, I know I crossed some boundaries . . . and I will apologize to you, but she is forceful in her own way . . . she got the better of me, you know how we are, I will try not to let it happen again." Talus replied defending himself. "Yes, I do know how you are . . . you are rather impetuous yourself." They turned and walked back to the clearing. "She will seek out Dominic Marchette tomorrow Talus and we will have another war on our hands." Said Daniel. "Perhaps, that's what we need." Talus replied. "She needs to conquer more battles on her own as she did today, before she can join us in a war against The Dominion, she is mortal after all and can be hurt." Daniel insisted. Talus stopped as they were now in the clearing again. "I will convince her otherwise, if that's what you choose, as she is under your dimension's guidelines, I will honor your decision." Talus waited for Daniel's response. Daniel was playing things out in his mind, before he answered. "I will depend then, on your good judgment to guide her away from The Dominion and Dominic Marchette, and Talus?" asked Daniel, "I will expect that you will not cross anymore boundaries, with Eden." He stated to Talus, as he faded into the forest. That was a firm directive, issued by a spirit leader that Talus had a great amount of respect for.

Talus walked back to his truck. Tomorrow he would meet with Eden, the impetuous one, first thing in the morning. It was hard to deny that he liked her spirit. Her grandmother would never have questioned Daniel's response or direction. Eden was another type of warrior entirely. She had the temperament for battle, though she probably didn't even realize it yet. She reminded him of Lillianna in her days as a Council member, when she was Sophia Basset and fearless. A big part of Talus wished Eden was part of The Council and immortal like him. Being a Warrior for The Path was so much harder.

One thing was certain, as he had been made aware of earlier in their friendship, Eden was a force to be reckoned with. Tomorrow he would see her again, and he would want her again. He had just made a professional agreement with Daniel, it was understood that his guidance tomorrow would be strictly professional. Knowing himself and knowing Eden, it wouldn't be easy. Talus checked into a hotel outside Hadleyville, he wanted to be at Eden's grandmother's house as early as possible. This conversation was going to take some time. However, he had made the commitment to be there when she needed guidance, and she needed it now.

Eden was up by daybreak, dressed and ready to begin her day. She had been unable to sleep very well, her mind was too full with thoughts about Dominic Marchette and The Dominion. She was sitting down at her grandmother's kitchen table, reminiscing about their days together when she heard a knock at the door. Looking through the kitchen window she could see it was Talus. She ran to the door and opened it. Throwing her arms around him and hugging him, she told him how happy she was to see him. He smiled and asked, "May I come in?" Eden immediately sensed this was not a casual visit. "Yes!" She replied, her voice was full of happiness and excitement. "How did you know I was here?" she asked, then she realized how foolish her question was. "Sorry, I am still getting used to things Talus." She apologized.

Talus looked over to the table and saw her breakfast. Cereal and a glass of orange juice. "Is that a healthy breakfast for you?" He teased. Eden laughed at his reference. "Yes, frosted flakes are my favorite." She replied. "Would you like some? . . . or coffee I can make you coffee!" She exclaimed, wanting so much to please him. "No, it's quite alright, I've had my coffee today." He sat down at the kitchen table, as Eden pushed her cereal aside. "Go ahead we can talk while you eat." He insisted. "It's fine I'm not hungry anymore." She answered him pulling her chair closer to his, so that they were side by side, rather than across from each other. Eden knew by his demeanor that she needed to settle down and restrain her emotions. She was failing miserably on keeping herself calm being so close to him.

"Talus, it meant so much to me that you were at the gravesite, thank you for being there." She said quietly looking down. It was hard for Eden to look in his eyes. She wanted to be in his arms and the internal struggle was killing her. "Your grandmother was a remarkable woman and I wanted to pay her my respect." Talus explained, in his very detached manner. Then he quickly continued with the point of his visit. "I understand it's your intention to pay a call on Dominic Marchette today." He said, his voice was very serious and all business. He leaned his arm on the table, rested his head on his hand and faced her. Eden was quiet. Finally she explained herself. "They almost killed my parents Talus." Her voice was low, as she spoke. "If you were to do that, you would be going against my assessment as well as Daniel's direction." Talus said as he studied her responses. Eden felt something close to embarrassment now as he sat next to her. "You need not feel embarrassed, Daniel and I both know you are learning and we both admire your strength . . . however, with strength comes weakness if the strength is not well directed and controlled." He told her wanting to touch her, to hold her and kiss her but he fought his instinct. "Talus, I don't understand, I am trying to defend myself and my family." Eden replied, confused and frustrated. "Eden, the dimensions exist to keep balance in the universe, we are part of that balance." He said pausing slightly and then continued. "There is a chain of command to be followed so that order prevails, our longevity depends on that."

"So, let me understand you, we are just supposed to stand by and let evil over take us." Eden snapped back. Talus realized that teaching was not something he was made for, and he was in his own way trying to be as patient as he knew how. "Now you are over simplifying...as long as mankind exists there will always be evil...and goodness." Eden gently placed her hand on his, knowing that he was trying and she was pushing him and testing him. "Please don't do that, it's not good for either of us." He replied coldly.

Eden rose to stand but Talus, put his hand on her arm. "Sit down . . . please Miss Evanharth we are not finished yet." His tone was stern but there was a hint of a smile on his lips. "Are you pulling rank on me Talus?" Eden asked sitting back down facing him full on. Talus turned to face her, resting his hands on his thighs. "Yes, I must because you are a stubborn and willful child." He replied the smile now forming into a complete one. "Child am I?" Eden teased back. His eyes were like large dark pools of endless wanting. "You will always be a woman child to me Eden." Talus was feeling something so unsettling, it was trying to consume him but he pushed it as far back as he could. Eden felt it from him and in herself. How would she get through this? Was it always to be this hard? How could they ever work together, wanting each other so entirely? "It will pass Eden, we have to give it time and soon you will be with Alestasis, you and I will become a faded memory." Talus was reading her completely and she loved it.

She wanted him to know her every thought, her every feeling. She wanted him to feel her heartbreak. "I cannot feel heartbreak, but I know mortals suffer from them constantly." He answered her thoughts. "We need to get beyond what we encountered with one another and focus on your abilities and training into The Path Eden, that's what's important here." His voice like always was controlled, direct, and unemotional. "You want me to feel nothing, like yourself and its hard, it's very hard. I know I've given my oath to follow The Path and marry Alestasis . . . I will see it through and I'll try not to cause you and Daniel anymore trouble." Eden replied solemnly. "Eden it's not about causing us trouble, it's about commitment and professionalism . . . and you are mistaken, I don't expect you not to feel things, you are mortal you should feel everything." Talus replied as he stood up, and walked into the living room. He didn't want to just walk out like this. It wasn't good for him and Eden in the long run. He could easily physically and mentally prevent her from going after The Dominion, but he wanted her to arrive at that decision on her own, by her own will not his.

He looked around the room, scattered everywhere were pictures of Eden from birth to High School graduation. He enjoyed looking at her as a little girl, and there were many with her grandmother. He prided himself on his strict and forceful communication style, which had waned greatly since he encountered Eden. Thinking back he had been harder and much more demanding of Lillianna, when she was with The Council and after that as well. Eden was different though, she was born mortal and she had been innocent until he came along. If he was feeling guilt, he didn't know it. Once again, very effectively he pushed it away . . . far, far away. Talus was a master of disguise, to himself.

Eden stood up and took her cereal bowl to the sink, she stood there almost frozen, her back to Talus. Inside she felt lost and alone. Why had she taken that stupid oath? Talus came up behind her and put his hands on her shoulders, turning her to face him. "Eden, you are not lost and you are never alone. You have Daniel, you have your family and . . . you have me." He spoke knowing she needed encouragement. "Right now you are all that I need . . . and all that I can't have." She replied. "I am always here for you as a friend, that's why I am here now, trying to guide you and direct you to understand our ways, and to understand our rules." He explained, sensing her insecurities, her fears.

"Eden think back before you became part of The Path . . . before Dante, before The Dominion . . . before me, what would you have thought then? . . . would you have gone out blindly seeking revenge?" he asked her, his voice soft as he looked into her eyes. Looking up at him, she was melting as the control over her emotions was slipping farther and farther away. "There is no before you . . . there is only you." She replied in a whisper as she fell into his arms.

Talus held her and kissed her passionately, throwing all caution to the wind. He wanted her, and his instinct to have her was battling his discipline to abstain from her. She clung to him and him to her, desperately not wanting to let go but Talus knew he had to. Finally, he pulled away from her, walking to the other side of the room. "I gave my word

Eden and both our reputations are at stake here!" He said raising his voice. "How can I give you support and guidance if you won't listen to me?" he admonished her. He knew this was mistake, why had he come? He walked to the door to leave, but Eden called out to him. "Talus, please don't leave like this, not after all we've been through." She pleaded, walking over to him. He turned to look at her. "Why do you continue to defy me Eden?" he asked frustrated at the situation and himself more than at her. "Because, I want you so badly, when you are near me it's hard to think straight . . . please, I don't want to lose your friendship . . ." she told him. "I'll get it straight, I promise I won't throw myself at you again." She said. "Eden, do not make a promise you can't keep, and I will try to do the same." Talus already knew that given the opportunity, it would happen again. They were both so physically drawn to each other, they needed to keep their distance. He knew it and so did she. In her he had found the redemption he didn't even know he was searching for. In him she had found knowledge and her womanhood. He was everything to her, a teacher, a lover, a friend and a wealth of experience and knowledge. It was hard to let go.

She searched his eyes for forgiveness. "It is I, who should ask forgiveness from you." He replied to her thoughts. "I was honest with you Eden from the beginning, I don't know what else I could have said to dissuade you from me." He said rationalizing. "Nothing, there is nothing you could have said or done . . . I cannot tell my heart who it should love or why it can't love, I only know that I love you, with all that you cannot give me, I still love you Talus . . . completely and unconditionally." Eden replied, her eyes filled with tears.

Opening the door he leaned against the door frame. "Eden, one day some mortal man will come along and sweep you off your feet, it might even be Alestasis." He smiled faintly. "I have already been swept off my feet, I don't expect it to happen again." She replied as he wiped a tear from her cheek. "It will happen, I would bet on it." He responded. "I opened the door for you into a new world, but some very lucky mortal man will fill it with all the love your heart can hold Eden, trust me." Talus spoke with complete confidence, but Eden wasn't buying it, not for a minute, he was her true love and he always would be.

"Just tell me what to do and I'll do it?" she asked slightly withdrawn from him. "Stay away from Dominic Marchette, those men were from Dante's regime, and you sent them all a strong message yesterday, and above all else follow Daniel's direction as he is your direct liaison . . . not I." He responded. Eden looked away from him. "Eden don't force me to seize your powers, I ask for your word as a warrior that you will follow protocol and the chain of command?" Talus asked her his tone direct and honest. "I give you my word, I will not seek revenge on anyone without Daniel's approval." She replied acquiescing. "Good, then we understand each other." Talus replied. Eden watched as he walked to his truck and drove away. She was about to close the door when she saw Father Clemmons walking toward the house. His step was quick as he approached the door. "Eden I'm glad I found you, we need your help, and we must be swift, as there is little time."

Talus was slightly frustrated as he drove back to New Hampshire, mostly because he knew he was stepping out of his genre by taking on Eden. He had given her his commitment to help her and now it was coming back to wreak havoc in his life. His only saving grace was that soon Alestasis would be coming into her life and he suspected that would deter Eden from her dependence on him. She would have a man to marry and build a relationship with. Talus knew he needed to create distance; he would make it a point to only communicate with her telepathically, if necessary. This morning had been amazingly hard for him, and if he had not had a gentlemen's agreement with Daniel, he would have caved in. The fact was that he was falling in love with Eden, but he would never admit to it, he was a Council member and that was his only belief system. As far as he was concerned that was not a possibility, so the idea would not occur to him, at least not yet.

He found it quite ironic that in a hundred and fifty years, the two women he had most wanted were not only related, but mirror images of each other. If that wasn't enough, they were both unattainable. What was the alternative . . . being mortal was not an option for him. It seemed it was time to go back to The Council's dating scene, which he had previously grown bored with.

As Talus looked in his rearview mirror, he noticed a car that had been behind him previously. He was always aware of his surroundings and today was no different. A sign for a gas station ahead caught his eye and he took that exit, so did the car behind him. As he pulled into the gas station, the car slowed down and then sped up continuing down the road. This was no coincidence, he was being followed. He was intrigued. Being a Council member had its advantages; nothing could completely destroy him, except expulsion from The Council. He got back in his truck and was on the highway, when he saw the same car in his rearview mirror. Talus focused his eyes on the driver, there was something familiar about him. He decided to take the next exit.

The car stayed behind him, following closely. Finally coming to an opened field, Talus pulled off to the side of the road, so did the black car. Talus sat there waiting for their next move, but his instinct had already told him it was Mortamion. Finally the driver got out, so did he. The driver of the black car walked towards him. As he had already anticipated it was Mortamion. The man stopped fifty or so feet away from Talus and stood still. "What is it that you want Mortamion?" Talus shouted. Mortamion walked toward him, stopping a few feet away. "Only your death." Mortamion snarled. "I apologized to Lillianna, as I know that I wronged you both." Answered Talus. "You are evil beyond measure and I mean to bring you down." Mortamion said seething. "Really Mortamion when did you lose your objectivity?" Talus asked sarcastically. "At the very sight of your existence." Mortamion responded. "What is it you propose?" asked Talus. "A duel to the death with swords." Mortamion replied. "I have expected you, but the scale must be balanced." Talus added. Talus knew his strength would over power Mortamion's. "It seems my wife, who's honor you took, did not bring you up to date . . . I gave up my soul and am now back with The Council Talus . . . so we shall see who wins and who loses, you will hear from my second by tomorrow!" Yelled Mortamion, as he walked back to his car and drove off. Talus should have known by looking at him that he was a Council member, for his features had not changed. This in fact would be a duel to the death, as neither would win, The Council would declare the winner by performance, and the loser would suffer expulsion from The Council and the universe.

In truth Mortamion did not have to fight Talus. He just needed to expose his lack of judgment and control with Lillianna to The Council Tribunal and there would be a hearing. More than likely Talus would be found guilty and sentenced to expulsion. Talus knew this, so did Mortamion. It was clear that Mortamion wanted revenge on a much more personal level. Either way, Talus drove home realizing his fate was looking quite dim as far as his tenure with The Council. He also knew he owed Mortamion the challenge, for forcing himself on Lillianna. Talus was up for the challenge, although it had been a long time since he had physically fought anyone. Mortamion was an expert with swords and Talus was all too aware of it. He wanted to uphold Lillianna's honor to the man who had taken it from her.

This gesture was honorable, and Talus saw Mortamion in a different light. If there was any righteousness left in the dimensions, Mortamion would slay him. Talus had grown jaded and cynical. He wanted the battle, and he needed it. All these years he had waited for it and now it had arrived. He knew that Louis would probably be Mortamion's second. When he thought about it there was only one person on earth that could serve as his second. The real question here was how did Mortamion remember? Council members supposedly had no memory of their lives as mortals, so how would Mortamion know he needed to fight for Lillianna's honor? By the time Talus reached home he had come to terms with the fact that Mortamion had indeed lied, a mortal trait after all, and was mortal, not a Council member. But then how exactly had he remained physically the same, without any change. As in all things, this too would be revealed . . . eventually.

Father Clemmons took Eden's hand, "hurry girl we must make haste!" He sounded frantic, taking hold of her arm. "Wait Father, I must gather up my things and lock the door." Eden insisted, pulling away. Father Clemmons waited outside as Eden grabbed her sweater and keys. As Eden locked the door Father Clemmons began walking toward the street. Eden ran to catch up with him. "What's wrong?" she asked keeping up with his quick pace. "Father Odell and I have been trying to release a child who has been taken over by a demon spirit." He said quickly and to the point. Eden stopped, and then he did as well. "I do not know anything about exorcisms Father." Eden said. "What you did with Dante, that my dear was an exorcism." Father Clemmons replied. "It was on a grand scale, but it was an exorcism which ended in death." Father Clemmons explained. "I didn't do it Father it was Talus and Daniel." Eden declared. Father Clemmons stopped and looked into her eyes, his eyes were piercing, "Are you a Warrior of God?" he asked her. "Yes, Father I am a Warrior of God, with limited experience." Eden replied truthfully. "That's all I need to know." The Father stated firmly and continued walking.

They walked a few more blocks to the church and then once inside down to the basement, which Eden was familiar with. However, Father Clemmons led her to a door at the far end of the hall, which was locked. It led to a long winding staircase into a sub-basement. Father Clemmons turned and locked the door from the inside. Eden noticed the walls were made of large stone bricks that looked old and some had cracks in them. When they got to the bottom, she saw Father Odell seated at a table with the Holy Bible opened in front of him. There were two other people standing nearby in the shadows. The only light was from two large lanterns and candles on small brick ledges that were built into the stone wall surrounding the sub basement. There were hundreds of candles illuminating the area. The room was large and in the middle of it was a chair with someone seated on it. Eden could hear growls and hisses from a young girl about seven who was tied to the chair.

Eden looked at her and immediately knew who she would be dealing with. The body and face was that of a child but, the eyes were inhuman. Eden could hear whimpering and sobbing, from the two people hidden in the shadows, they were obviously the parents. Eden walked up to the child, standing only a few feet away. The beast inside the little girl was growling at Eden like a wild animal. The fathers had gagged the child, and Eden could see that there were a lot of bruises and cuts on the hands and arms of the child. Eden took her cross off and placed it on the neck of the girl, as she did the head of the girl turned completely around to face her.

As alarming as it was for the parents to see, as Eden could hear their gasps and cries, she herself was not intimidated. "You will not win the battle over God." Eden spoke out loud to the demon. She would have tried to bite Eden, and succeeded had she not been gagged. Still the girl fought hard against the restraints and the gag, her eyes were red in color and distorted and followed Eden's every move. Through the gag she spit and swore obscenities. Immediately the skin of her neck began to burn where the cross rested. Eden started reciting The Lord's Prayer, in unison with Father Odell and Father Clemmons who were both standing not far from Eden. She walked around the the chair which was vibrating and lifting off the ground, with the girl still strapped to it. Eden willed herself to levitate to meet the chair in mid air, calling out in a great voice for the demon to be cast out. The demon in the child howled, its force pushing against Eden and trying to knock her down.

Eden fought back, her own force of will fighting against the demon who had taken over the child. Some of the cracked stone in the basement fell onto the ground from the energy force of both Eden and the demon. Eden raised her voice calling out for God's mercy to cleanse this mortal soul, and release the child from the evil spirit that had taken over her spirit and soul. Eden's hair rising up and flying about as if there were a great wind as the two Fathers prayed out loud from Revelations, 12.10 and then when they were finished Eden lead them into the Apostles Creed. Slowly they began to win the battle and the chair started to fall back to the ground.

Eden then went to one of the cracked stones that had fallen on the ground and looked for one with a sharp edge and picked it up. Sliding it hard against the inside of her arm, she cut herself. The demon was now like a dying lion, still unpredictable, internally raging. She took the sharp end of the stone and cut the child on the inside of her forearm, she could hear the mother of the child gasp again. Eden knelt down and placed her cut arm against the child's cut so their blood could mix. The demon inside the child screamed, as its death came quickly. As it left the body of the child it flew around the room.

Its essence appeared to be something between a human, a dragon and a gargoyle, a horrible stench filled the room as Father Odell opened a door in the floor where the demon spirit sunk into the dirt and was buried. Eden wondered how many spirits had been buried under the church, in all the years the church had been in existence. She suspected a lot of spirits. What kept them down there? Did any sneak out and take some other mortal's unsuspecting soul? Had this spirit been one of them? She couldn't deal with all these questions right now. She had to finish the task at hand.

Then both Father Odell and Father Clemmons slammed the steel door shut and bolted it with steel rods that went across the entire width of the door. Father Odell and Father Clemmons came over to the child who was still gagged and strapped to the chair. Eden was knelt down in front of her. Slowly the child raised her head, Eden looked into her eyes. They were clear and normal. The child's mother came running to her daughter, but Father Clemmons held her back. Eden knew they were waiting for her assessment. She studied the young girls face closely. Tears began to pour down from the child's eyes as she searched for her mother. The cuts and bruises were already beginning to heal and disappear.

The cleansing had been successful. Eden untied her gag as Father Odell unstrapped her and her mother cradled her child in her arms. Making her way upstairs, Eden knew this had been a rather easy exorcism. Father Clemmons came up the stairs behind Eden, returning her cross to her. "No, Father Clemmons the child must keep it on . . . tell her parents it is a gift and she must wear it." Eden replied as the Father unlocked the sub-basement door, letting her out. Eden didn't know how she thought to cut herself and the child and mix their bloods. It was just instinctual. All of it had been instinctual. She had nothing to draw from except what her heart and mind told her to do. Walking home she thought about Talus, she wanted to communicate with him desperately.

Through her own determination she stopped herself. As the demon had been cast down into the dirt below the basement of the church and buried, so would her love of Talus be cast down and buried. There was no choice and no turning back. Talus had made that perfectly clear and he was right. She had given her word at the battle with Dante. Her future was with Alestasis and the sooner she accepted it the better. Eden resolved to keep a distance from Talus, for a while anyway until she got over him. If . . . she could get over him. She knew that she would always love him and want him, but she had to accept the new direction her life had taken.

As she approached the front lawn she noticed a car parked outside in front of her grandmother's house. Seated on one of the porch chairs sat the detective from yesterday. He greeted her as she walked up to the front door. "Hello Miss Evanharth." He said with a slight edge of inconvenience. "I'm sorry I wasn't able to come down to the station this morning, I forgot I was scheduled to help out at the church." Eden offered quickly. "What happened to your arm?" he asked noticing the cut, when she put the key in the lock. "Oh I scratched myself on a piece of stone . . . it's nothing serious." She replied.

He followed her inside to the kitchen were Eden washed her arm off. Then she went into the bathroom and grabbed a bandage out of the cabinet, putting it on the cut she walked back out to the kitchen toward the detective. "I can go with you now to the station, if you would like." Eden said, smiling slightly. "Yes, I would like that, that's in fact why I came here . . . I'd like to get this case wrapped up." He responded. "Have my parents already been there?" Eden asked. "Why yes, they were there first thing this morning, I thought you would be there with them." He told her. Eden did not respond or make any more comments, she waited, she knew he would speak again. As they got in the car, he looked over at her. "I went to the rectory and it was locked, then I came here again." He said. Eden met his eyes, smiled and replied. "Oh, the two Fathers and I were doing some cleaning in the basement." The detective started the car and headed for the station house.

Eden had never been in a police station before. Fortunately things in her past had not led her there. However, she had spoken with several police officers and detectives when Sienna disappeared. The station house wasn't very large and rather old. The detective's desk was a mess with paperwork and files everywhere. He indicated that Eden should have a seat. Many of the officers and other detectives smiled at her and offered her coffee, or water as they passed by which she declined graciously. "Your coworkers are all very friendly." Eden commented. "Well, it's not every day a beautiful girl comes into this station, that's for sure." He replied as he arranged his desk. "Here's the drill . . . you tell me what happened in your own words and I print it out and you sign it." The detective explained. "Will I get a chance to read what you print out, before I sign it?" asked Eden. "Yeah, absolutely." He answered.

Eden told him the same story she told him when the break in happened, referring back to his handwritten notes, he mentioned to her that it was almost verbatim. "You have a good memory, Miss Evanharth." He commented as he typed.

"Well, it's easy to have a good memory when you are telling the truth." She replied. He looked up at her after he had finished typing. "Alright, as soon as it prints you can read it." He told her and walked across the room to the printer which was about as old as the building. Turning in her seat, she saw photographs of all the people that were wanted for crimes or missing. Then one that caught her attention. Eden stood up and walked over to the wall. There was a picture of Sienna hanging along side of many others. The detective came over to her. "Do you know her?" he asked. "Yes I did once, we went to school together and then she disappeared." Eden replied. "Yeah too bad, the case has gone cold on her." He said as an afterthought handing Eden the printed statement.

Eden signed the statement and asked for a copy which the detective provided. Leaving the station house, she had decided to walk home, she thought it would help clear her mind. The detective had offered her a ride if she needed one, but as nice as he had been, being there had unsettled her and all her feelings about Sienna and Dante came rushing back to her. Then Joshua and Talus . . . it had all been too much. She walked through the town of Hadleyville and looked at it from a new perspective. She wasn't a girl anymore, innocent to love and the evils of the world, overnight she had become an adult woman.

The seriousness of her new life was having a major impact on her. She thought about her grandmother and how she managed through all of it. She knew that the world was simpler back then, but fighting evil must have been just as hard as it was now. Being adult and responsible was not easy and taking on the commitment to be a Warrior of God was and would be the hardest thing she would ever have to do, or so it appeared.

"And in the end the love you take is equal to the love that you make."

The Beatles

Honoring the Oath
Chapter Twelve

By mid week, Eden had begun tutoring, three days a week. She had missed some time, without negative consequences, due to her grandmother's passing, and the break in to her home by the three thugs. It had already been six days since Dante's death and she had received no word. Life went on as normal for the most part, with the exception that her parent's questioned her daily, on whether she had heard anything about her future husband. Then, on the afternoon of the seventh day, Nia and Leah were waiting for her as she left school in the late afternoon. When she approached them Nia said, "Daniel would like you to come to the clearing." Eden nodded and replied, "Take me to him."

They drove for a few miles and Leah pulled the car off to the side of a dirt road. "Follow us." Leah said getting out of the car. Through the brush and trees a small clearing lay ahead, in the distance Eden could see Daniel in human form. She walked toward him. "We will wait for you by the edge of the clearing." Stated Nia, as the two walked back in the direction of the car. Daniel spoke first, "With the approval of The Highest Realm, The Legions of The Path and in direct law set by The Council . . . Alestasis has found a home." He announced smiling. Eden was impressed because Daniel didn't smile very much, it made her smile back. "You will be contacted by him directly tomorrow . . . let nature take its course Eden and leave the rest to us." He told her. "What if he is more Dante then Alestasis?" Eden asked. "We will pray very hard that he isn't, but take note, his name is Sebastian Joshua Kolten, not Alestasis." Daniel replied, trying in his tone and mannerism to comfort her. "You must remember your bravery and your direction in The Path Eden, to help you with any uncertainties that you may have." Daniel said, looking deeply into her eyes.

He wasn't smiling now instead, the serious nature of the situation demanded his calm focus to her concerns. "How do we know what is right and what is wrong . . . all of the time?" Eden asked him. "This is too hard a question for me Eden." Daniel replied, the smile faintly returning. Eden stood surprised by his answer. "I don't understand . . . I thought you were the all knowing?" she asked aghast. "Me?" Daniel asked. "No, I'm just an angel, for questions like these, only the Devine One knows the answer." He responded earnestly. "But what are we fighting for then, and why do we struggle to save lives and torture ourselves saving souls?" Eden was completely taken aback and her voice illustrated it. Pausing, Daniel gave his answer. "I suppose we try to follow The Path as we believe that we do it for the good of mankind." Then he continued, "Eden, we are all souls, trying to inhabit this vast universe . . . together. I suppose right and wrong depends in which dimension you are in and the truest nature of your being." His voice began to fade as his body became cloud like.

"We believe in the journey, to take us where we need to go . . . whether it is with The Highest Realm, The Dominion or The Council, we are all in need of a home, and the greatest of these is The Highest Realm." It was hard to hear his last words, but Eden was able to understand them. Now, she was alone in the clearing, with only her own thoughts and conscience to guide her. Her fear and frustration was building, the inward struggle had begun and she felt lost and alone. Here she was eighteen years old, on her way to marry someone she didn't know, quite possibly Dante, pretending to be Sebastian. Why was she doing it? How would she survive? Who would save her soul? Eden dropped to her knees and felt the cool moisture of the grass on her skin. Doubt and fear were creeping in, how would she get through this? She asked herself.

Suddenly, she heard something . . . rather it was like words forming thoughts in her head. They were interrupting her own thought process. Slowly as she concentrated, the thoughts made sense. She realized she was receiving a telepathic communication. "Follow your own truth, and the nature of who you are, that will answer your questions . . . as for me I follow my instincts." She knew it was Talus sending her a message. She concentrated and sent her love to him, saying she doubted she would ever be able to communicate telepathically as well as he and Daniel did. This time she heard him loud and clear in his response. "Sure you will, I've had a lot more practice." As she began to stand, her eyes fell on a familiar pair of black boots, she looked up to see Talus standing before her. He held out his hand to help her up. "You see all your abilities are getting stronger every day." He said smiling faintly. Eden contained her want and desire to sink into his arms. She waited for him to speak again.

Moments passed with both of them just standing there in silence. Then in his direct manner, Talus spoke first. "I have come to ask you a favor actually . . . I am asking you to serve as my second." As was his nature, it sounded more of a direction then a question. "I will do anything you ask of me Talus, but what is a second?" Eden's youth and inexperience made Talus laugh slightly. "I'm not laughing at you, I am laughing at myself." He replied quickly before she took offense. "Mortamion has come back, and is seeking revenge, it will be a fight to the death." Talus explained. Eden stood silent as it sounded so dramatic and ancient, and he stated it so casually. "Talus these are modern times, isn't there a more civilized way to settle the misunderstanding?" she asked with childlike innocence. Talus was silent for a few seconds which made Eden uncomfortable. "Eden, Mortamion was Lillianna's husband." He replied simply.

Now it was all making sense. They were both from the past, still living in the past but existing in the present. "But you are immortal, you cannot be killed . . . can you?" her voice now sounding afraid and shaken. "We will fight, till Mortamion has had his revenge and then The Council Tribunal will make the final decision based on the infraction I committed." Talus explained. "What does that mean . . . I'm new to all this, Talus you have to explain it to me." Eden implored. "You will be my witness and representative, to make sure the rules of the duel are followed, it is part of the formal procedure." Talus replied calmly. "What happens if you lose?" she asked him, her voice reacting, to the tears forming in her eyes.

"Eden, I will lose, do not let your emotions over take you . . . you are a Warrior of God and the person I have been closest to, which is why I am asking this of you, besides it is excellent training for you." Talus put his hands on her shoulders and kissed her forehead. She slipped her arms around him and he held her. "What will happen when you lose?" she asked still wrapped in his arms. "I will cease to exist." He answered her still holding her, his eyes looking off into the forest, where becoming blurred, by what he realized were tears. "As in death? Physical death?" Eden asked losing all control. "Yes, as in physical and spiritual death." Talus answered softly. "Is there no other way?" she whispered. "No, it must be as it is, I owe it to him as a Council member and as a man." Talus replied, he wasn't going to fight against his feelings anymore not with her, not ever again.

Eden pulled away slightly to look at him, tears streaming down her face. "Take me with you! I want to go with you! I know you have that power!" She cried. He pulled her closer to him, her face buried in his chest. He caressed her hair with his hand. "No, you have a full life ahead of you, Eden your place is here on earth, you are human and have the gift and honor of life, never take that for granted, but I will be no more." Talus replied his voice low and filled with the acceptance of his demise. "No. this isn't happening . . . I can't lose you forever!" She sobbed trying to pull away from him, but Talus held her firm. He had to, until she calmed down and he knew she would. She pulled at his jacket and his shirt as if she wanted to be a part of him, to be one with him. Eden sobbed into his chest, unable to comprehend everything that he had said, and yet knowing deep within herself that it was going to happen, as he said it would. How would she survive without knowing he was there for her? She loved him so completely, exactly as he was.

With all that he could not give her, she loved him totally. Now he was telling her he was going away forever . . . never to exist again. He held her until the the shock wore off. Finally, she stopped sobbing and Talus eased his hold. Still she held him, his shirt crumbled within her fists. She didn't want to let go, not now, not ever. No one could give her what he had, make her feel the way he did. He knew her inside and out, he was her rock, her balance, her everything. It was impossible to lose everything at one time. Talus telepathically communicated everything he was thinking to Eden as he held her. He knew that would be the best way for her to comprehend what was going to happen and he did it slowly, so she could absorb what was going to take place.

Eden slowly realized it was all out of her control and all the crying in her world would not change what was going to happen, in their world. Once she needed his strength, she still did. But now he needed hers. "I'm not a very good warrior." She said desperately trying to control her tears. Her face wet and swollen from crying, she began wiping her face with her hands. Talus removed a handkerchief from the inside pocket of his leather jacket, and wiped her face with it. He lifted her chin with his hand to meet his lips. He kissed her gently and tenderly, very uncharacteristically for him. "One day not far from now, you will be one of Daniel's best warriors." He whispered to her. "Talus there must be some other way . . ." she cried looking into his eyes. "Not for me there isn't." He answered her softly. "I will love you always." She said as her heart was breaking. "Eden, you have given me something that no one ever could have, or would have cared to." He answered without pause or hesitation. "What did I give you Talus?" Eden asked surprised. "Unconditional love." He told her caressing her face.

"So, Eden the Warrior, will you be my second?" he asked again, trying to keep it light. Her voice now in control, as they let go of each other. "Yes." She replied half heartedly. "Very well then, thank you, I will be in touch with the details." He responded in his usual controlled and unemotional way, just as a negotiator for The Council would respond or so he'd have her believe. Walking away, he paused briefly to look at her standing there and put the handkerchief inside his shirt, close to his heart. Then as Eden watched him, he disappeared into the forest. Eden stood still for a few moments to regain her composure and then returned to Nia and Leah who were waiting for her by the car.

The next morning Eden started her tutoring class as usual. Her concentration had been difficult and she found it hard to focus. Her thoughts were of Talus and the terrible future he faced. Somehow she needed to think of a way to change the outcome but, it seemed impossible. Her heart was breaking and now she knew that his was as well. When the lunch bell rang, she sat motionless, looking out the large school windows. She decided to skip lunch and correct homework papers. She thought if she could focus on something else she could forget Talus if only for a moment. She suspected he had been standing there for quite some time before she looked up and saw him. "Are you Miss Evanharth?" the handsome stranger with the broad smile and hazel eyes asked. "Yes I am." Eden answered. "Well, it's nice to meet you Miss Evanharth, My name is Sebastian Kolten."

He reached out to shake her hand, it felt warm when she touched it. "I hope I'm not getting you at a bad time?" he asked. "No, I was just correcting some papers . . ." she replied with pause, knowing this was Alestasis. "Well, I would have come here sooner to see you, but I was in a terrible car accident last week." He explained. "Oh . . . are you alright?" her concern was genuine. "Oh yeah, I'm fine it was touch and go for a couple of days, then finally I opened my eyes." He said as he searched his backpack for some papers. "Why don't you sit down Mr. Kolten?" Eden offered her chair and brought it around the desk. "Oh no that's fine, you sit . . . I've been sitting all morning, I drove down from Maine." He was still looking for something in his backpack. "What brings you here Mr. Kolten?" Eden asked. He stopped and looked up at her. "You do." He replied, staring into her eyes. "I'm actually a college admissions counselor, and I'm not sure how I got your paperwork . . . perhaps you faxed it, anyway it landed on my desk." He paused and then continued. "Anyway Miss Evanharth, your grades and SAT scores are really quite good."

Finally he pulled out an application form and handed it to her. "Really I am never this unprepared, I suppose I'm still a little shaky from the accident." He admitted. "Maybe you should go home and we can meet when you are feeling better." Eden suggested, with concern as to his well being. "Oh no Miss Evanharth, I drove all the way down here today to see you in person and answer any questions you might have." His enthusiasm shinning through. Eden looked over the application form as Sebastian studied her. He could tell this young woman had a very clear and definite path to her future. She handled herself in a very mature and serious way. He was also taken with her exceptional beauty and the professional way in which she spoke. Not to mention her eyes which captivated him the moment he saw her. "The application is pretty standard . . . if you have any questions don't hesitate to ask."

He was trying to stay focused, but the truth was he was a driven man. He was driven to her by a higher power of which he did not know or recognize. "Well, Miss Evanharth, as I said your grades and SAT scores are exceptional . . . I am here today to offer you something that few students have the capabilities or grades to receive . . . a full scholarship." Eden looked up and studied his eyes, there was something hauntingly familiar in them that found its way to her, both emotionally and spiritually. "What school?" Eden asked. "Oh didn't I mention it . . . its Laramont University?" Sebastian replied. "Isn't that a Christian College?" she knew that it was. "Yes it is, but we don't force anyone to pray." Sebastian replied, joking. "I'm a little bit thirsty, do you mind if we talk about this while we walk to the cafeteria?" Eden asked as she opened the drawer in her desk and retrieved her wallet. "Sure I'm actually thirsty myself." Sebastian agreed as he looked for a place to rest his backpack. "Is it ok if I leave my backpack here?" He started to place it on a student desk but Eden took it from him. "Hmm, why don't we leave it under my desk?" she suggested. "Good idea." He replied.

They both arrived at the doorway at the same time which was too narrow for both of them to fit through together. Sebastian indicated for Eden to go through before him. "Ladies first." Sebastian said smiling. As they made their way to the cafeteria, Eden spoke first. "Have you ever been to Hadleyville before Mr. Kolten?" He looked over at her and she could feel his eyes take her all in. "I don't believe so, I don't get down to the Boston area very often." He replied. "So Mr. Kolten tell me about the school." Eden's curiosity was peeked and she wanted to hear him speak and express himself. "Oh you don't have to call me Mr. Kolten, it sounds like you're talking to my father." He laughed. "Everyone calls me, Josh." He was smiling again. Eden responded quickly. "Josh . . . I thought your name was Sebastian?" her voice signaled her surprise. "My first name is Sebastian, but since I was a kid everyone has called me by my middle name, which is Joshua—Josh for short." He explained. "I see, your name is Sebastian but you like to be called Josh . . ." Eden replied quite seriously. He took it in stride. "Oh really its fine . . . ask me anything about me or the school." He suggested with a warm and easy air. Eden liked the way his full head of soft brown curls danced about when he talked or moved.

There was more than just a similarity to Joshua . . . her Joshua. "How is the journalism department . . . Josh?" she asked. "See? That's much better." He responded teasing her slightly. "Our journalism department is excellent, and it's run by one of my favorite professors." Josh answered with true excitement adding, "Why don't you come up and visit or I can drive you up and back, if you'd like." He offered in earnest. "All the way to Maine?!" Eden was shocked. "Sure, you could stay over . . . with my parents. We have a huge house, seriously . . . five bedrooms, and then I could drive you back." He was too nice Eden thought. They were now at the cafeteria and all the summer school kids were making a racket. "You've gotta love em." Josh said loudly over the noise. "Do you like children?" she asked. "Oh yeah, I have a bunch of nieces and nephews, my family is pretty big. I have two sisters and an older brother who has five kids! His poor wife." Josh proceeded to insert coins into the soda machine "Which one?" he asked. Eden looked at him pensively. "I'm sorry what did you say?" she asked coming back to the moment, "Soda, which one?" he asked again. "Oh coke is fine." She replied handing him a dollar. "No worries, I've got lots of change, for the tolls, you know." He handed her the can that fell out of the dispenser, then thinking out loud he said, "I think I'll have a root beer."

"So you were saying about your brother?" Eden persisted. Josh took a long drink from the can of soda and then answered. "He has five! And their all great little kids, well one is only six months." He replied in a way that Eden sensed that he was close to them. "You should really consider coming up for a visit I think you'd really like it." He was staying focused, the truth was he really liked Eden and wanted to see her again, soon. "Well Josh I have to get back to class, lunch is over." Eden told him. "Sure I understand I've taken up a lot of your time already." He replied, the disappointment was evident in his voice. As they walked back into the room most of the second graders were already seated, Josh waved to them as he walked over to Eden's desk.

Eden handed him his backpack, and he handed her his business card. "It was a pleasure meeting you Miss Evanharth." He said as he shook her hand. "Are you going to be around later?" she asked him. "I certainly could be." Josh replied. "Well why don't we meet about three o'clock outside the school? You could follow me to my parent's house and have dinner with us." Eden said, hoping he would say yes and of course he did. "That's a swell idea and I can tell them all about the school, hey maybe you can all come up for the weekend!" His excitement was infectious. "I know it's only eleven thirty now but we have a nice library across the street . . ." Eden suggested, realizing that three o'clock was a long way off. Josh looked deeply into her eyes and winked. Then he said, "no worries, I'll see you at three." Eden smiled as he walked to the doorway, he turned and waved. Eden looked up at the ceiling and whispered. "Thanks Daniel." "Who is Daniel? Was that Daniel?" asked Lucy in the front row. Someone from the back yelled out, "Miss Evanharth has a boyfriend."

Eden looked at the class and smiling said. "Never mind, please open your math books to page thirty-six." Eden had made a commitment to The Path, which she fully intended to keep. However, her heart was with Talus. Somehow she needed to find a way to save him from expulsion . . . but how? At their last meeting yesterday he had told her he would contact her with the details, he never indicated how long it would be. She would keep her plans with Sebastian, introduce him to her parents and discuss the college in Maine, which would make everyone happy. Tomorrow she would find Mortamion, Daniel had to already have known about this, Talus would have told him as a replacement would need to take his place. Daniel would have to help her, after all he was fond of Talus. Surly he would help her. She would find Mortamion and plead for his mercy on her own behalf.

She could not loose Talus completely, just knowing he was around somewhere and could hear her was enough. She could live off that the rest of her life, even being married to

Sebastian, as long as she knew that somewhere, Talus was there and she could still communicate with him. If she had to fall down at Mortamion's feet and beg, she was prepared to do it, to save his life . . . for she would be saving her own. Was this action worthy of a warrior? no it wasn't. Was it worthy of a woman in love? Yes.

Sebastian made his way down the steps of the school to the outside parking area. He opened the back door of his black SUV and threw his backpack on the seat. Then he got into the driver's seat and reclined the seat as far back as it would go. He removed his watch and set the alarm for two o'clock and then placed it back on his wrist. A nap was just what he needed after that long drive down from Maine this morning. Hitting all that morning traffic hadn't helped the commute. Closing his eyes he felt a headache coming on. Sitting up he pulled down the cosmetic mirror and looked at his eyes, they were irritated and blood shot. He thought about the impression Eden must have had of him with his eyes looking so bad.

Feeling around in his glove compartment for his saline and contact case he finally found them. Squirting some saline in each eye he removed the colored lenses and put them in their container, placing it on the passenger's seat, he intended to put his contacts back in after his eyes rested for a while. Then he looked at his eyes in the mirror again, the saline had helped a bit. His violet eyes looked back at him, they weren't as blood shot. After his nap he would put his hazel colored contacts back in. For now he settled back for a much needed rest.

As she entered the garden she saw Talus seated on the stone bench, his back to her. His eyes intent on the statue of Lillianna as a child. Eden sat next to him and placed her hand on his. "Why do try and deny me an honorable death as a warrior Eden?" he asked not looking at her. "Why do you continue to read my thoughts?" she asked in response.

"It is a trait I was created with and it is the one way I can be close to you." He replied. "Your dinner with Alestasis went well this evening, but I understood you to have reservations." Talus said changing the subject. Eden paused and took a deep breath. "I saw something in him, some very small gesture that reminded me . . . of Dante." She answered. "You may be seeking something that is not there, because you are not fully committed to the oath." Talus explained as he stood and slowly walked around her grandmother's garden, admiring all the flowers, he sighed. "What is it you seek from me Eden? Your thoughts are filling me with doubts about your commitment to The Path." Talus spoke wisely as usual. "I seek your salvation as without you I will not survive, I can't live without you in my life . . . knowing that you will be gone is completely unimaginable to me." Eden spoke as tears filled her eyes, as was usual she was becoming illogical and emotional just being near him.

Eden stood and walked over to him. "I cannot lose all of you, I would rather deny my lineage and denounce the oath, I don't care about any of it, not if I am to lose you." Eden spoke with sheer determination and conviction through her tears. "To do so would be horribly foolish, immature and not worthy of you or your namesake . . . lacking the dignity of a warrior." Talus scolded. "I don't care, there is no dignity when you love someone." Eden cried, "I can't live on this earth without a part of you near me . . . I'd sooner die and let The Council ravage my body from my soul, I cannot live without you." She was wrapped in his arms, which he did not resist. "I do not want to live without you, for me it would be like a kind of death." She whispered as she held on to him. He knew his time was ending soon, and he wanted to give her everything she needed from him while he still could. "Eden, how can I explain to you all that you are and all that you will become . . . nothing great has ever been accomplished without great sacrifice and total commitment." He replied, his face nestled in her hair. "Then, let me sacrifice myself for both of us." She said looking into his deep brown eyes. "To do so would leave me less than a man, is that how you see me?" he asked her. "Is this what you are asking of me, to be less than what I am?"

The question threw her, as she then realized the depth of his own strength and conviction. Pulling away, she looked at him. How could he put his manhood above the love she felt for him? "Eden, a man, any man that would allow a woman to fight his battle is not a man." Talus told her, his face somber. "This is not the seventeen hundreds Talus, this is now . . . today! Women stand up for their loved ones everyday . . . it doesn't matter if they are men or women." Eden argued. He walked over to her and took her in his arms and she rested her head on his chest. He held her as tightly as he could without hurting her. "You are an impetuous and willful woman child, and I fear that you will let your emotions rule your better judgment." Talus told her. Lifting her in his arms, he took her inside. Talus had a plan, a plan that would leave her with a part of himself, after his extinction from The Council. He knew that his virility would serve him well. A part of him would live on in Eden.

Eden opened her eyes and immediately felt that dawn had arrived much too quickly. Talus stood in front of her grandmother's mirror, adjusting his shirt and then putting his jacket on. She sat up in bed and caught his eyes in the mirror. He smiled at her as he pulled his hair back. Sitting down next to her, she caressed his face, such a youthful face with a mind that spanned one hundred and fifty years of life's experience that she would never have. "Eden, you are with child." He said and kissed the inside of her palm. "How do you know?" she asked, her voice hushed. "I made it so." He replied. "You can do that?" she replied stunned.

Talus looked at her with a raised eyebrow. "I can do many things, and have done some that have proved unfortunate." He contended. "Without asking me?" her voice indicated disappointment. She looked away from him. "I thought it would please you . . . if you do not want the child, you must tell me now and I will stop it." He replied in his directorial way. Eden moved closer to him. "Of course I want the baby . . ." She explained. "It's a male child." He interrupted. "Do not concern yourself with time, I have already communicated with Daniel and your engagement will begin swiftly." He told her as he stood up. "I want the baby and I want you, can't you communicate that to Daniel?!" Eden began crying. "Why is it so impossible to have both?!" She implored.

Talus walked over to the window, and studied the beginning of the sun's rise to form the day. "Woman, why do you constantly test my patience? I am giving you all that I have to give!" His voice was raised as his frustrations with all the recent events were taking a toll on him. "Because, I love you and my heart is breaking . . . how I wish you could feel what I am feeling." She covered her face with her hands. "I do feel it, somehow I feel it, I didn't think it was possible . . . Eden our destiny is taking us in two different directions . . . it was from the very beginning." Talus replied calmly and walked out of the room. Eden wrapped in only a sheet hurried after him. She found him standing still by the door his back to her. She came up behind him and put her arms around him. He took her hands in his and placed them over his heart. He had never wished to be mortal and now at this moment, that was all changing. For this one and only time and as never before he had the longing to be mortal. Yet the part of him that was untainted and honorable knew that he had to answer for his transgression with Lillianna.

Slowly he turned to face her. "I am only a mortal Talus, a mortal woman in love." She tried to explain. "I know this, all mortal women in love are dangerous." He replied smiling. She smiled back. How crazy this was, she thought. I will be marrying one man and carrying the child of another. Again he read her thoughts. "Not so unusual for mortals, as I've come to see." He answered. "I will miss that most of all . . . how you read my mind and know from near or far what I'm thinking." Eden mused. "It's possible Talon will have this ability, as he will be mortal and immortal." Talus considered. "Then I am to name him Talon?" Eden asked. "If I were here, that would be his name, yes." Talus confirmed the decision. "If Alestasis be a good man, he need never know about me." Talus instructed. " . . . and if he is Dante?" Eden asked. "Fight him with every means you have, above all cost protect our son." He kissed Eden and opened the door. "Do you remember where I live?" he asked her. "Yes, I think so." She replied. "Tomorrow then you must be there, in the woods in back of the house by dawn." He said simply and walked to his truck. "Talus!" She called out to him and he came walking back. She threw her arms around him, kissing him all over his face. He kissed her back not wanting to leave but knowing he must.

"One last thing, I have transferred the house into your name, there are funds in an overseas account that you will have access to, once I'm gone. I will give you all the papers tomorrow." His speech was direct and focused as he spoke. "Listen to me carefully . . . don't let Alestasis know about the house or the funds until you are sure he is Alestasis and bares no trait of Dante. If need be, that will be a place to secure your safety and the child's safety. I was going to tell you this tomorrow Eden but, perhaps you will rest better knowing it now." He kissed her lips and walked toward the street. "I will never rest better, . . . never again, not without you." Eden whispered, watching as he walked to his truck, got inside and drove away.

Walking back to her bed, she caressed her stomach with her hand, trying to imagine what the baby would look like. Wondering how she would get through tomorrow. First she needed to get through today. She was now eighteen and pregnant. He would have stopped it, he had told her so. She couldn't have, she loved him too much, and she wanted his child. His child would carry in him all the love she had for his father. If nothing were left, she would always have his son. As she lay down on the bed, she saw that he had left his watch and her purity ring on the bedside table. It was not that he forgot, of course he wanted her to have them, because this was truly the end. Tomorrow was just ceremonious. Mortamion unleashing his anger which he had a lot of, rightly so. If only he could know that Talus was no longer the same man who had taken Lillianna against her will. There was no way for her to tell him that. She knew that it would not make a difference, if he did know.

They were both from another time and place, and she had no right to interfere in this business between men. What she came to understand was this day had been the finality of their love. He was never again to return to her. Never would she feel his kiss or his arms around her. She buried her head in her pillow and cried until there were no more tears left. She could fight all forms of evil, but losing Talus was going to kill her. He knew that as well, which is why he had given her his child, to try and quell her pain and despair.

Eden had begun to drift off to sleep when she heard the doorbell ring. Putting on her robe, she made her way through the living room and opened the door. Sebastian stood there, smiling at first, then obviously taken aback by her tear stained face. "Hi Miss Evanharth, I stopped by your parents house and they said you'd be here." He waited, but

Eden did not reply. "Perhaps, tomorrow would be a better time to see you . . ." he said awkwardly. "No, no it's alright, come in." Eden replied coming out of her vague demeanor. Sebastian walked into the room and Eden closed the door. "I'm sorry about your grandmother's passing . . . your mom mentioned it this morning, when I stopped by your house." Sebastian fumbled. "Would you like something to drink Alestasis?" Eden asked still filled with grief and distress. "Sorry I didn't catch what you said?" Sebastian replied. "I'm sorry Sebastian, that was someone from my past . . . that just came into my mind." Eden recovered. "Miss Evanharth, why don't you get dressed and we'll go out and get breakfast, unless you want to be alone." He suggested with hesitation.

"No, we could go and have breakfast." Eden agreed, knowing he was her future. "Just give me a few minutes." She said walking down the hall to her bedroom. "Take your time." Sebastian replied. Eden took her clothes from the bedroom and went into one of the bathrooms locking the door behind her. Looking in the mirror she knew why Sebastian felt ill at ease, her face and eyes were swollen from crying. Splashing cold water over her face repeatedly, she tried to bring the swelling down. Looking at her face she knew only time would help . . . then there was tomorrow to deal with. Her eyes were going to be swollen for a long time. She readied herself, as best she could, Combing her hair, she fastened it up with a pink crystal barrette her mother had given her. She put on her black jeans and a black eyelet peasant blouse with a scalloped hem. Staring at herself in the mirror she knew this was as good as she could look considering the circumstances. When she came out of the bathroom Sebastian was gone. How odd she thought. What was going on?

She opened the front door and saw him driving up in a car and parking in front of the house. As he walked toward her, she smiled. He had a floral bouquet in one hand and a pair of sunglasses in the other hand. "These are for you." He said handing them to her.

"Thank you, Sebastian . . . that was really nice of you." She replied. "I liked the flowers and I thought you could use a pair of sunglasses today . . . it's so bright outside, my eyes are really sensitive to light." He explained.

Eden put the flowers in a vase in water, while Sebastian sat on the porch. Then she put the sunglasses on and locked the door. He looked at her. "They look good on you." He said, as they walked towards his car. "Didn't you have a truck yesterday?" Eden asked. "Yeah this is my dad's car." He replied. "Wait, you mean you went back to Maine last night and came back this morning?" She questioned him as he opened the car door for her. She slipped into the seat and he shut the door. Opening the driver's side door he got in and sat down. Buckling his seat belt he started the engine. Sebastian lowered the windows and turned to her. "Yep that's exactly what I did, because I needed to see you again." He told her putting on his own sunglasses. "Why?" she asked, snapping her seat belt into place. "Well it's like this Miss Evanharth, I'm pretty sure I'm in love with you . . . I know it sounds bizarre and crazy, it does to me too!" He laughed. "I've never experienced anything like this before, really you can ask my family." He urged. "All I ask Miss Evanharth, and I know I have no right to ask, but just give me a chance, I'm a pretty nice guy . . . I'll grow on you." He said sincerely. Eden leaned her head back on the seat and remembered Talus' words. "Your engagement will begin swiftly."

"So, where would you like to go, Miss Evanharth?" he asked turning his signal light on. "You can call me Eden." She responded. "Only if you'll call me Josh." He replied. "Well Josh, why don't we just drive for awhile . . . just drive to nowhere." Eden answered as a faint smile crossed her lips.

"To understand everything, is to forgive everything."
The Buddha

Absolution
Chapter Thirteen

"If I may love, let it be fully and completely. Perfectly envisioned as the birth of each new day, with the simplicity of the gentle August breeze which blows through the delicate leaves in the summer trees . . . herein lies these truths, that I will love you with that perfection and that my heart be directed only to that end." Sebastian told Eden as he placed the solid gold wedding band on Eden's left hand ring finger, kissing her on her cheek. Her eyes looked up at the man who had gained her hand in marriage. Father Clemmons put his hands over Eden's and Sebastian's hands and spoke. "Eden do you take Sebastian as your lawful husband, in holy matrimony to love and honor him all the days of your life, in sickness and in health, for richer or for poorer as long as you both shall live?" Father Clemmons asked. "Yes, I will." Eden answered. Father Clemmons turned to Sebastian and asked, "Sebastian do you take Eden as your lawful wife, in holy matrimony protecting her, loving her and honoring her in sickness and in health, for richer or for poorer as long as you both shall live? "Yes, with all my heart I will." Sebastian replied. "Then, if there be anyone present who has just cause as to why this union should not take place, let them speak now or forever hold their peace." The congregation heard footsteps walking down the isle of the crowded church and a voice deep and clear called out, "I take exception to this union as that woman loves me and I her, therefore she belongs to me." Eden turned to look out into the crowd and saw Talus walking towards her. She lifted the bottom of her wedding gown and ran to him. He picked her up off her feet and carried her out of the church . . . no one followed. Why would they, this was Eden's dream and she would have it her way.

She awoke startled thinking she had missed the alarm, which she had set for three in the morning. It was only two thirty. It wouldn't matter if she was early, but she could not be late. She had showered when she had returned home from her afternoon with Sebastian, and had gone straight to bed. Crying for Talus most of the night, she had not really slept. By three o'clock she was already on the highway, driving in her grandmother's car which had not been used for some time. Surprisingly the engine started without any problem and the gas tank was full. She had asked for Uncle Eli's car in case she needed it, which was parked in front of the house. It was dark and lonely on the road. Lonelier still was her heart as she knew what today would bring.

The mountain leading up to Talus' house reminded her of their first night together. As she reached the top, she could see that there were lights on in the house. Two cars were there already, one was Talus' truck and the other a black sedan. She pulled up next to Talus' truck. She knew all too well what the black Sedan represented. It was still quite dark as dawn had not begun. Walking up to the house, she looked in the window and saw Talus sitting in front of the fireplace. He appeared to be alone.

Eden opened the door as she knew it would be unlocked and walked inside closing the door behind her. "Good morning Eden," he greeted her with a faint smile, as he turned to look at her. She walked over to the couch and sat down next to him. Talus stared in to the fire light. "Is Mortamion here?" she asked, the thought crossing her mind as to why he seemed so illusive toward her. "Yes, he's in the back with his second." His tone was different Eden noticed. Finally, he turned his body to look at her. "Eden why are you crying so much? You are spoiling your beautiful face." He told her putting his hands around the back of her neck, he touched his forehead to hers. Then he kissed her face and her lips. "How can you ask me why I am crying Talus, when you know I am dying inside?" Tears falling from hers eyes as she spoke. "Don't do that Eden you have our son inside you, emotional stress is not good for humans." He told her standing. He was shirtless, wearing only tight black pants and tall boots that had thick black straps around them. Around each of his wrists was a thick wide black leather band. "Come with me." He said, holding out his hand. She followed him into the bedroom and watched him as he opened the closet door.

On the top shelf he removed a small black leather box, which showed considerable wear. It resembled a very austere jewelry box. Talus placed it on the bed and opened it. "Here is the deed to the house and the account numbers to my funds that are in a bank in Geneva." He looked up at her his long blond hair falling across his face. "You mean Geneva, as in Switzerland?" Eden asked. "Yes." He answered her, laughing softly. "I have instructed them to move the funds to a bank in America at your discretion . . . but I would wait until you are married and comfortable with Alestasis, before you make any decisions on that."

He put the box back up on the shelf, closing the closet door. “After this is over today, take the box with you and keep it in a safe place as you may need it.” He said simply. Eden put her arms around him and he held her close to him, he wanted to feel her heart beating against his. “His name is not Alestasis, its Sebastian.” She cried. “Names are not important Eden, it’s who you are in your soul that matters.” His voice choked as he spoke and Eden looked up at him. “You seem different today . . . so unlike yourself, your eyes are different.” She told him holding his face in her hands. He took her hands in his and kissed them. “I am . . . The Council has made me mortal for the purpose of the duel.” His eyes felt wet and he did not want Eden to see his tears, so he pulled her in close against his body. “Mortamion is a Council member who has also been made mortal for the purpose of the duel, it was his desire to fight me as he was the last time he saw me, which was as a mortal man . . . I agree it is, as it should be.”

Talus had completely accepted his fate and his resolve was evident to Eden. But she fought him anyway. “You are mortal now and you could be with me Talus, we could talk to The Council Tribunal and Daniel, this could be handled a different way Talus! We could try!” She pleaded. Talus grabbed her hands tightly, holding them in his. “Eden! Listen to me!” His voice was quiet yet fueled with urgency. There was passion and determination in his eyes. “Pull yourself together, this is how I want it . . . this is how it must be.” He insisted his eyes locked on hers. “Eden, in all these years I never thought I could be loved . . . or that I could feel love and to my surprise I found it in you and truly I am not worthy of it.” The humanity in his voice was coming through and Eden felt it. She listened for once saying nothing. “Let me become worthy, let me die honorably and in this, you will know that I have felt the everglow of your love into eternity." Suddenly, a resolve came over her, a wave of serenity took hold of her and Talus saw it happen, and he was pleased. Pleased, that she was taking control of her emotions under the most difficult of circumstances.

Talus took her by the hand and led her to the bathroom. There he washed her face with a cold cloth and taking his brush he combed her hair. "There now you look like as you should, the woman of a warrior sending her man into battle." Talus handed her a bottle of oil and asked her to cover his back, chest and arms with it. "Why?" she asked. "It is a pagan ritual, which Council members follow and I have been a Council member longer than I have been anything else." When she was done caressing his body with the oil, she kissed his back and chest, tasting the oil with her lips. "It is time now Eden, are you ready?" he asked. "Yes." She replied. Talus bent down and kissed her one last time, deeply and with undeniable longing.

Outside dawn was upon them. She saw Mortamion, his body glistened as well, his pants and boots were similar to what Talus wore. His hair was long and black, his looks very appealing, but in his eyes was a hatred that was visible to Eden. A short imposing man stood next to him and there to her surprise stood Daniel. As she and Talus walked towards them, Talus whispered in her ear. "I asked Daniel to be here for you Eden." "Thank you." She replied quietly, completely composed. Twelve men appeared in the distance, coming out of the woods. "Do not be afraid, they are The Tribunal." Talus explained. Dressed in black they all looked identical, they looked normal except for their eyes . . . they didn't seem to have any. Large holes were where they eyes should be. The short man spoke first. "I am serving as Mortamion's second, are you ready to do battle Talus?" he asked Talus. "Yes." Talus replied and looking over at Eden, he nodded his head to her. "I am serving as Talus' second, are you ready to do battle Mortamion?" she asked Mortamion with a touch of arrogance. "Yes, with pleasure and longing." He replied, giving her back the same attitude.

In unison The Tribunal stood back and nodded their approval. Mortamion's second, Louis picked up a sword from a long leather case, which lay on the ground and handed it to him. Then Eden picked up the other sword which was left in the case and handed it to Talus. It was very heavy, but she willed herself to lift it and hand it to him. Talus was very proud of her at that moment, for she used her warrior powers to lift it. Its weight was quite considerable even for a man of strength. Louis picked up the case and stepped way back, at least forty feet, Eden and Daniel did the same, only in the opposite direction. Talus and Mortamion held their swords in both hands, vertically at waist level, the swords rising way above their heads. Suddenly, Louis called out "On Guard!" Mortamion took the first strike, and Talus blocked it sideways, coming back at Mortamion he swung his sword in long swift movements. It was clear to Eden that Mortamion had better speed and accuracy, but Talus had more brute strength. "Is there no way to prevent Talus from his fate Daniel?" Eden asked keeping her eyes on Talus as she spoke. "Ultimately it is up to The Tribunal Eden." Daniel answered her. "However, they are being as fair as possible, for both men are equally matched." Daniel added. Mortamion had the advantage and it was evident as he drew his sword back and then sideways with incredible speed, sliding it on the outside of Talus' arm drawing blood. The gash was long and deep. Now Talus came at him, with great gusts of fury, both men grunting and yelling as the metals collided.

"Eden you must understand that Talus will lose this battle one way or another." Daniel reminded her. Eden did not respond. She couldn't, the idea left her inconsolable and hopeless. Why had she fallen in love with the one man she could never have? Why were these two men fighting over the honor of a woman who had died over a hundred years ago? Though she was there in the middle of it . . . it was surreal and dream like, to Eden. Unimaginable and yet happening before her eyes. Daniel read her mind and knew he would need to step in and control her emotions . . . he knew under these circumstances she would not be able to. If for no other reason, it was necessary and instrumental that Daniel should be there for Eden at this moment in time.

Finally the duel took a turn as both men were becoming tired and began to stagger. Daniel explained that if they were fighting as Council members, this could go on for hours. However, as mortals the sheer weight of the swords would begin to slow them down.

Suddenly, Mortamion lost his footing as Talus forced his bodily strength against him, knocking him down. Falling to the ground Mortamion lost his grasp on his sword. Talus placed his foot on it, pushing it out of Mortamion's reach. Then Talus held the tip of his sword to Mortamion's throat. "Do not move Mortamion for you will bring about your own death." Talus yelled, gasping for breath. His chest rising and falling as he breathed. His long blond hair finally settling, as he stood over Mortamion. Eden had never even seen him perspire once. "Do with me what you will Talus, plunge the sword or by all that is in me, I shall come after you again!" Mortamion said seething.

Talus stepped away from Mortamion and flung his sword into the wind, and then he turned his back on Mortamion and walked away. Eden's instinct made her run to him, but Daniel stopped her and she could not move. Her body was frozen, by Daniels will. Mortamion rose and called after Talus. "Pick up your sword and kill me or fight me, do one or the other." He took his sword in hand and ran after Talus. Talus stopped walking and spoke, with his back to Mortamion. "Will you slay me from behind Mortamion?" he asked slowly.

"Then turn and die like a man." Replied Mortamion. Talus turned, his eyes fixed on Mortamion's eyes. Both men knew why they were there, both accepted their own measure of responsibility.

Mortamion drew his sword back and then sent it plunging into Talus' stomach. Talus fell to his knees, his head lowered looking down at the blood which gushed out of him. Mortamion pulled the sword out, covered in his blood and Talus fell. It was then that Daniel released his hold on Eden, and she ran to Talus.

Mortamion stood close by watching him die. Eden cradled his head, kissing every part of his face and neck, crying uncontrollably and then screaming his name. Slowly his body began to convulse. He tried to focus his eyes on her. "I have loved you Eden as I have loved no other, you are all that is right in the world . . ." These were his last words, his hand reaching out to touch her stomach, fell and rested there.

His body began to disappear slowly turning into dust until only a small ball of light remained in her hands and dispersed into the atmosphere. Mortamion began to walk away, as Eden stood and called after him. "Take up your sword Mortamion and fight me!" She screamed. "I should like nothing better madam, for any friend of Talus is my enemy." He yelled back. Eden ran in the direction where Talus had thrown his sword, picking it up easily.

She ran across the field, to attack Mortamion. "No!" Daniel commanded, standing between them. "The Tribunal does not sanction this, nor do I . . . lay down your sword Eden." He said with his right hand raised. Eden obeyed his command, but continued to argue. "I plead with you Daniel and The Council Tribunal to let me avenge Talus' death." She spoke with controlled emotion and with complete clarity as she was fueled with anger which had replaced her sadness.

"Woman you would have no strength against me." Mortamion said chiding her. "She is Eden Evanharth, a Warrior of God Mortamion, her power would overtake you, as you are still mortal." Daniel reminded him. Mortamion was clearly shocked. "Is her lineage from Lillianna?" he asked Daniel. "Yes it is . . . and there will be no battle between the two of you." Daniel ordered. "Daniel please, I am begging you, let me fight him!" Eden implored. Daniel stopped her bluntly, with his mind and directed her towards the house. "This was between the two men Eden, you have no just reason to do battle here and The Tribunal has forbidden it." She turned to look at The Tribunal as they walked back into the woods and disappeared, and Mortamion gathered both swords and handed them to Louis to put back in the case.

Daniel expected this, so had Talus which is why he had asked Daniel to come to the duel. Daniel would have anyway as he had a fondness for Talus, and would miss him. Daniel knew Eden was passionate and would make a great warrior one day. Daniel also knew that she had to be guided and trained and he knew just the person who would accomplish this . . . Mortamion. Sebastian would make a good foundation in her personal life, and his soul would be saved in the process. However, Eden needed a man of strength and breeding to take her to the next level in The Path. Mortamion would be that man.

Daniel walked with Eden to the front of the house, stopping at the front door. Mortamion came up to Daniel and thanked him for his intervention in helping convince

The Council to keep him mortal, for the duel. Eden chose to ignore his presence. She felt him look at her but would not even turn her head in his direction. After Mortamion drove off with Louis, Daniel spoke to her. "Eden, your heartbreak is one Mortamion feels and understands; release your pain as it will do you no good to bear it." Daniel looked into her eyes, forcing her to look at him. "Now . . . I want your word as a warrior and member of The Path that you will not try and hurt Mortamion in anyway." Daniel's voice was as it always was, filled with understanding, wisdom and reverence. However, Eden knew what he was capable of. "I give you my word Daniel, I will not interfere or harm Mortamion, in anyway." She replied in earnest. "You are with child now, you must think of your son and your future marriage to Sebastian." He said as he turned into a cloud like form and began to evaporate in to the atmosphere. Daniel had disappeared, but Eden could hear his voice in the distance as he spoke. "Hate has no place in the heart of a true Warrior of God."

Eden entered the house, it was impossible to think that Talus was not there. The fire in the fireplace that had been there this morning, was now just a smoldering pit. Looking around the large room visions of him raced through her mind. She went into the bedroom and fell on the bed, crying, pulling the sheets to her and wrapping them around herself. "I cannot bear this, I cannot bear this . . ." She cried out. She could not stop her tears or the pain that was ravaging her heart. She longed for him with every part of her body and to the very depth of her soul.

Hours passed before Eden finally stopped crying and took the box down from the shelf in the closet. Talus had showed her what it contained but she opened it anyway. Looking at the envelope on the top, she turned it over and it read Eden on it. It was not sealed, only the flap had been turned in to it. She opened it quickly. Inside there was a letter addressed to her.

Eden,

"You are an impetuous woman child, whom I truly loved. Even though, if I were there with you now, I would deny it completely, for I would be immortal. I know it is the evening of my death and you have cried for many hours, I am telling you to stop and go home to your grandmother's house. Take the box with you, do not live it behind. I ask one thing of you, only one. If you ever speak to our son about me . . . if you so deem to tell him I was his father. Tell him two things, that I loved his mother and that I died honorably in battle. For these are truths." It was signed, Talus.

His penmanship was strong like he was, and his words direct like he was. Eden folded it and put it back in the envelope and then in the black box. Gathering her thoughts, she poured water over the smoldering ash in the fireplace. She locked the front door with the keys that were left on the kitchen table and got into her grandmother's car. Looking at Talus' truck, she wanted to make sure it was locked, so she got out again. Upon opening the passenger side door she saw that resting on the seat was a single red rose, surrounded by baby's breath. Picking it up, one of the thorns pricked her finger drawing blood, she closed her eyes and thought of Talus. Their relationship had been like a rose, beautiful, short lived and not without its thorns.

The sun had begun to set, as Eden pulled into her grandmother's driveway. Unlocking the door, she stepped inside the house. She remembered the disagreement she and Talus had here the the other evening. Their relationship, though extremely short had taken many twists and turns, but Talus was the most dynamic, effectual and stubborn person she had ever known. Yet, he was also the most honest, magnetic and logical person she'd ever know. Talus had been a force in the universe. Now he was no more. Eden opened the sliding glass door which led to the garden, it comforted her being there. The garden was alive with roses and daisies, chrysanthemums and daffodils. She placed the rose Talus had left her in front of Lillianna's statue. She thought it fitting, as he had lost his life due to Lillianna. Eden knew Lillianna would have protested the duel had she been living on the earth, but it didn't matter as now she and Talus were gone, Lillianna to uncertainty, Talus cast into infinity.

Eden heard the doorbell ring and thinking it was her parents or Sebastian she opened it promptly. It was Mortamion on the other side. First she felt anger rise inside her, as she fought to keep her composure. She remembered her oath to Daniel. She did not invite him in. "What do you want here Mortamion, to gloat at my misery?" she asked coldly. "I would like to speak with you . . . if you would grant me a few moments of your time." His voice was a lot lighter than Talus' voice. In general he was not as imposing. "Come in then." Eden widened the entrance for him to pass, as he carried a long wooden box with him. He looked around the room as she waited for him to say something. "Obviously Daniel told you where I live . . ." she told him. "No, I actually followed you here." He answered her. "You waited all those hours for me to leave?" Eden asked in disbelief. "I went home and washed, then I came back . . . I knew you'd be there for some time." Mortamion responded. "Why? What is it you want?" Her voice filled with controlled anger. "Today, I didn't know who you were, I want to say first, I apologize for being rude to you earlier . . . Talus asked that I not harm you as you were his woman, and I gave him my word that I would not harm you in anyway."

He explained. "Well you have harmed me in every way you possibly could!" She shouted, holding back tears. "I know this has hurt you deeply and for that I am sorry, as I have been in pain as well, so I understand how it feels." He told her, placing the wooden box down on the floor.

"What is that?" Eden asked. "I bring you his sword, and wish to pay my respects to you." Mortamion replied. "Why?" Eden's shock was evident. "Were you not his woman?" asked Mortamion, confused. "Yes . . . yes I was his, I still am." Eden answered, hardly able to speak. "I don't understand your ways, this is all so uncivilized." Eden said through her tears. "Do you not honor your dead . . . I believe it is your custom to present this country's flag to the dead soldier's woman . . . is it not?" he asked her. "Yes it is, but not from the enemy!" She shot back at him. Bending down on her knees she opened the box and there it was, some of the dirt, oil and blood from him still hung on to the metal. She ran her hand across it. "I am not your enemy Eden." Mortamion said softly as he watched her. Eden ignored his comment.

"I lost my life and Lillianna who I cherished more than life itself . . . any life, mortal or immortal." His said. "Talus did not kill your wife!" She came back at him raging. "Yes he forced himself on her, which was a terrible thing to do, but I know he regretted his actions and he personally spoke to her spirit in my presence and asked for her forgiveness and she gave it to him." Eden lashed out at him with her words, because she was bound by her oath to Daniel, not to do otherwise.

"You didn't know him now, the kind of person he was now, how I loved him, how much he meant to me, he was and always will be my first and only love!" Eden fell to her knees sobbing. "I would have given up my own life, my own soul for his." She couldn't go on, it was not humanly possible for her to handle this grief that surrounded her. Mortamion walked over to her and handed her a handkerchief, which she accepted.

He bent down next to her. "I am sorry for your grief and heartbreak Eden, I think today when I saw you standing next to Talus, the anger rose inside of me, as you remind me so much of Lillianna. I thought you were just a woman he was dating because, you looked like Lillianna . . . it sounds unbelievable, but it is how I felt . . . I didn't know you were mortal, I thought you were a Council member." Mortamion held out his hand to help her up. "Thank you but I can get myself up." She replied standing. "It doesn't matter; who you thought I was, you were not justified in taking his life." She said, wiping her eyes, which she could barely open now as they were so swollen. "The Council would have taken it, if I hadn't . . . can you find no comfort in the fact that he died honorably, in battle?" he asked. "Talus asked for expulsion, it was he, himself that notified The Tribunal." Mortamion explained. "No, I don't believe you!" Eden yelled. Mortamion grabbed her shoulders, forcing her to look at him. Eden saw the truth in his eyes. "Can you not understand what I'm telling you Eden?" he contested. There it was, she thought.

These two men Talus and Mortamion, they were from another time and place, where the rules were different. Both lived by a code that did not have a place in the modern world. For them it did, but not for anyone else. "Eden, Talus died the way he chose . . . he asked The Council Tribunal to make him mortal for the battle, this is why I was made mortal." Eden looked at him with complete shock. "Talus had been with The Council for over one hundred and fifty years, other then what he did to Lillianna he had no other transgressions." Mortamion continued upon seeing her surprise. "Why could they not spare him?" she asked through her tears. "The punishment for a Council member to take a mortal woman against her will, is expulsion." Replied Mortamion. "We were both made mortal, so that he could die a noble death . . . they granted him that privilege and tomorrow I will become immortal again as I have been." Mortamion walked to the door, "I have spoken all the words I came to speak." His back was to her. "Wait." She said stopping him. "Would you like to see something?" Eden asked him as she wiped her eyes. He turned to look at her. "Follow me into the garden." She said leading the way.

Mortamion's eyes looked around, at all the flowers and then they rested on Lillianna's statue. "That is a statue of Lillianna as a child, a friar at the mission created it when she disappeared from the village . . . my grandmother was her half sister and brought it here from the village of San Michelene in France." She said sitting down on the bench in front of the statue, Mortamion sat down next to her. "San Michelene yes, I remember now, San Michelene." Mortamion said as tears welled up in his eyes. All the memories of Lillianna, Alestasis, the castle and George were crashing back into his mind all at once. "Did you not remember your life Mortamion?" she asked him, calming down and confused by his reaction. "No . . . The Tribunal told me very small amounts of what happened . . . I know that Talus told them everything, about Lillianna and what took place between them and he asked for expulsion from the Council very recently." Mortamion could not stop his own tears, as he spoke.

Eden handed him back the handkerchief, which was all crumbled up and wet from her own tears. "Then you did not know that Alestasis was Talus' son?" Eden pressed on. "No, not that I could remember, when you are with The Council most memories are lost. It was not until four days ago that some memories started to come to mind. I was told about Lillianna and Talus, less than a week ago and I knew she had been my wife, but today when I became mortal it drove me beyond what I could tolerate." He paused, wiping his tears with the back of his hand. "I remembered my own death and Lillianna's face as I died. Today when I became mortal I wanted to fight him . . . I wanted to kill him . . . . yet I have felt no satisfaction in the result. We had been warriors together, many many years ago, I was his captain." Mortamion let his head fall back and looked up at the sky as if searching for a star or constellation. Then he looked at Eden and continued on with his account.

"They made it clear to me that Talus was the father of my son and that he took Lillianna my wife by force . . . It was so hard for me to comprehend what he had done, as I had trusted him as my brother. The Council brought him to serve under my command. I trained him and taught him to fight and negotiate. He betrayed me, by his actions . . . then Daniel made it possible for me to communicate with Lillianna and she confirmed what happened to me telepathically. She told me she thought I knew all these years, and that I had come to earth to be mortal because of my anger toward her. This was not true, I would have never abandoned her. Instead I chose The Council, as I would only want to be mortal if she was alongside me, and because she took her own life and left a child behind, she can never be mortal again." His despair was genuine and Eden began to feel his pain and sadness. Daniel was indeed correct when he said that Mortamion knew and understood her pain and her heartbreak.

He was pouring his heart out to Eden, human tears falling from his eyes. "Now sitting here Eden, I know everything, I feel everything as a mortal and I remember that only this kind of love can break your heart and torture it in the process." Eden looked at him and replied "I wish

I could stop feeling everything." Mortamion turned his body to her, he greens eyes saddened and shocked by her comment. "Don't wish that Eden, as much as it may hurt, to be mortal is to be touched by The Devine One." He answered her, his voice gentle, and soft spoken. She knew that his love for Lillianna, equaled her love for Talus, in its entirety.

"How do you know that Talus told them everything?" she asked him. "Talus told me this morning, when we were allowed entrance into the mortal world to do battle." Mortamion replied. "Can you tell me everything he told you Mortamion, please . . . it is so important that I know everything?" she pleaded. "I know that I will be taking his place as lead Council negotiator in the east." Mortamion explained.

"So, . . . that was the purpose of this visit . . . to manipulate me, so that we could work together." Eden stood up, her voice angry and hurt. "No!" Mortamion contested. "I wanted to talk to you and apologize, because I took the life of your loved one in battle!" He raised his voice to her. "When I learned you were mortal and an Evanharth, my heart opened up to you, I could feel your pain and I thought if we spoke, you could feel mine!" He had lost his control, as a mortal would. "This I can tell you, and all of what I speak is true." Mortamion walked over to her and placed his hands on her shoulders. She turned her head, but the truth in his words made her eyes connect with his. Eden had no recourse but to see him and hear him, because her instincts did not lie. "The purity and strength of your love saved Talus, and The Council Tribunal and I gave him an honorable death." He stopped and rested with those words.

"I saw you plunge the sword into him Mortamion, he was defenseless!" She yelled at him, a part of her still did not want to accept the truth. "He was not defenseless, he threw down his sword as that was his salvation . . . he wanted death! Oh yes, I know you wanted my death, that would have pleased you . . . but that is not why we were there today Eden." Mortamion protested her inference. They were silent for a long while and then Eden spoke.

"I would not have wanted your death, all lives are sacred Mortamion." She answered him, her voice calmed. "Well, you made a very good show of it, when you challenged me seeking revenge this morning." He said in awe of her bravery. "You have been very brave coming here tonight, Mortamion . . . to tell me why you wanted my loved one dead." Eden said her voice filled with anguish.

"I can't ride this emotional rollercoaster with you Mortamion, You come to me, that I may comfort you? That you might find forgiveness? I have lost my grandmother, Talus and Joshua in the same week. I have had to fight Dante and The Dominion and their thugs . . . my heart is broken beyond my own comprehension, and I made an oath to marry a man I don't love so I could save his soul, which is Alestasis, so I'm sorry if I can't mire in your pain . . ." she cried out to him. "I'm tired and I'm lost and I have no place to turn to for comfort."

Now, Eden was pouring her heart out to Mortamion. She stood silently, her hands covering her face, waiting for him to leave. Mortamion walked over to her and took her in his arms, "Let me be your comfort then, for no one's heartbreak is less than anyone else's, and no one's heartbreak is more than anyone else's. You will be my Lillianna and I, your Talus this night . . . this one and only night, as I will exchange my love for yours and in this shall we be comforted." He said, kissing her on the lips. Eden did not fight him, somehow she needed to be close to Talus . . . even if it meant being with the man who had taken his life.

"I don't want to leave you." Mortamion whispered to Eden. "You must go back." Eden responded quietly, resting in his arms. "You have become my sanctuary . . . I can't go back to the nothingness of immortality." Mortamion sighed deeply. "I never thought I could feel this way again, you have been my salvation." His voice was soft, gentle in its tone. Eden lifted herself up and resting on his chest, faced him. "I have given you all I can Mortamion, and soon you will become a Council member again, your emotions will recede and you will begin to forget all that you have felt here with me tonight . . . and seeing me won't be as hard anymore." Eden told him, caressing his face. "You took Talus' life, but I have seen inside your soul tonight and I know you as a different man, and there is goodness in you." Eden said standing as Mortamion took hold of her hand.

"Do not go from me, stay with me a while longer, as leaving this place and you, will be my darkest hour." He pleaded. "You are talking this way because you are mortal, and we both sought the comfort of those we have loved through each other." Eden replied. Mortamion rose up from the bed and took her in his arms. "Why did you save me from my torturous misery just to throw me back again?" he asked her. "Out of compassion for your loss, I did seek comfort for my own." Eden replied. "Did you find your solace then?" he asked her. "Yes Mortamion, you did comfort me and I released my pain, my anger." Eden answered quietly. "Eden, I want to be with you, to take care of you, I can speak with The Council, I have great favor with them . . . I can ask for my mortality back." Mortamion said as he closed his eyes and held her close to him. "I have vowed to marry Alestasis, by Council oath Mortamion, it would never work, I gave my word as a Warrior of God." She looked into his eyes.

"Mortamion . . . you must hear what I am saying, this too shall pass." Eden searched for his comprehension. "So, you are now to be ripped away from me as well?" he asked her, as tears appeared in his eyes. "No, I will still be here . . . but we have different roads to take you and I." She answered him, smiling faintly. "It seems I am always on the wrong side of the argument." She mused. "What do you mean?" he asked her. "Nothing, I remember a conversation I had with someone that was very similar." Eden replied. "Are you referring to Talus?" he asked. Eden nodded. "Yes, because he was immortal, he could not give you all of himself . . . but I can and want to!" Mortamion insisted. "No Mortamion . . . it would never work between us, my heart belongs to only one man, even though he is dead." Eden said as she turned away from him. "Yet, you are willing to give your heart away to Alestasis in marriage, whom you don't love . . . I can't understand this Eden, by all that is in me as a man, I would protect you and love you, and yet you discard me away?" Mortamion asked in a raised voice. "Mortamion I gave my word to The Council, what recourse do I have?" Eden pulled away from him, trying to think, to clear her mind. "You have the recourse of my love." Mortamion replied, wrapping his arms around her. "Tonight was a gift of my forgiveness and compassion for you, but I cannot give you the kind of love you seek from a woman." Mortamion stepped back from Eden. "Then tonight meant nothing to you as a woman . . . is that what I am to understand?" he asked her.

"No, it meant everything, in our love we cleansed our souls and released our pain." Eden was trying desperately to find the right words. Her eyes intensely fixed on his. "And I gave you, the man that took from me my truest love, forgiveness and and comfort, for blessed are those who mourn for they shall be comforted . . . Mortamion did I not comfort you in your sorrow?" Eden asked him. "Yes, you have comforted me and through that I have found peace . . . which is why it is so hard to leave you." Mortamion said wanting her again. Eden read it in his eyes and turned away from him. "I carry Talus' child inside of me and maybe now it would not bother you . . . but I know that later you would not treat him as your own, and I couldn't handle that." Eden said the words she needed to say, that would dispel his longing for her.

Mortamion sat down in the bed, surprised at her confession. "Why did you not tell me this before? Your honesty is admirable Eden but your timing leaves a lot to be desired." Mortamion snapped back at her as he got dressed. "What gives you the right to get angry with me?" Eden asked. Mortamion pulled his black turtleneck over his head and stood up. "I'm sorry," He exhaled. "I have no cause or incident to affront you and I am wrong in doing so." He replied sadly, still shaken by her news. "Now that I know, it was with just cause that you wish us only to be friends." Mortamion replied as he kissed her forehead. "In truth I would love any child of yours, whoever the father might be." He told her with sadness in his voice. She believed him. "Before the light of day, this will all become a very far and distant memory Mortamion, you may actually forget me completely." Eden replied. "Not if I became mortal and truly that is what I would wish for, to be with you and to love you." He replied, with hopeful longing. Yet Eden knew all too well, he was just being human and emotional.

Eden put on her long satin pink robe, as Mortamion looked at her and remembered the color pink. She went to him and hugged him. She could feel the sadness of her rejection inside him. "Thank you for forgiving me with your love Eden, I will try never to forget this night, the love I have for you, now as we are, in this moment in time and the beauty of your soul." Mortamion said and kissed her one last time. She watched as he walked away towards his car. Closing the door, she leaned her back against it and her eyes fell on the box containing Talus' sword. Eden knew that by the light of dawn Mortamion would no longer feel for her what he felt tonight. As he would be immortal again, becoming emotionally detached and The Council Tribunal would erase his memories. She resolved then, that she had felt his heartbreak and loss, and absolved it with her own.

Eden walked over to the box that held Talus' sword and opened it again. She ran her hand across it slowly and felt something on the bottom part of the handle. It seemed to be some sort of inscription. Why had she not felt it before, when she challenged Mortamion? Perhaps in her temper she didn't realize it was there.

Using her powers she lifted it easily and took the sword into the kitchen and laid it length wise on the table. Turning the kitchen light on wasn't enough, the writing was too small and was inscribed circular around the handle. She knew her grandmother always kept a flashlight under the sink and true to form it was there. The inscription was very worn, but she was able to make out the words as she rotated the sword. "For he who lowers his sword for his own salvation, will be granted forgiveness for his sins." It read. Could it be that Talus still existed somewhere? Perhaps, The Council Tribunal had spared his soul? Maybe through the compassion of The Highest Realm, Talus still existed somewhere. Somewhere, in the vastness of time and space and the dimensions . . .

The Beginning

We are one, after all, you and I, together we suffer, together exist,
And forever will recreate each other.

Teilhard de Chardin